ACCLAIM FOR . . .

MALICE DOMESTIC 1

"Pull up your coziest armchair, brew yourself a pot of Earl Grey, and settle in to enjoy as these sleuths, both amateur and professional, solve crimes of murder and mayhem."

—*Prime Suspects*

MALICE DOMESTIC 2

"The second very solid volume in this series of mystery short stories offers ample evidence that a skillful writer can deliver a worthwhile read in pared-down prose. . . . A variety of styles and settings offers an apt reminder of the vitality of this genre."

—*Publishers Weekly*

MALICE DOMESTIC 3

"The quintessential cozy anthology."

—*Mystery Lovers Bookshop News*

Elizabeth Peters Presents MALICE DOMESTIC 1
Mary Higgins Clark Presents MALICE DOMESTIC 2
Nancy Pickard Presents MALICE DOMESTIC 3
Carolyn G. Hart Presents MALICE DOMESTIC 4

Published by POCKET BOOKS

CAROLYN G. HART
presents

MALICE DOMESTIC 4

An Anthology of
Original Traditional
Mystery Stories

POCKET BOOKS

New York   London   Toronto   Sydney   Tokyo   Singapore

An *Original* Publication of POCKET BOOKS

POCKET BOOKS, a division of Simon & Schuster Inc.
1230 Avenue of the Americas, New York, NY 10020

Copyright © 1995 by Martin Greenberg

ISBN: 0-671-89631-8

First Pocket Books printing May 1995

10 9 8 7 6 5 4 3 2 1

POCKET and colophon are registered trademarks of
Simon & Schuster Inc.

Cover art by John Zielinski

Printed in the U.S.A.

Copyright Notices

Contents

Contents

Real People, Real Passions

Carolyn G. Hart

I adore the opening segments of the Agatha Christie television mysteries because they capture the essence of the kind of mysteries—Malice Domestic mysteries —celebrated in this anthology.

If you recall, in the opening segments we see a figure peering out a window into the street and two women with sly faces in close conversation. There is an air of secrecy, covertness, and, most of all, intimacy.

Neighbors watch.

Friends—and enemies—gossip.

There are lies and deceptions, misunderstandings and misapprehensions, passion and pain, fear and fury.

In a word, all kinds of Malice Domestic.

Christie once compared the mystery to the medieval morality play. It is a brilliant analogy. In the medieval morality play, the trades-fair audiences saw a graphic presentation of what happens to lives dominated by lust, gluttony, sloth, and all the deadly sins.

This is precisely what readers of today's mysteries are offered in a more sophisticated guise.

The traditional mystery provides readers with parables. The distant mother creates a child who cannot love. A tyrannical boss engenders hatred and frustration. Slyness evokes distrust. A man who cheats on his wife—or a woman who cheats on her husband—cannot be trusted in any relationship. If this, dear reader, is how you live . . .

Critics who do not understand the dynamic of the traditional mystery inquire, "Why do you want to write about murder?"

The answer is simple.

Murder is *not* the focus of a mystery. The focus of the mystery is fractured relationships. In trying to solve the crime, the detective searches out the reasons for murder by exploring the relationships between the victim and those around the victim. The detective is trying to find out what caused the turmoil in these lives. What fractured the relationships among these people?

And readers, being the intelligent creatures that they are, extrapolate the lessons observed in fiction for their own use, their own lives.

When readers observe the lives around them, they can see the torment of an abused wife or husband (and abuse can quite often be mental and verbal rather than physical), the despair of an unloved child, the anger of a betrayed spouse, the jealousy of a less-favored child, the hatred of a spurned lover.

Usually these emotional dramas do not end in

murder. In fact, they do not end. The violent emotions created by fractured relationships corrode the lives of every person involved. Often forever.

This is what Malice Domestic is all about.

Malice Domestic reveals the intimate, destructive, frightening secrets hidden beneath what so often seems to be a placid surface. Malice Domestic offers even more to readers. Malice Domestic explores not only the passions in everyday life but the foibles and mishaps and humor that make life entertaining as well as stressful.

Once again, Agatha Christie comes to mind. No one ever captured the destructive power of greed any better than she did in *The Murder of Roger Ackroyd.* But, equally, in book after book, she punctures pretension and wryly observes the human drama. In *The Body in the Library,* Christie notes with humor the stuffiness and class consciousness of Colonel Bantry, but she also observes with compassion how a suspicion of wrongdoing, if not resolved, could destroy his life.

It is no accident that Christie has outsold every writer, living or dead. It is because her people are real. Readers recognize them at once. Oh yes, that's just like that fellow in the office. Or yes, that's just like Aunt Alice.

Truth to tell (and fortunately), most readers do not spend every waking moment trying to escape from a serial killer.

But they do spend their lives in moments of stress and confrontation with those around them. They know the jealous mother, the miserly uncle, the impossible boss, the woman who confuses sex with love, the selfish sister. These are the realities of life with which they must cope.

So this is why Christie's mysteries and all Malice Domestic mysteries are so popular.

What could be more everyday, more humdrum, than life in a remote English village?

Miss Marple can tell you.

I've always been amused by those who dismiss traditional mysteries by saying, "Oh, how absurd. All those bodies in a little village. Isn't that silly?"

No.

It is reality.

There may not be a body in the library, but there will always be heartbreak and passion, fear and denial, jealousy and revenge, in every society everywhere.

It is how these emotions destroy lives that fascinates the writer of traditional mysteries.

So join us as we plumb once again the heights of goodness and the depths of evil as they are played out every day in ordinary lives.

Welcome to Malice Domestic, the greatest reality of all.

MALICE DOMESTIC 4

Mister Smithereens

Ralph McInerny

I awoke, the sole occupant of a king-size bed, in a hotel room cold enough to accommodate sides of beef. The remote control was on the table beside the bed. Swaddled in a blanket, supported by three pillows, I turned on the television. A Barbie doll woman looked sincerely into the camera and gave me the news.

I was dead.

Killed in an explosion the night before.

Cut to street scene. A mildly curious crowd was being kept back from the charred chassis of the car in which I had died. Supposedly. I pinched my still-living flesh. Awake, I can imagine myself asleep and I might pinch myself in a dream. But one way or the other I had to be alive.

"The victim has been identified as Daniel Lloyd, a

resident of Wheeler, where the explosion took place. Next of kin have been notified."

Victim? News of one's death should concentrate the mind, but my head was a balloon from all I had drunk the night before. I pressed gently on my closed lids and brought back the psychedelic lights of the bar off the lobby where I had misbehaved the previous night. My tongue was furry and thick. I turned off the television and, in an intricate maneuver, managed to get my legs over the side of the bed and my feet on the floor without having my head roll off my shoulders. No one with such a hangover could possibly be dead.

I shaved in the shower so I wouldn't have to confront myself in the mirror. The bathroom filled with steam so that when I emerged, the mirror was too cloudy to reflect me. It was all unreal. Perhaps I really was dead. With a washcloth I cleared a small circle on the glass. I stooped and put in a cameo appearance. Dead men do not see themselves in mirrors.

By the time my breakfast was brought up, I was ready to confront the astounding news item.

I was having breakfast in a Chicago hotel room. The television had informed me that ninety miles away in Wheeler, Indiana, I had been blown to hell in my car. The car in the hotel garage below was a rental. I checked my pocket and found the keys. I had taken a commuter flight from Wheeler to Midway field, where I rented a car and drove to this hotel. Last night, a red-meat dinner, the White Sox, and then back to the hotel and the bar downstairs. I had closed it down at two o'clock and come directly to my room. No matter how I thought of it, it was clear that I was not dead. What next of kin had been notified? They must mean my lawyer. Halfway through my second cup of coffee, I put through a call to Andrew Broom.

Andrew Broom is the premier lawyer of Wheeler, Indiana, which may not sound very impressive, but he could practice law anywhere he wanted. In Wheeler, he could remain a generalist in the law, he probably outearned most senior partners in the larger Chicago firms, and there were two tournament-class golf courses in the vicinity.

"Yes?" Andrew said when he came on.

"Andrew, this is Daniel Lloyd."

There was a pause. "Go on."

"The most amazing thing. I just heard on the television that I'm dead."

"Where are you?"

I told him. I realized that as much as anything else, he wanted to hear me talk and reassure himself that it was indeed a supposedly dead man on the phone. A few minutes later he gave me instructions I was happy enough to follow. Using the rental car, I was to return to Wheeler and come directly to Andrew's building. He would meet me in the garage and take me up in the freight elevator.

"Who am I avoiding?"

"Whoever thinks he already killed you."

Driving out of Chicago and into Indiana, taking lesser roads, I wondered who Andrew Broom would be casting for the role of my assassin. The life of an accountant is not one of maximum danger, though many of my clients regard the monitoring of their financial affairs as a life-or-death matter. Would Andrew seek among my clients the one who had sought to kill me?

Following Andrew's instructions, I entered Wheeler from the east and took the street parallel to Tarkington downtown. When I nosed my rented car into the garage entrance, I felt that I had accomplished some daring feat. Andrew was standing beside the driver's door before I had turned off the motor. He pulled open the door and looked down at me with a grim smile.

"I thought the next time I saw you, you'd be laid out."

Going up in the freight elevator, with Andrew Broom looking at me as if I were Lazarus raised from the dead, I felt posthumous. How would people react when I really died if they expended all those emotions on this false alarm? This feeling increased when Sussanah, his wife as well as his secretary, greeted me with a little cry, tears in her eyes. But finally we were settled in Andrew's office.

"All right, Daniel. Who wants you dead?"

"You made out my will."

He tipped back, a large athletic man, white hair, face bronze from hours on the fairway. He thought about the document he had drawn up. Whatever money I left would go to institutions and causes, not individuals.

Sheriff Waffle, who had been summoned by Sussanah, arrived, his officious voice audible in the outer office before he came in. He had a frown for Andrew, the frown of an officer of the law interrupted in the midst of important business, and then he saw me.

"My God!"

Andrew waited while Waffle adjusted to the shock. The sheriff, as he repeated over and over, had just come from my barbecued remains, and here I was, bright as a penny.

"Except for a headache."

"Headache?"

I told him of my riotous night in Chicago, and that led on to the tale of leaving my car at the airport, flying to Midway, renting the car. Waffle wanted exact times, taking notes, but through it all the big question was eating at him.

"Who the hell was in your car when it exploded?"

A rhetorical question. I said nothing. Andrew told Waffle he wasn't going to wait until the sheriff or, more accurately, the state police discovered who the victim was.

"I can't have a client running around dead, Earl."

"It's bad for business," Sussanah said.

"Mine or Andrew's?" I asked.

Thus did my presumed violent murder become an occasion for joshing. Only Earl Waffle went on frowning.

"What hotel were you staying in?"

I told him, beginning to be irked by his dour doggedness. Waffle seemed almost disappointed that a living and breathing me had turned up to complicate his life.

"In Chicago on business?" His eyes dropped to the briefcase I had propped beside my chair. I looked down at it too. The initials embossed on it seemed to enlarge and converge on my bloodshot eyes. Meanwhile Andrew, having run out of patience with the sheriff, was urging him on his way. I hung my arm over the side of the chair and covered the initials with my hand. J.T.C.

After he had gotten rid of Waffle, Andrew returned.

"Andrew, this isn't my briefcase." I showed him the initials.

"Where did you get it?"

"Apparently I had it all along. I never opened it. I told you how I spent my time in Chicago."

"J.T.C.," he read.

"Tom Collins?" Sussanah asked.

I lurched in my chair. "My God!"

"What is it, Dan?"

I looked at Andrew and then at Sussanah. "I met with Tom just before leaving for the airport."

Sussanah was on her feet and hurrying into her office. "I'm going to call Kay."

"Maybe you should just go over there."

"Good idea," came from the other room, and a moment later the outer door opened and closed. That quickly Sussanah had put it all together. The victim of the explosion had been identified by the briefcase that had been found more or less intact, my briefcase. But I had Tom Collins's briefcase, apparently the result of a mistake when I hurriedly left a meeting with him to go to the airport. Sussanah was on her way to be with the presumed widow, who would not yet know her changed status.

"Tom was a client of yours, wasn't he, Daniel?"

"They both are."

Collins Ford Toyota was the largest dealership in the county. I was Tom's accountant, both for business and personal finances, and I knew how much he made despite the narrow margin of profit he operated on. Volume, that was the key. Volume. Kay Collins would roll her eyes when her husband repeated his familiar creed. Of course, he made his own television commercials. Tom Collins had been a blustering overweight guy who had been phenomenally lucky in getting whatever he wanted.

"Where did you and Tom meet?"

"At the dealership. I downloaded last month's accounts onto my laptop."

"Onto your computer?"

I looked at him. He nodded slowly. "That was found along with your briefcase. How did you get to the airport?"

"Tom drove me!"

My head was finally clear. How vivid the scene formed in my mind. After I downloaded the data from Tom's computers, we sat on in his office. I told him of the minor trouble I was having with my new car—the dashboard lights were erratic—and he boomed, "I'll give you another car, if you'd like. What've you got on it, a thousand miles?"

"I like that car."

"So leave it. We'll fix it."

"I have to get to the airport."

"I'll take you. You can show me what's wrong with the car. You say you know Emily?"

"I said I know who she is."

Tom's eyes rolled toward the ceiling. Emily was his latest conquest, and in the manner of the swashbuckling seducer, he wanted to tell me all about it. There was no way to stop him. I knew Emily, all right, and it was painful to hear her spoken of as just another notch on Tom's belt or wherever he recorded his triumphs.

"He drove you to the airport?" Andrew asked.

"I drove. It was my car. But he came along to take the car back to be checked."

"And was blown to hell."

"It doesn't make any sense."

"Where was your car while you were meeting with Tom?"

"In the garage of his dealership. I asked them to look at it while I was in the office, check those dashboard lights."

I could see Andrew thinking of the maintenance operation at Collins Ford Toyota. How many employees would be there? And what better place to wire a car than a garage?

"That bomb was intended for you, Daniel."

"Andrew, I have no enemies. Who would want to kill me?"

"Could any mechanic have known Tom intended to take you to the airport?"

"I don't see how."

"Who was in the office when you and Tom were meeting?"

"It was his private office."

"No secretary coming and going."

I thought about it. "I don't remember. There was only Kay."

"Kay!"

"She stopped by to show me her checkbooks."

"How long was she there?"

I shrugged. "A couple minutes."

Andrew got up and went to the windows that gave a commanding view of Wheeler and the country beyond. He stood there for a full minute, only turning away when the phone rang. It was Sussanah, telling him that Kay was at the golf course.

"I'll meet you there."

He asked me to come along and I tried to get out of it, telling him I would look to Kay like the guy who should be dead rather than her husband. Andrew dismissed this. His mind was still full of whatever thoughts he'd had standing at the window.

"Didn't you date Kay when we were kids?"

"I took her out a few times."

"How'd they get along, Kay and Tom?"

"I'm not much of a judge of happy marriages, Andrew."

The person blown up in my car was identified as Tom Collins by his dental work. Andrew got the news on his car phone while we were on our way to the country club where Sussanah had located Kay Collins. We checked out a cart and drove to the fifteenth hole, where Sussanah and Kay were seated in a shelter. Pretty obviously Kay had already been given the news. Andrew bent as he entered the shelter, then sat next to Kay and took her hand. Kay looked up at me with widened dry eyes and suddenly burst into tears.

"Tell them, Dan," she sobbed.

Sussanah and Andrew turned to me. There was a water fountain in the shelter and I turned it on, sending a great arc of water through the air. Andrew managed to get out of the way, but some of it got on Kay.

"You did that on purpose." She tried to laugh, but it

came out as a strangled sound. "For God's sake, tell them."

"You mean about Emily?"

"Whatever her name is."

Kay had confided in me what I had already known, Tom's affair with Emily.

"It's because it doesn't mean anything that it infuriates me so," she had said. "It's not as if he intends to leave me and run away with the little tramp. He'll use her and discard her and go on to another. Of course, people know and I get such looks, but he doesn't care. He doesn't care at all how it embarrasses me."

Emily had been a temporary diversion for Tom and only an embarrassment to Kay. Or so she thought. Had it been unfriendly to tell her of the amounts of money Tom was transferring to Emily's account?

"I don't believe it!" she'd said.

I had to show her then, I couldn't have her thinking I would make up something like that, but I had to explain the bank statements to her. How easily she was deceived. If I hadn't blurted it out, she would never have known. The amount of money involved made Tom's affair with Emily a very different thing.

"You have to stop him, Daniel!"

"Oh, I've talked with him. But I can't prevent a man doing with his money what he likes."

"His money! It's our money. Mine. And he's giving it to that little slut. Yes, slut. Isn't that what you call a woman who does it for money?"

"It's not her fault, Kay."

"Don't take her side. I doubt you even tried to talk Tom out of it."

"Kay, if I could have prevented that from happening at all, I would have."

She had looked at me, put her hand on mine, calmed down. "Poor Dan," she said. "Sometimes I wish I had married you."

Was she remembering how Tom had swept her off her feet, eclipsed me in a matter of minutes? For him she had represented diversion, conquest, excitement, but of course, Kay played for keeps and they married. I knew that she imagined I still half loved her. If I did, I half hated her too, her and Tom and their life together, hellish as they made it for one another.

"What does she do, the girl?"

"Her name is Emily. Emily Trout."

Kay would have preferred to keep her anonymous, the other woman, a role, not an individual. I told her Emily had a computer consultant business. "She's in the same building I am."

"So that's how you know her. Did you introduce Tom to her?"

What contempt she unconsciously felt for me. Did she imagine I would pimp for her husband? But I *was* responsible, however accidentally, for Tom's meeting Emily. His computer went down one day and I suggested Emily, and the rest, as one might say, is history.

"Tom had a girl," I said now to Andrew and Sussanah.

"And you found out?" Andrew asked Kay.

I sat on the bench across from the three of them. Twenty-five yards away a very fat golfer wearing a white hat stood motionless over a putt as if he were on video and the hold button had been pressed. Finally he brought back his club, slowly, then stroked the ball. His head remained motionless until well after he had struck the ball. Suddenly he erupted in ecstacy and the men with him shouted and cheered. Andrew, the consummate golfer, ignored it all.

"He never really tried to keep it from me."

"There were others?"

Kay turned to Sussanah. "It was nothing personal. They were just toys."

"Until this one?" Andrew asked.

I was conscious of holding my breath. But Kay said, "This one was no different."

"I'll close that account," I said to Kay.

"What account?" asked Andrew.

I looked at Kay; she must know Andrew should be told. She shrugged and I told Andrew how Tom had created an account for Emily Trout and instructed me to transfer money into it regularly.

"Trout?" Sussanah said. "The computer consultant."

Kay got up, as if any reference to Emily except as a tramp was unacceptable to her. Sussanah got into a cart with Kay and we followed them back to the clubhouse.

"Kay was there when you and Tom met yesterday before you left for Chicago?"

"She was around, sure. But mainly Tom and I talked."

"She would have known Tom would be driving your car."

"I don't know that she did."

"Dan, someone rigged your car with a bomb. Unless you were the intended victim, it had to be Tom."

"What does Kay know about cars?"

He looked at me. Kay knew all about cars, and often made a nuisance of herself in the maintenance garage of Collins Ford Toyota.

"Okay," I conceded. "But what does she know about bombs?"

"She's a product of the sixties, Dan. We all are. Lots of people learned a lot about bombs."

I dropped it. It was Andrew's theory, not mine.

Andrew suggested that we all have dinner in the clubhouse, but Kay declined. Sussanah didn't want to leave Kay alone, so the two women went off and Andrew and I had dinner by a window, watching the sun go down and twilight settle over the golf course. At least I watched it. Andrew seemed lost in his thoughts. When we parted, he said he thought he'd stop by the sheriff's office and have a talk with Earl Waffle.

After I got into bed, I stared at the ceiling for a long time and then must have suddenly dropped off. I woke at two in the morning, with the light still on. What luxury to turn it off and roll back into the warm darkness of sleep. The next sound I heard was the telephone beside my bed. It was Andrew wanting me to come by his office at midmorning.

The outer office was empty when I arrived and Andrew called me into his office.

"Sussanah's running an errand."

"Did you talk to Waffle?"

He nodded.

"What did he think of your theory?"

"He thought it had merit."

"What's he going to do?"

"I told him I wanted to check out something first and then he could act."

"Andrew, I've told you all I know. If you expect me to say I know Kay rigged up my car because she heard Tom say he would drive me to the airport, forget it. Maybe she did, maybe she didn't hear him say that."

He laughed. "You think my theory depends on your proving it?"

"It better not."

"How about coffee?"

"Why not?" Andrew became philosophical. "I think the only proof I'll get is from the killer."

"Don't try to trick Kay into anything."

The door in the outer office opened and there was the sound of voices. Sussanah and another woman. I suppose I thought it was Kay because we had just been speaking about her. But suddenly Emily Trout appeared in the doorway with Sussanah. Andrew rose and went to her and it wasn't until he had taken her hand and brought her to a chair that Emily became aware of me.

"You!" she cried, her face distorting. "What are you doing here?"

"I think you know, Emily," Andrew said in a low voice.

Emily stood, arms akimbo, her hands forming fists, staring at me with eyes full of hatred. Then she rushed at me and began to pound on my chest. I tried to grab her wrists, but before I could she began to scratch at my face, a feline infuriated woman.

"You killed him," she cried. "You killed him. Well, it's not going to do you any good, do you understand?"

Andrew pinned her arms to the sides of her body and pulled her away. She looked at him over her shoulder. "He said he'd do something. He said he'd kill him and me too, if he had to."

The simple truth is a terrible thing. I felt naked with the three of them looking at me. I tried to act sadly surprised, I tried to laugh. Denials formed in my mind, but I could not voice them. Andrew and Sussanah knew it all. That was painfully obvious. Andrew could see me as I saw myself. I slumped into my chair.

"Tell me about it, Daniel."

I had not realized what pride a killer takes in his craft. I found myself explaining to Andrew how I had managed it. It was planned down to the minute. If my plane had been delayed and Tom had remained with me at the airport, the bomb would have exploded ineffectually in the parking lot. But everything went off like clockwork.

"I could still deny it," I said, with a pang of regret. But I was more reluctant to forgo credit for what I had done. Given Emily's reaction, it was the only satisfaction I was likely to get. Sussanah took Emily away, leaving Andrew and me alone. "I was a damned fool to admit it. I could still deny it and nothing could be proved."

"But you lied about Kay."

"Kay?"

"She wasn't in Tom's office yesterday, Dan. She was

playing bridge at the time of your appointment with Tom."

"That's her story."

"It's true. That's when I decided to bring Emily here. When I talked to her last night I realized that she was the only one who really mourned Tom Collins or gave a damn that he was dead. You didn't. Neither did Kay. But Emily was devastated to hear he had been killed. That's when I realized what an extraordinary thing you had done, Daniel."

His admiration seemed genuine. It swept away the anger I felt at hearing of Emily's reaction to Tom's death. She was just a little fluff to him, but apparently she had felt more for him. Andrew Broom's appreciation of what I had done made up for that, at least in part. So I told him all about it again, embellishing the story.

"There is a bank account in Emily's name. I opened it without Tom's knowledge, and transferred money of his into it. Emily knew nothing about it."

"So I gathered."

"You asked her."

"Very obliquely."

I was momentarily irked. But then Earl Waffle arrived and I found myself explaining to the sheriff what I had done. He too listened in rapt attention. Was this my fifteen minutes of fame?

Andrew said, "If you hadn't made such a point of Kay's being there, I'm not sure I would have guessed."

"That's unimportant," I said impatiently.

He shook his head. "Maybe if you had just said she was there and she wasn't."

"What difference does it make?"

"I asked Kay. You tried to get her to come there. But calling her and demanding that she bring her checkbook to Tom's office and going into a snit when she told you she was going to play bridge and you could see her checkbook anytime—that was a major mistake, Dan. Of course, you needed her there if your scheme was to be perfect."

Had Kay realized what telling that to Andrew would do to me?

Earl Waffle stood. "Congratulations, Andrew."

"Congratulations, Andrew!" I was furious. What the hell was Earl praising Andrew Broom for? I was the one who did it. With one deed gotten revenge on Tom Collins for ruining my life. He had taken Kay from me, and then Emily. But I had stopped him finally, blowing the sonofabitch to smithereens. And I wanted recognition. But neither Andrew nor the sheriff seemed impressed anymore. When I was led away it was as a common criminal.

"You're my lawyer," I cried out to Andrew Broom.

"Not this time, Daniel. I'll be called as a witness."

Regrets Only

Rochelle Majer Krich

Maggie lies curled on her side in the king-size bed. It is seven o'clock in the morning, but the room is still gray, and the oppressive heaviness in the sunless air tells her it will probably rain. She closes her eyes, but she cannot find her way back to what she senses was a pleasant place.

Through the bathroom door she listens to Bill's morning sounds—the seven-minute rush of water cascading in the shower; the sandpaper toweling of his body; the hiss of Right Guard deodorant (its acrid scent will linger in the air to assault her); the methodical swoosh as he brushes his teeth to the accompaniment of water streaming from the faucet; the crackling whine of the electric shaver; the brisk slapping of hands as he applies aftershave on his broad, handsome face and neck.

She hears the door open. Through almost sealed

eyelids, Maggie watches as he puts on boxer shorts
and a ribbed white T-shirt. The boxer shorts were her
idea—Bill wore briefs, but she bought him two pair of
boxers because she liked the way Bruce Willis looked
in them on "Moonlighting"; she told Bill she found
them sexy and he grinned and said, "What the hell"
and bought half a dozen more. Bill in boxer shorts is
tall and lean and, after twelve years of marriage, has
almost no flab, but he is still Bill. The boxer shorts
didn't work whatever magic she'd expected.

And now briefs are back. The other day she saw
Marky Mark in an ad for Calvin Klein's.

Maggie stretches a sigh into a yawn.

"Did I wake you?" Bill asks, turning toward her.
The boxer shorts and T-shirt have been covered by
gray wool slacks and a white cotton shirt with thin
blue stripes.

"I have to make Sarah's lunch." Noah spent the
night at a friend's, and the friend's mother will
prepare his.

"You're going to Cynthia's luncheon today, aren't
you?"

"I don't know." She doesn't like her sister-in-law
Cynthia or the affairs she hosts—ostensibly to raise
funds for a myriad of worthwhile causes, but Maggie
knows better.

"Did you tell her you were coming?" Bill asks as he
fixes his tie. A note of worry has crept into his voice.
"If you didn't, she won't have a place for you, and her
tables will be off."

"The invitation said 'regrets only.'" The ivory
linen-weave square is on the nightstand, tucked into
the slim volume Maggie is finishing for the fifth time.

"I'll probably go," she says, not wanting to worry Bill, who is sweet and kind and has worked hard to maintain harmony between the families.

"You don't have other plans, do you?"

"Nothing special." She rarely does anything special. She exercises at the gym three times a week. She has her nails done once a week and a facial once a month. She reads *The New Yorker* and *Vanity Fair* and *Cosmopolitan* and the *L.A. Times* and *People*. She makes biweekly trips to the market and is expert at selecting fruits and vegetables and never brings home a leaking milk carton. She is a class mother for Sarah's class of six-year-olds and Noah's class of eleven-year-olds.

She was a French major who dreamed of spending a summer, if not a lifetime, in the French countryside; instead, she married Bill and worked as a legal secretary until she had Noah, and Bill's accounting practice was established enough so that she could stay home and be a mother. She is a good mother and Bill is a good father and loving husband and she wishes he would kiss her good-bye and leave. She reaches for the book on her nightstand.

"Hi, Mommy."

She looks at the doorway and feels a rush of love. "Hi, sweetheart."

Sarah, her face tinted pink and creased from sleep, slips into the bed and insinuates herself against Maggie's side. It is their morning ritual. Until recently, Noah would snuggle with Maggie mornings, too, but he has told her he is too old for "that stuff."

"How're my two favorite women doing?" Bill asks. Leaning over, he tickles Sarah, who shrieks with delight; then he kisses Maggie on the mouth. It is a chaste kiss because Sarah is in the bed and because passion has been relegated to evenings behind locked doors after the children are asleep. Bill's mouth tastes of mint toothpaste and he smells wonderful. Maggie flirts with the idea of waiting for Sarah to leave the room and asking Bill to undo his carefully assembled outfit and come back to bed. He will do it, she knows, unless he has an early appointment.

"Do you have an early appointment?" She fingers his tie.

"Nope. Why?" He glances at Sarah, then at Maggie. A different question flickers in his kind brown eyes.

"Just wondering when I can reach you." Releasing his tie, she realizes that, more than wanting to make love, she wanted him to be late. The thought was provocative, exciting, and now it is gone. She shoves him gently away.

"They're saying thunderstorms," Bill tells her. "Noah took his jacket, didn't he?"

She nods. A moment later he is gone and Sarah is in her own room, getting dressed. Maggie showers. Wearing jeans, a sweatshirt, and running shoes, her dark brown hair pulled back in a ponytail, she walks downstairs to the kitchen to prepare Sarah's lunch—a cream cheese and jelly sandwich, a cherry Fruit Roll-Up, carrot sticks, and a small carton of apple juice. She places a heart-shaped sticker for Sarah's album collection on top of the plastic-bagged sandwich and shuts the Barney the Dinosaur lunch box. Noah gave up "babyish" lunch boxes along with early morning snuggling. Maggie always draws a happy face on his paper lunch bag and wonders when he will tell her he has outgrown that, too. She phones him at his friend's and wishes him a great day.

"I love you, sweetie. I'll pick you up at five-thirty. Make sure you wear your jacket, okay?"

"'Kay, Mom. 'Bye."

Twenty minutes later, Maggie buckles a lavender-slickered Sarah onto the backseat of the tan Volvo station wagon. Most of Maggie's friends have car pools, but she prefers driving her children to and from school, being their first audience, making certain they're safe. Today Sarah is going to a classmate's for a birthday party. Maggie will pick her up when she gets Noah.

When Maggie parks in front of the school, it has started to rain. Sarah unbuckles herself and plants a wet kiss on her cheek. Sarah is a dear child; so is Noah. And Bill is a dear, sweet man and a tender lover, though not a shaman, and she is lucky to have him and doesn't know what is wrong with her, what has been wrong with her even before she read the book for the first time.

"I was beginning to think you wouldn't show," Cynthia says when Maggie enters the elegantly decorated room at the small Westwood hotel on Wilshire. "Almost everyone's here."

The tables, set with mauve cloths and white napkins, are occupied by expensively groomed women, some of whom Maggie knows from Cynthia's other fund-raisers (today's will raise money for an orphanage). Cynthia is wearing the winter white Valentino she told Maggie about. Her blond-streaked hair, cut and styled like Princess Di's, is perfect, though her face is not. She has had it buffed and made up professionally, but her small eyes are still hard and her thin, coral-painted lips look pinched.

"Sorry I'm late." Maggie spent almost an hour before she settled on a hunter green silk dress that shows off her narrow waist and hips and, judging from Cynthia's stare at the vee of her neckline, a little too much décolletage, accentuated by the lacy black push-up bra she bought at Victoria's Secret. She is also wearing the matching panties and garter belt.

"I put you with Bethany and Clarise at table six," Cynthia says, looking somewhere behind Maggie. "We're going to—Oh, here he is!" She rushes away in her Bruno Magli pumps, her voice as breathless as a schoolgirl's.

Maggie turns toward the tall, handsome man who is the object of her sister-in-law's attention. The guest speaker, no doubt; Maggie doesn't remember his name. Cynthia holds both of his hands and lifts her lips to his cheek. Then she leads him, like a prize bull at a fair, into the room. Not having looked for her table, Maggie has the advantage of heading the line of women who have pushed back their seats and are hurrying to meet the star.

"This is Robert Brissard," Cynthia simpers. "Robert, may I introduce my sister-in-law, Maggie. Maggie majored in French in college and is a great admirer of yours, as are we all."

Up close he is even more handsome. Prominent cheekbones. A strong chin. Wavy dark brown hair, a little too long. Inscrutable gray eyes. "A pleasure to meet you, Monsieur Brissard," Maggie says, feeling pretentious about the "monsieur" yet being careful not to pronounce the final *D*. "I love your work," she adds as she extends her hand, though she has no idea what work he does or why she supposedly admires it—is he an artist? a writer? a composer? She wishes she'd paid attention to the invitation and to Cynthia's ramblings about him.

"The pleasure is mine." He lifts her hand to his mouth. He isn't wearing a wedding band. His lips are soft against her skin. "Maggie is short for Marguerite, *non?*"

"Yes." She loves the way her name sounds on his lips, so musical. "I—"

"Robert, this is Gwen Richley," says Cynthia, who is an equal-opportunity hostess. "She's one of our foremost . . ."

Maggie turns and breaks out of the dense circle that has formed around Robert and Cynthia. She talks to two women she knows casually from other luncheons, but her attention is focused on Robert, who stands tall above the crowd of fawning women and, she senses, is looking at her from time to time.

Seated at her table, Maggie picks at the berries and sliced fruit in the hollowed papaya on her plate. She doesn't dislike Bethany or Clarise or any of her other tablemates, but she has little in common with them, and she tells herself that, though Cynthia will be irritated and Bill pained, this is the last one of these luncheons she will attend.

Through the wall of rain-spattered windows facing her, Maggie watches the sky darken to a threatening purple. Cynthia is talking animatedly to Robert.

Maggie sips white Chardonnay and wills him to look at her. She is eating a slice of kiwi when, suddenly, his eyes meet hers; she holds his glance for a moment, smiles, then turns away, flustered and pleased. Pink tints her face and neck, and she says, "Yes, thank you," to the waiter who offers to refill her wine goblet.

Lately she has taken to flirting like this. Bill tells her that he loves her and that she's beautiful and she believes him, but his admiration is casual, seasoned by twelve years of marriage and certainty. He has seen her stretch marks and unshaved legs and her early morning face, and she knows he will never again be startled when she walks into a room, never catch his breath, feel his heart pound. Just as her heart will never again pound when she sees Bill—dear, sweet, kind, handsome Bill—who will always be the same, in boxer shorts or briefs.

So she stares at good-looking, well-dressed men she doesn't know and doesn't care to know and enjoys the moment when they turn and look at her appreciatively and smile. It makes her feel young and attractive and seductive and there is no risk or harm because, unlike Francesca and her photographer lover in the novel on her nightstand and unlike the women she reads about in her magazines, women who invariably seem to be leading lives more exciting and colorful than hers, she will never take the next step. She has stared at men at Gelson's market, at Brentano's, at Saks, at a restaurant while having lunch with her girlfriends, at the movies sitting next to Bill. She does it when she takes Sarah and Noah to the library to check out the books she will read to them at bedtime. She does it in her

Volvo, stopped at a red traffic light, her foot ready to press on the accelerator to speed away as soon as the light turns green.

The main course is poached salmon with a cucumber sauce. The food is delicious, but she eats only a few bites. She wonders whether women flirt with Bill. The idea interests and pleases her and renders him more appealing.

The rain is battering the windows, as if demanding entrance into the room. At the podium Cynthia introduces Brissard as an internationally acclaimed, award-winning French novelist, ". . . the Flaubert of our time." Maggie thinks of Emma Bovary, unhappy woman, and her many lovers, and her suicide. She sips her wine and listens to Robert discuss his *oeuvre* and feels a tingling warmth whenever he looks directly at her, which is often.

After the questions and answers, after the exuberant applause echoed by a sharp clap of thunder and lightning, after the rum-laced chocolate mousse and brandy aperitif, Maggie joins the queue of fans to congratulate Cynthia and fawn over Brissard, who is sitting at a table, signing copies of his latest novel.

Now it is Maggie's turn. "It was a lovely luncheon, Cynthia." Aware that she has probably had too much wine, she kisses her sister-in-law's cheek, then turns to Brissard. "I enjoyed your talk. I look forward to reading your book."

Brissard picks up a glossy red hardcover from the depleted pile on the table and opens it to the title page. "To Marguerite, is that not right?" His smile is warm, his Mont Blanc fountain pen poised to write beautiful words.

"Yes." She didn't intend to buy a copy. Now she has no choice, but she doesn't mind. She takes out her checkbook.

"Twenty-five dollars, made out to the orphanage." Cynthia points to a placard bearing the orphanage's calligraphied name. "Maggie, I planned to take Robert back to the Beverly Wilshire, but it'll be a while before I'm through here. Can you do it?"

"Yes, of course."

"It's no imposition?" Robert asks. "I can call a taxi."

"No, really. I insist." She wishes she had Bill's Maxima instead of the Volvo wagon—it's so middle-class suburban—and is immediately embarrassed by her pretentiousness.

"Alors, I have no choice but to accept." His smile lights up his face and accentuates his cheekbones.

Maggie steps away from the table and reads his inscription. *Pour la belle Marguerite—je peux voir votre âme à travers vos yeux pensifs.* For the beautiful Marguerite—I can see your soul through your pensive eyes.

In the rest room she freshens her lipstick and dabs perfume behind her ears and just below the hollow of her throat and studies her eyes in the mirror.

After Robert has signed his last copy and said his good-byes, he walks with Maggie to her car, holding a wooden-handled black umbrella over both of them. He looks debonair and cosmopolitan in an olive green trench coat, and she wishes her raincoat were newer and more fashionable.

Inside the Volvo the air is close and humid, the windows fogged. She turns on the defroster and the windshield wipers and, feeling light-headed from the wine and brandy, pulls away from the curve slowly and carefully.

"I appreciate very much your taking me to the hotel," he says. "It's so kind of you."

"It's nothing, really. The hotel's on my way home." She hesitates, then says, "Thank you for the inscription."

"You are not upset? After I signed your book, I worried that you would think me presumptuous."

"No, not at all. I like what you wrote." She keeps her voice light and her attention on the road, which is slippery.

"I am glad. So many people have empty eyes, eyes that say nothing. Yours speak of a certain loneliness, a certain *mécontentement*—I don't know how you say it in English."

"Dissatisfaction," she tells him. "I'm not dissatisfied," she lies. "I just don't enjoy luncheons."

"As a rule, I don't either. Even if they are for very good causes. Your sister-in-law loves good causes, does she not?"

She darts a glance at him and sees his smile. She smiles, too, and quickly turns back to the road.

He is silent for several blocks. Then he says, "But it's a necessity, you know. You write the book. You must promote it. You never know about the audience —will they like you? Hate you?"

"They loved your talk. I found it fascinating."

"But you didn't ask any questions. Why not?" His tone is suddenly playful.

"I was busy listening to your answers."

He laughs. "Well, I have a question for you. Tell me where I can buy a special scarf. A gift."

"For a girlfriend?"

"For my mother."

She has just finished listing shops near the hotel when she pulls into the Beverly Wilshire driveway. "Ask the concierge," she says, wishing she could prolong their conversation. "He'll direct you."

"I'm sure. Thank you for everything, Marguerite." He leans forward and kisses her cheek, then opens the door. Suddenly he turns to her. "Come have a drink with me. It's too gloomy a day for either one of us to be alone."

There is nothing special awaiting her at home, and there is no harm in having a drink with an interesting man. "Just for a short while," she tells him, and is warmed by his smile.

Seated in the booth in the hotel's cocktail lounge, she tries to listen intently as he talks about his family, his career, the previous stops on his seven-city tour, his yearning to return home, but she is too aware of the musk of his aftershave and the nearness of his thigh. When he rests his hand on hers and says, "Now tell me about yourself," she is excited and flustered and a little alarmed.

"There's not much to tell. Compared to you, I lead an ordinary life." She doesn't want to talk about Sarah or Noah or Bill. Certainly not about Bill. Forcing a laugh, she removes her hand and makes a show of checking her watch. "It's three o'clock. I have to go."

"Of course. I hope I didn't take up too much of your

day." He stands and helps her on with her raincoat. "I'd like to give you a book of poems I wrote, a small thank you for this delightful afternoon."

"It's not necessary."

"That's the definition of 'pleasure'—that which is unnecessary, spontaneous." He smiles. "I have a copy in my room. Or I can send it to you—whichever you prefer."

She is not naive. She has no illusions about where this is leading—Robert's "book of poems" is no more original than someone else's etchings—but she finds herself walking with him to the elevators, his hand guiding her elbow. On the elevator, crowded with people, he is silent. She feels self-conscious and wonders if she is making a mistake. Then he smiles.

In the living room of his seventh-floor suite, he drops his raincoat and umbrella onto a sofa. "I'll be right back," he tells her, and disappears into the bedroom.

She knows he has gone to change into a robe and will present her with an excuse instead of a book of poems. She is flushed with excitement and nervousness and too much wine. A minute later he returns, still wearing his suit, and hands her a slim volume.

"I had no time to gift-wrap it." He has removed his tie and undone the top two buttons of his shirt. "I hope you like it."

"Thank you." She feels silly for having misread his intentions. And a little disappointed. She looks down at the open book to hide her face. "It's beautiful."

He lifts her chin and kisses her mouth. The shock to her body is electric. So this is what it is like, she thinks.

"I meant what I said about your eyes, Marguerite," he whispers. "I hope we can make each other a little less lonely."

He takes the book from her trembling hands and puts it on the table, next to the umbrella, then slips off her raincoat. He kisses her again. Even with the lights off and the drapes pulled, the room is too bright. She closes her eyes and loses herself to the touch of his hands and the murmur of his beautiful words in her ear. The blood is pounding in her head and her heart is racing and she is undressed, except for her black lace Victoria's Secret underwear, when she realizes with a sickening jolt that this is not what she wants, not what she wants at all. She feels suddenly humiliated, ashamed, cheap in her nakedness.

"I'm sorry," she whispers, breaking away.

He looks at her, startled. "I don't understand. Did I do something wrong? I thought . . ."

With her back toward him, she struggles into her dress, fumbling with the zipper.

"Marguerite, please. Tell me what's wrong. Maggie?"

She grabs her raincoat and runs from the room. The elevator takes forever to arrive, and as it stops on each floor, she is certain that the people entering are staring at her, that they know her sordid secret.

When the valet brings her Volvo, she tips him and speeds away, almost skidding on the slick asphalt. Slow down, she commands herself, but she is desperate to put miles and time between herself and the hotel, and even as she nears her neighborhood, she is still driving more quickly than she should.

The rain has stopped, but the sky is an angry black.

She is crying and her head feels as if it is going to explode. She doesn't see the Stop sign until she is halfway into the intersection, and though she tries, her reflexes are too slow and the ground too wet and she cannot brake fast enough, cannot stop the Volvo from slamming into the bicycle and the yellow-slickered child riding it.

Maggie screams even before she hears the thud, before she sees the child being tossed up into the air, then landing several feet away with a loud thump that chills her heart. She wants to stop the car and run to the child, wants to ask a neighbor to call the police, but the police will smell liquor on her breath, she has had so much to drink, too much, and they will arrest her, and her life—the life she has found so mundane and pedestrian, the life that is suddenly so precious—will be over.

She is shaking and whimpering and hates herself for running away—what if it were Noah or Sarah lying injured or dead?—but with each passing block she knows there is no going back.

From a phone booth at a corner, she calls 911 and reports the injured child and hangs up when she is asked to identify herself. Then she drives home. She checks the front of the Volvo but can't discern any damage to the fender. She starts to cry again and hopes the ambulance has arrived and taken the child away. She refuses to replay in her mind the sights and sounds of the accident and tells herself there is no reason to think the child is dead.

She has almost two hours to compose herself before picking up Noah and Sarah. She cannot imagine how she will fill the time. She lies down on her bed and turns on the radio to a news station, and that is where she is half an hour later when the doorbell rings.

She has known all along that they will find her—a neighbor probably saw the accident and jotted down her license plate number, or maybe the injured child did—so she isn't surprised when she looks through the peephole and sees two uniformed policemen. Still, she stiffens.

"Yes?"

"Mrs. Lorimer? May we come in, please?"

"Of course." With shaking hands she opens the door and steps aside. She shuts the door behind them. "Can you tell me what this is about?" she asks, wondering why she is prolonging the charade.

The two policemen look at each other.

"Mrs. Lorimer, I'm afraid we have some bad news," says the older of the two. "Apparently your son, Noah . . ."

She doesn't hear the rest because an unearthly scream is piercing her ears. The room starts to spin. She clutches air, then falls.

In the hospital waiting room she sits with Bill.

He has learned from Noah's friend that Noah decided to bicycle home after school for a Nintendo cartridge. He borrowed the friend's bike and slicker.

"I hope the police find the son of a bitch who did this," Bill whispers, stroking her hair. His eyes are red and swollen.

Maggie nods.

"I can't understand how anybody can leave a child lying in the street like that, can you?"

"No." She has contemplated telling him the truth,

but she has learned today, among other things, that she doesn't have the courage.

When the doctor finally enters the waiting room, she clutches Bill's hand, and he helps her to her feet.

"He's going to be all right," the doctor tells them.

Maggie listens, disbelieving, to the report: Noah has a broken leg and cracked ribs, but no head injuries because he was wearing a helmet. It's a miracle, the doctor tells Maggie and Bill, and she nods in agreement, too numb too speak.

Bill is weeping, the tears streaming down his dear, kind familiar face. She loves his face and his comforting solidness. She loves his goodness, his tenderness, his strength.

"You can see him now," the doctor says. "But just for a few minutes. He's one tired little boy." He smiles.

She wishes she could take back everything—the wine, Robert, the hotel room, the accident—but of course, she can't. She feels betrayed, seduced by the romance of Francesca and her photographer, who love illicitly with impunity, and by the women in her magazines who are searching for something that may not exist. She knows she has no one to blame but herself.

She will live with regret forever.

Bill draws her close. "Let's go see our son," he says, his voice hoarse.

She cannot imagine why she has been given a second chance.

Dirty Dancing

Carole Nelson Douglas

———

The orange flyer featured drawings of balloons, cock-tail glasses, and confetti, its centerpiece a crude picture of a fifties-vintage convertible. Words angled here and there: "Drinks" "Dancing" "Disco."

"'Portnoy's.' Sounds like a place my kids would go against my best advice," I complained when the girls at work flourished the flyer for the monthly employees' club outing. "What is it?"

"Oh, a singles' bar, really," said Mary Lou, "but our group booked it earlier in the evening, before the rush." She is an outgoing bottle redhead who is becoming pleasantly plump now that menopause has come and gone. "It'll be fun. They have a huge buffet, and drinks, of course, and pool tables and stuff."

"Sounds like a blast," Connie said, her choice of words revealing her own fifties generation and taking me back to my single years, which had suddenly come again.

Connie was younger than Mary Lou and I, a thin, forbidding-looking fashion plate who was actually a cream puff at heart.

"Why not the usual daytime outing?" I wondered. "I don't even know what to wear to that kind of place."

"Oh, we'll dress up, I imagine," said Mary Lou. "You know, something middle-aged-respectable but a little kicky. Listen, we old broads would never dare go to a place like that if it weren't under company auspices. Some guy in accounting is program chair and he set it up. We can see how the aerobic set lives."

"You make it sound like a strip bar," I fussed. My upbringing always inclined me to step wide around the unrespectable.

"It's not," Mary Lou assured me. "My kids have been there. Do you think I'd let them go anyplace tacky?"

I wasn't keen on going to a place that appealed to my friends' kids: Unlike many parents, I knew that kids like to do things that their parents would never approve of.

But I'd never missed a company outing, so I went.

I didn't expect to be nervous, any more than I had expected to be suddenly single. And I know I'm out of touch with the modern-day cult of the deliberately crass, but the smooth, unexceptional course of my life has isolated me from the ruder realities. I grew up in the Midwest, and attended college long enough to acquire a degree and a fiancé.

His name was Jim, and he was, of course, a gentleman.

We had two children, who never gave us more than the expected minor trouble. When they were both in high school, I entered the working world. College loomed, and while Jim was doing well working for the city, additional income was nothing to sniff at. Besides, we wanted other things than the necessities; we weren't getting any younger.

I was as giddy as a girl graduate to win my first paid position at a large bank in town, and while the ins and outs of finance are more arcane than most, I thrived on the challenge and a new circle of work friends, many women like myself, either single parents or working wives.

Despite one or two women vice presidents—who avoided fraternizing with the other women employees, not wanting to be mistaken for less than what they were—women filled most of the firm's support jobs and had the sort of easy camaraderie that made going to work stimulating.

The kids moved on to college in that smooth slipstream all middle-class families dream of. Everything was wonderful. Jim and I were even planning a modest cruise for Christmas.

Then he died. Suddenly, at work. I was notified at my desk, but my rush to the hospital was a mere formality. The heart attack had been unheralded and immediate.

At fifty-two, I was a widow, a bewildered widow who'd had no warning. Everything I'd done, everything I'd assumed, had been Jim and I. Now "I" was at sea. The cruise seemed pointless, although the kids urged me to go anyway. The kids were always urging me to do something atypical after Jim died, as if they worried that I would wither if not exposed to stimuli.

Work proved to be a blessing, of course, especially my women co-workers. Women form a certain sisterhood because of the unspoken fact that they expect to last the longest, and live alone the longest.

So Mary Lou and Connie, my middle-aged girlfriends, made sure I went now and then to movies I didn't really like, and out shopping for clothes, and to the monthly office outings.

We met at Connie's house at seven-thirty, then she drove us in her Taurus to the highway that looped the city. We moved through a river of black asphalt shimmering with the head- and taillights of heavy traffic.

"I had no idea the Loop was so clogged this far past rush hour," I said from the front passenger seat.

"You've been in a rut, Linda." Mary Lou, in the backseat, sat forward to talk to me, bracing her hand on Connie's headrest. "This section of the Loop is teaming with superstores and trendy restaurants. That's a pretty dress; where did you get it?"

"Mallow's." I touched the full chiffon skirt figured in a floral swirl of dusky rose, purple, and green. "I bought it for the cruise."

They were silent for a bit. I noticed the streetlights glinting off of Mary Lou's wedding ring as we passed under them. I still wore mine, of course; it had never occurred to me to take it off.

Portnoy's announced itself with racy outlines of red and lavender neon. Except for that garish decoration, it resembled the nearby upscale franchise restaurants that squatted on black islands of asphalt parking lots all along the freeway—a one-story sprawling building tricked out with ersatz Art Deco architectural details. The facade's wavy glass block windows reflected the red neon, making it look as if bloody, agitated water washed against them.

Inside the place was dim and barnlike, the bar a neon-outlined altar winking with glassware and bottles. A wooden dance floor adjoined the bar, and the only other seating was the far banquettes that rimmed the perimeter and a few tiny round tables on stilts.

I recognized a sprinkle of faces there as we headed for the banquettes. Unused to wearing high heels except to weddings, I stepped gingerly over the polished parquet dance floor.

Everyday faces had altered in that lurid nightclub atmosphere. The other women had chosen dressy clothes as well, thank God; the men, of course, looked the same. Suits are suits.

After the women complimented each other on their outfits, our group hunted for a table. I realized that the banquettes had to be mounted by a step, and that the only occasional chairs were actually high stools.

"This is silly." Mary Lou giggled, hopping up on a stool despite her high heels. "I'm too old to do this without jiggling like a bowlful of jelly in all the wrong places."

"Maybe this is the wrong place," I suggested.

A willowy woman definitely young enough to hop on and off a hundred barstools without jiggling anywhere but where it draws applause passed our table. "Drinks, ladies?"

We eyed each other. "A margarita," Connie ordered with aplomb. Mary Lou rolled her lively eyes. "I can never make up my mind—how about a . . . lite beer?"

The girl nodded, then eyed me with the bright, expectant look of a begging squirrel that I assumed was her workaday mask. I can never decide either.

"A Bloody Mary," I finally said.

She sashayed off with the round brown empty tray and I noticed then that her skirt barely covered her bottom.

"The men will love this place," Mary Lou predicted in a low, laughing voice.

"I like the family outings better," I said. "With our failing eyes, we can hardly see in this barn. Wasn't the sleigh ride in December fun? Or that June trip to the water park? What are we going to do here, except drink and talk to only the people we know?"

"It's good to see how the other half lives," Mary Lou said. "And I hated wearing a bathing suit in front of all my co-workers. Some things are meant to be kept between an older woman and her Maker, like cellulite. Gosh, look at this place. I forgot what it was like, being meat on the hoof and single."

A few young customers were edging into the cavernous space, all dressed with casual care and all wearing a wary, hopeful look in their eyes. The place was otherwise deserted except for our group, but suddenly the music system shuddered into loud life.

"Goll-y." Mary Lou clapped her palms over the red curls covering her ears. "I thought our hearing was supposed to be going too."

Already the cigarette smoke from a banquette behind us was drifting into my nostrils, tickling my allergies. The pounding bass beat made the stool legs and the tabletop vibrate, a slight, shrilly annoying sensation that made me move my hands to the boxy black satin evening bag sitting on my perilously slanted lap.

Then an odd thing happened. I found my feet tapping the stool's wooden rail to the thunderous beat. Jim and I used to dance when we were dating, standing apart but near, gyrating to music not quite as loud but just as insistent. Married life and responsibilities had made that phase less than a memory. Now, here, unexpectedly, it came back. The Jim of those days came back—tall, thin, a bit raw, but so likable . . . and ultimately, so lovable.

I would not dissolve into more widow's tears; not in public. Jim's death had shown me how repressive the fifties had been: A public place was nowhere to display affection, fears, tears, or even opinions that might ruffle someone.

I wished that I had been less inhibited, and had gone to work sooner, had not neglected myself while I fulfilled the roles of wife and mother. Now husband and kids were gone, and I was like some gawky, awkward spinster despite my devotion to husband, home, and family. I was alone and aging, linked by telephones to my nearest and dearest. If I hadn't had work . . .

A new song—if you can call contemporary music that—came on. No, not a new one—an old one. The forgotten but familiar guitar twangs snapped my senses like a barrage of rubber bands. "Johnny Be Good."

"Oh," I said impulsively to Mary Lou. "Jim and I used to dance to that all the time when we were young. That rhythm makes me want to beat my feet on some floor all night."

Mary Lou glanced around the dim room. "Too bad there aren't any suitable partners in the employees' club—unless you want to ask the night security guard to dance," she added with a snicker. "He's here alone."

Harvey was a retiree past seventy—genial and paunchy, with a slight limp.

I jerked an elbow into her side. "Shhh!" With the music so blaring, I had to talk loud even to urge discretion. "I wouldn't ask anyone to dance, but I sure love that music. Uh! Listen to it! Doesn't it get your blood pumping? I loved to dance to that song." The deserted dance floor begged for some young people gyrating on it, even if they were only ghosts.

"Say," came a voice from the nearest banquette. "Jerry likes to dance and I don't. Why don't you two hit the floor?"

She was a beautiful young woman—dark-haired with classic features, and more, a kind face. Startled, I eyed her escort, a man I'd never seen at the company. He was perfectly presentable, a classic thirty-something with curly blond hair and the eager, energetic smile of a born salesman. Maybe his slight buckteeth enhanced that notion.

"I couldn't! I haven't danced in years."

"Go ahead," the young woman urged. "I hate to deprive Jerry."

He was getting up and coming toward me, his

friendly grin as unwelcome to me as a sinister leer. I was appalled. I wasn't used to making an unrespectable spectacle of myself: For thirty years, not doing that had been my vocation. How was I going to untangle myself gracefully from the damn high chair?

And still, at my back, the music's beat beckoned, making me giddy, making me reckless.

Who cared what a woman past fifty did? Jim and I had planned to dance again, a little, on the cruise. This unknown young man couldn't possibly be construed as anything but a "safe" sexless partner for a woman my age.

Besides, he was pulling back my stool. Before I knew it, I was tipped onto my tottery feet—the shoes were new—and we were threading past the empty tables to that empty, garishly lit dance floor where a ghost of a me I'd forgotten was urging, *Hurry up, the song will end. This is your last chance.*

"Do you whoosh dance?" he asked from behind me.

"What? I can't hear over the music."

"Push dance?"

"Push? No, I never heard of it—"

We were on the floor and I turned to my providential partner, hoping I wouldn't look too silly doing the gyrations of thirty years ago, the Swim and the Jerk. Maybe I would pick up some updated moves from my dance-loving partner.

He grabbed my hand.

No! We danced alone, in the old days, without touching, without accommodating ourselves to a partner. Didn't they still do that? Isn't that what was on MTV all the time nowadays?

He swung me behind him, his strength, unexpected in such a wiry short man, jerking me around like a Raggedy Ann doll. I turned, dazed, and he jerked me in the opposite direction. I was dizzy already, and disoriented, and the soles of my untried high heels skidded over the slick floor.

He never let me go. He never let me stand in one place. It didn't matter what I did, I was an object he manipulated. He twirled me under his arm and I felt the underarm seam of my new dress rip. I wasn't dressed for this kind of workout, this kind of wrenching.

Around me, the seductively throbbing music had become a relentless cage of lyrics and never-ending beat.

Way down yonder in New Orleans . . .

Spun, turned, twisted, jerked in unanticipated directions, then snapped in the opposite direction . . . dizzy . . . as if trapped for endless minutes on a state fair ride you regret going on the moment it starts hurtling you in some unnatural motion . . .

This wasn't dancing as I knew it, as I had expected, where I stood alone on my own two feet and was in control of myself. This was like a French Apache dance. The only hand-holding dance I had ever done was the sedate lindy hop as a preteen; this was a frenetic jitterbug. I could only hope he wouldn't lift me off the floor and throw me around like they used to.

Then, midway through a powerful jerk, his fingers released mine. I saw his grinning face. In the lurid light it looked demonic.

He had released me in midmotion. Like any thrown object, I kept moving, out of control. My shoe slipped on the floor. I was spinning, downward. To the floor. Hard.

The music—I had thought it was a short song, but perhaps it had been a shorter dance than the forever it felt like—twanged on. I was sitting on the floor looking like a fool, an incompetent old fool, breathless with the shock of the fall.

He came to help me up, but I pulled away, feeling my face redden as it hadn't in years, and struggled gracelessly to my feet, my high heels snagging in the full chiffon skirt.

When I turned, trying not to look beyond the dance floor to my watching co-workers, I saw him waiting for me.

"I wanted to dance alone," I shouted over the scream of the sound system. "Separately." My arms gestured apart.

He grabbed one.

I couldn't believe that he wouldn't stop, wouldn't let me go.

Jerk. I was pulled beyond him into the dark, noisy outer space beyond the shining neon planet of the dance floor, where people I knew and didn't know were grinning at the spectacle I made.

Just when I thought I would hurl into merciful darkness, his arm jerked me back into the vortex of noise and neon and his grinning face. Twirl. Pull. Spin. Jerk.

Dizziness had escalated to utter disorientation. I didn't know where dance floor or watchers were, where dark and light began and ended. I just tried to keep on my feet until the damn, driving music ended and freed me.

It did just that far too late. He released my hand.

"What were you doing?" I demanded in the quiet moment before another selection began.

"Dancing," he said, still grinning.

"I didn't know that dance."

He shrugged. Was it a matter of pride with him, that he was a short man strong enough to jerk even an inexperienced partner around the floor? You would think a good dancer, a gentleman, would not want to try anything so athletic with an unknown partner that it would send her to the floor. You would think.

I was steady enough to walk back to my table, imagining what my friends thought, or would say, but I was too numb to say anything more. Our drinks had arrived. Connie and Mary Lou were studiously sipping away before their sympathetic eyes met mine.

"We'll have to try it again sometime," he said blandly in parting. I couldn't believe his nonchalance about it all, like he tossed women to the floor every day.

"I don't think so."

He smiled again, grinned. "Sometime when we haven't been drinking."

"I was perfectly sober," I said indignantly, knowing that such assertions always sounded like their opposite, but my Bloody Mary hadn't even arrived until now.

His smile smug and disbelieving, he vanished back to his young woman, who was also smiling. I understood now why the lovely young lady with the kind face wouldn't dance with him.

"Forget it," Mary Lou said in the ladies' room at work the next day, fluffing her moussed curls with a metal pick. "He's just a jerk."

"But he made me look like a fool! Why? And then he acted as if it was *my* fault, like I was a lush or something."

She shrugged. "Nobody will remember that you fell in a few days."

"Everybody will think I'd been drinking."

"Maybe. But hey, you've got reason to let loose a little. They've all done something like that."

"I don't even know who that young couple was, where they work."

"Accounting, I think, both of them. Those people come and go."

"Not soon enough."

Martha in Personnel was an elevator friend of mine; we only chatted going up or down together, but we did a lot of that.

"Jerry in Accounting?" She frowned, her darkly penciled brows drawing together. She had the lacquered hair and nails of a woman groomed to greet the public, a longtime receptionist. "We've got more than one. Why are you interested?"

I lowered my voice and told her. Martha was about my age. She raised an irked eyebrow.

"What a dirty trick! And you didn't even know that push dancing is a cousin to slam dancing. You don't do that kind of a dance with a partner you haven't practiced with, or who doesn't know the dance pretty well."

"Slam dancing," I said in horror, for even I had heard of that violent exercise. "How do you know about this push dancing?"

"My kids, of course," she said. "It's like jitterbug, and it's getting popular again, but it's not for amateurs. Tell you what, I'll look him up in the computer."

Her nails clicked on her clacking keyboard. "Got a Jerry Snyder . . . or a Kimball."

Inspired, I asked, "Which one is on the employee club board?"

"That info wouldn't be in here."

"I don't suppose his description is in his file."

"This ain't police headquarters, honey. But . . ." She glanced around. "You could always go down to Accounting and check it out."

"I don't want to see him again," I said between tight teeth. "I just want to tell him off from a safe distance, so I don't kill him. If I had his phone number, I'd tell him what he did so he doesn't do it again to anyone else."

"Don't you think he knows what he did?"

"No! I think he's a thoughtless creep without any manners who imagines himself God's gift to dancing women."

"Tell you what." Martha's lethally long crimson fingernail tapped the edge of her keyboard. "You make sure it's the right Jerry, and I'll get you his home phone number."

* * *

Accounting was foreign territory to me; my work never called me down there. The place was a maze of the latest office cubicles, sleek, neutral-colored, and impersonal. I wandered through, feeling like an awkward intruder, ready to jump if my particular bogeyman popped up from a cubicle like a jack-in-the-box. Every cubicle I peeked into was a potential bomb of unwanted recognition for me.

"Oh."

I had not found him, but I had found her. The nameplate on her inner cubicle wall read "Misty Weatherall."

"Hi." She looked as surprised as I did.

"I'm . . . looking for your young man."

"Jerry?"

"Yeah."

"He's not my young man. I just went out with him a couple of times. I won't anymore."

"Why not?"

"He's kind of . . . got a chip on his shoulder."

"Why did you suggest I dance with him?"

"I overheard you saying you wanted to dance, and I don't dance."

"You don't push dance?"

"No."

"Have you ever danced with Jerry?"

"Once. The second time we went out."

"And?"

Her eyes evaded mine. "I didn't fall, but I didn't like it."

"Is that why you sicced him on me?"

"Listen, you said you wanted to dance. I thought

49

you knew how, that you could handle that kind of thing. And I sure didn't want to dance with him."

"Is that the only reason you aren't going out with him again?"

"Well, there's you. Once you two hit the floor, it was obvious that you weren't up to his speed. He should have stopped."

"Thanks."

"And he's awfully bitter about his ex-wife. It gets tiresome hearing him going on about it. Actually, I dated him because I felt sorry for him; then I felt sorry for me." She frowned. "He doesn't take no for an answer. He's going to be hard to cut loose. I guess we both made a mistake."

"Do you have his phone number?"

"Never needed it."

"What's his last name, anyway."

"Snyder."

"Is he on the employee club committee?"

"Sure, he's program chairman now. Why do you think we all ended up in his favorite venue?"

"Wait a minute, if you overheard me wishing I could dance, did you both overhear me complaining that a singles' nightclub wasn't a great place for a meeting?"

Her dark eyes shifted to her computer screen, where a complex table of numbers stood frozen in their amber rankings. She tapped a key and the screen went black. "I heard it."

"Could he have?"

"I guess, but it was my idea to suggest the two of you dance."

"You didn't suggest the kind of dance, though."

She shrugged again and looked at me. "Jerry doesn't do any other kind of dancing."

I went back to Martha and got the phone number.

It did me no good.

I called it in the evenings, several evenings. All I ever got was an answering machine and a smarmy recorded message that "Jerry was out having fun."

I never left a message. I wanted to hear him respond when I told him what he had done; how irresponsible he had been. How my dress was too fragile and my shoes too new for such gymnastics, how boorish it was to hurl a strange woman old enough to be his mother around a dance floor in such a violent manner. I wanted to tell him what a cad he was to blame my fall on alcohol. All right, "cad" was a melodrama word. I wanted to tell him what a jerk he was.

"He never answers his phone himself," I complained to Connie one day. "Probably people are standing in line to tell him off."

"Why not confront him at work?"

"I've made enough scenes in front of my co-workers."

Mary Lou had overheard us and bustled over, waving papers. "I told her to forget the jerk," she explained to Connie. "He doesn't care anyway."

"Yeah." Connie's smooth blond head nodded without disturbing a hair. "Some guys are like that; they get a kick out of rattling women's cages."

"That's just it. I felt like I was caged with a wild animal out there on the dance floor. I could have seriously injured myself when I fell, broken a leg. It was . . . social assault."

"God, you women." Gene, the assistant manager, was suddenly behind me. "Everything's rape nowadays."

Speechless, I watched him walk away before I could answer, feeling rage boil over.

"He's a jerk, too," Connie said softly. "Mary Lou's right. Forget it. There isn't anything you can do about it."

Some acts in life are too uncivil to be borne, and sometimes they seem very small things on the surface.

I can't help feeling that way. I was reared in a generation in which children were to be seen and not heard, when politeness was an expected feature of daily life, and when most people were assumed to mean well. If knighthood was no longer in flower (I'm not that old), men—except for the most illiterate types who still spat in the street—were expected to behave like gentlemen.

I began calling Jerry Snyder impolitely early in the morning when he would be getting ready for the office, and even on weekends. Always the answering machine. Jerry was out having "fun." I even tried calling at three in the morning, one night when I couldn't sleep. I was having trouble sleeping; I kept going over and over the incident in my mind, wondering if he did it deliberately because I had criticized his idea of entertainment, deciding what I would say to him when I finally cornered the rat. He deserved a good dressing down.

Martha got me his address as well, with only a lift of her eyebrow for comment.

I looked it up on the city map: deep in a nest of new apartment complexes for young singles on the city fringes.

I drove by one Saturday, looking for his unit. The buildings suggested Swiss chalets. A flashy fountain spit high into the air in an artificial pond near the complex's center. Complex was the name for the place, although it was pretentiously called Wood-winds. Laid out at angles, each building's numbers hid discreetly. I finally found number 66—a second-story unit reached by both exterior stairs and an internal elevator.

If all else failed, I could waylay him; confront him in person at his door. That meant I had to park our '85 gray Honda Civic and wait. He would have to come back to that apartment sometime.

But he didn't, not all day Saturday, and not as late as ten o'clock, when I finally gave up and left.

I needed more information than Martha's user-friendly personnel files would provide. I thought about it. With his car license and description, I could find his car in the employee section of the parking ramp and follow him home after work, just like a lost dog.

The telephone again. Stomach fluttering, I called the Motor Vehicles department.

"I have a problem," I told the woman who answered, wanting to sound flustered and innocent and having no trouble doing that. I wasn't used to extracting possibly confidential information. "A gentleman and I got into a fender bender the other day. He gave me his card, but I'm in sales and call on a lot of people who give me cards, and the accident shook me up. Now my insurance company needs the information. I think I know which card it is, and have a likely name. Could you tell me what the car looks like from your records, and then I'll be sure it's the right person?"

The pause made my heart beat triple time. "I'll transfer you to someone who can help."

I repeated my spiel to a man this time, my nervousness all the more genuine. I'm sure he was thinking, "just like a woman," when he looked up the name. The computer, he told me, would take a few moments to sift through all those names for the right one in the right town.

"Two cars, ma'am. A yellow eighty-six Corvette and a black seventy-two Chevrolet Impala."

"Oh, it was the black Chevrolet. I remember it was an older car," I exclaimed with honest relief. "I certainly would have remembered the Corvair."

"Corvette," he corrected in a weary, condescending tone.

Good. I had been made to look like a fool on the dance floor, and now I was discovering that it could serve my purpose to look like one elsewhere. The clerk would never be suspicious of such a ditsy middle-aged woman.

I didn't have the license numbers—I didn't want to stir doubts by asking for too much. Better safe than sorry; I knew that from recent experience.

On my lunch hour I prowled the employee parking levels. Parking ramps are eerie, echoing places. Women are always urged to be wary in them, but now I relished the deserted air, the scrape of my shoes on cement and the squeal of cars turning down the exit ramp the only sounds. Our employees invariably ate at their desks or downtown.

Not being an expert in cars, I had purchased a Blue Book and went down the rows, proud when I stood before the broad black rear of the correct-vintage car. I jotted down the license number on my notepad.

I always got off half an hour earlier than Accounting employees. All I would have to do is drive out and park on the street near the exit—not easy during rush hour with limited spots, but if I went round and round until something turned up, it should work. And I should . . . wear a hat or scarf, so he wouldn't recognize me. Tonight. I would put the plan into operation right after work tonight.

Everything went perfectly. I bought a nondescript scarf on my lunch hour. I looked like a grandmother, but all the better. *Oh, what big eyes you have, Grandmother!* I thanked God now that Jim and I hadn't been able to afford a flashy new car someone might notice. My hands gripped the Civic's wheel, even though I was parked; the motor was running and I was ready.

As cars poured in a relentless stream from the parking ramp's mouth, I had only a moment to identify the right vehicle. This was the hardest part. Cars all looked alike to me, except for the most flagrant. And so many people had black, gray, and white cars these days. With dirt and dust, they all faded into one monotonous neutral stream.

Then—a large, dusty-black silhouette, a flash of blond curly hair. I wrenched the steering wheel and checked the traffic stream in my left mirror—a truck coming fast in my entry lane.

I pressed the accelerator and spun out of the parking place. Behind me an angry trucker honked. I didn't care; I was only a car behind the black '72 Chevrolet.

I stayed behind, but it never went onto the Loop towards Woodwinds. That unnerved me. I knew how to get there. I didn't know where the car would take me now.

Then, after we left the crowded downtown and I did get an idea, I didn't like where it was leading me—out to the dingy circle of deteriorating neighborhoods that ringed the downtown, we drove. Out where makeshift Vietnamese restaurants stand next door to pawnshops and laundromats and missions, and even big, belching city buses drive by fast. Out where gangs wage war and men lie like the dead in alleyways, drunk or drugged or even really dead.

It was still broad daylight, but driving through that area dimmed my vision; I was as nervous as if nightfall veiled my senses.

Jerry stopped his car before a seedy-looking three-story brick apartment building from the twenties. He vanished inside. Too scared to venture after him, I decided to wait for him to come out again.

And, again, he didn't, at least not by eight o'clock, which was as long as I dared stay, even with all the car doors locked.

I decided I had to follow him again, and I needed more protection than locks. I was able to purchase a can of pepper spray from the gun section of the local mall's sports outlet. Standing at the glass counter with all the mechanical black and silver weapons laid out on shelves beneath me was . . . nerve-racking. The young man behind the counter even assumed I wanted to buy a gun.

"Can just anybody do that?" I asked with an uneasy laugh.

"Yes, ma'am. Just fill out a form and wait a few days. Want to see anything?"

I eyed the foreign instruments. That's what they looked like, instruments for some strange manufacturing process. "No, thanks. The human bug spray should do it."

"How about a movie tonight? *Jurassic Park* should be running out of hordes of kids by now at the cheapie theaters."

Connie and Mary Lou stood beside my desk like the Bobbsey Twins, radiating innocent eagerness.

"No . . . uh, thanks. I have to volunteer at the old folks' home tonight."

They finally left, after more idle chitchat, which I had no time for. I had things to do.

Driving behind Jerry after work that day was a picnic. In fact, I had brought along a thermos of coffee and had packed a sandwich and raw veggies with a cookie in an Igloo cooler—I hadn't made lunches like that since the kids were in grade school. I was prepared for the long haul. He was not going to elude me this time. Besides, it was so fascinating to watch the smartly suited young accountant vanish into that disreputable building. Why?

This time I didn't park the moment he went in. I drove around the block, undeterred by overflowing Dumpsters and a ragged man shuffling down the alley behind Jerry's place. Alley! On the next cruise through, I turned down that narrow way lined with dented silver garbage cans and littered with trash.

I counted the buildings as I drove and—yes! A shambling wooden garage for four cars hunkered behind Jerry's building. The alley was narrower, dimmer, meaner than the street, but I found a deserted garage to park by. Then I slumped behind the wheel and waited.

None too soon. A dirty door in Jerry's garage began crawling upward on its tracks, screeching with age. Shortly after, a sleek, low yellow rear edged out. Jerry backed the Corvette in the absolutely wrong direction to the way I was facing. Frantic, I balled up my fists, then started the car and seesawed it out of the cramped spot. The Corvette was gone when I was once more pointed down the alley, but I hit the accelerator and sped at forty miles an hour down the lane. One wasn't supposed to drive more than twenty in an alley, I remembered from my long-ago driver's test, but this was an emergency.

My car paused for the side street as I peered right and left. A yellow glint at my right made me jerk the wheel that way. The old car squealed at such treatment; Jim would know why a steering wheel always did that when cranked too hard. I didn't care. I followed the car back onto the street in front of the apartment buildings.

The Corvette was attracting greedy street glances now, but Jerry was impervious, fleeing this sad neighborhood. My car attracted no notice, from the street men or from Jerry.

We headed for the Loop at last, and I was mentally

rehearsing my diatribe against him, which by now had become quite a production. He would finally face what he had done and realize his behavior had been thoughtless at best and caddish at worst.

But the yellow Corvette did not take the exit for Woodwinds.

Instead of entering an affluent apartment complex, I finally found my car sitting in the parking lot before a big, boxy building identified only by a big, boxy, cheap-looking sign high on a pole beside it.

"Foxy Chix," it read, none too legibly. "Topless dancing. Beautiful babes."

I sighed, and set about eating dinner and drinking coffee and waiting for dark, which no longer scared me, because then I would be invisible.

With the pepper spray in my right hand, I waited past eleven. The yellow—atrocious color for a car, and yet how fitting to his poisonous personality!— Corvette was impossible to miss, even at night in the dimly lit parking lot. Sinister customized vans hiding who-knows-what in their roomy, secret interiors, pickup trucks, junkers and sports cars whose names I didn't know, and massive motorcycles sprinkled the lot around me. It was only a weeknight, after all.

About eleven-thirty I noticed movement by the Corvette and sat up straight.

I dared to roll down the window a bit. Voices, abrading voices, drifted in through it. A man's and a woman's.

"I told you to leave me alone, Jerry! Damn it, why do you come here!" Her voice was ragged, raw and on the verge of sobs. "I'm working."

"I pay for my drinks like anybody else. I can watch you like anybody else, Tiffany." He sneered the name, obvious pseudonym that it was.

"I don't want to see you anymore."

"But I can see you any time I want, all of you. Come on, get in the car."

"No! I just want you out of here. Get a life, get another girl, get one who wants you. I don't."

Something rang in the air, the clap of a hand on a face. I started the motor, thinking of my own two daughters, who would never be caught dead in a place like this, yet . . .

I shifted into gear. I didn't want to . . . to blow my cover, but I could see the two figures interlocked, and this time the push dancing was serious.

I pulled on my headlights and pointed my car at them. They were framed and frozen by lights like deer on the highway.

Jerry's face wore the same leer/sneer I knew so well from my one nightmarish dance with him. The girl who was shaken in his grasp, being pulled this way and that, now suddenly jerked to face the lights. Her expression was unforgettable, fear and struggle masking her pretty, made-up features. I was aware of long, bare legs and arms, of white boots and some skimpy sort of cover-up, of flying long red hair etched into flaming tendrils against the car's garish yellow background.

"Let me go, Jerry," she begged as she saw her opportunity. "Just let go and don't come back."

He glared into the corona of my headlights, looking for someone to blame behind the wheel. Then he released her so quickly that she fell, fell hard against the car. My foot pressed the accelerator as he jumped into the Corvette's low front seat.

In a moment he had roared away with taillights as red as the devil's eyes glaring back at us. I slowed to cruise past the dazed and shaken girl. She stared mindlessly into my driver's window as I passed. I knew that in the dark it was only a blank, black grease-blob of glass, and that I was nameless and faceless, just another passerby in the night.

The phone was ringing when I got home.

"Linda! Mary Lou and I were worried sick! If you're going to be out so late, let us know."

"What did you call for?"

"Well, we wanted to take you out to dinner. You've been keeping to yourself so much lately. You dash out of work every night like a rabbit scurrying home to its burrow. We're worried that silly incident at Portnoy's is turning you into a hermit."

I tried not to laugh.

The next day, I decided my investigation needed to take a new tack. Martha could help me again.

"Ex-wife?" She frowned at her computer screen. "I doubt we'd have that."

"She wasn't always 'ex.' Maybe she was listed as next of kin when he applied for work here."

"Why do you want it?"

"Oh, it's silly, but I thought . . . maybe if I understood him, if I knew why he was so hostile to women that he took it out on me, a complete stranger—old enough to be his mother, for heaven's sake—I'd be a little more understanding of what happened."

Martha grinned up at me. *"Cherchez le* shrink, huh?"

"Who knows a man better than an ex-wife?"

Maybe an ex-dance partner was beginning to.

I looked so respectable that she let me into her apartment almost immediately. Her name was Karen. She was a tiny woman almost overwhelmed by her cloud of bouffant brown hair, the painfully thin kind who always look cold, hunched somehow, but pretty if habitual anxiety hadn't sharpened her face. When I told her I was there about Jerry, her haunted features grew even starker, all cheekbones and big eyes and soft, scared mouth.

"Oh, God, I can't even stand to hear his name. I just want to forget him, I just want him to—please, God—forget me."

I told her why I couldn't forget him, and she just nodded. "Listen . . ."

"Linda."

"Listen, Linda, he is such bad news. You're lucky that all he threw you around was a dance floor. And his hate just escalates."

I glanced at the impressive battery of locks and chains on the front door.

She nodded. "My name's not on the mailbox and I have an unpublished number. Every time it rings I'm afraid it might be him anyway. I'm just grateful he found that stripper. I had a lawyer who was trying to represent my rights in the divorce, but Jerry got so ugly that I finally just took the divorce papers and ran, left him everything. God, I am so glad to be out of there."

"So now she's got him," I mused. "Looks like the only way to escape him is if he finds another victim."

"Look, it's not like that. I wouldn't wish him on anybody. But he doesn't let go easily." She shook her head and bit her already raw lip. "And I don't understand the creepy apartment near downtown, the two cars . . . although I bet he got the 'Vette with what would have been my part of the divorce settlement. All I know is that he was meaner than a junkyard dog, abusive, obsessive, and he was just getting worse. I'm lucky to be alive."

I stood to leave. "Thanks for the insight. I'm shocked but not surprised. This puts my dance from hell into a different light."

When I left I kept seeing Karen's old-young face and hearing her soft, tremulous voice. I thought about my two distant, happily married, wholesome daughters and their dull textbook husbands and suburban houses. I thanked God, and I knew I couldn't stop now.

The sleazy street in front of Jerry Snyder's apartment building was never deserted. I wore an old raincoat I'd kept for yard work in cold weather and the dowdy scarf and tennis shoes. I parked a half block away and shuffled toward his building ignoring the men on the street, my pepper spray clutched in a fist tucked into a pocket.

The building's deserted lobby was like a movie set: peeling gray paint, cigarette butts and advertising flyers stuck to the vinyl tile floor, a battered rank of painted gray metal mailboxes. Tattered pieces of paper identified some of the units as occupied; last names were the only clue to who lived there. Once this tawdry puzzle-board with half the words missing would have stymied me, brought me to the brink of tears with frustration. Now I wasn't so easily put off. Of course, "Jerry Snyder" was nowhere listed. One word caught my eye. Rider. It rhymed with Snyder and sounded like a C.B. radio handle, a second, secret self-identity a macho-man would take. Rider. Maybe a man with two cars and two lives.

The landlady was what I'd expected—buxom, blowsy, indifferent, her television baby-sitting four fussing kids in the background. Her aquiline nose and challenging eyes didn't promise easy cooperation, but I softly told her that I'd come to town to tell my son that his daddy had died and I didn't know anywhere else to reach him and who knows where he was during the day . . .

My sad tale didn't soften her heard-it-all facade, but she didn't care about apartment house rules anyway. When I told her my name was Rider, she nodded.

"He doesn't hang around here much anyway, but he always pays his rent on time."

"Oh, I'm glad to hear that, about the rent, I mean."

She looked at me as if I were the most naive mother in the world. Obviously she found Rider's long absences suspiciously criminal, as did I. But she gave me the extra key. I trudged up three flights of filthy stairs and finally stood before door number nine.

The place was as grim inside as the untended hall outside. An ugly plaid sofa on its last legs was the only furniture in the living room. The tiny kitchen beyond was relatively clean, and equipped with a small microwave. The cupboards were sparsely stocked with instant coffee and discount-store eating utensils, glasses, cups, and dishes. The microwave dishes looked new. A bottom cupboard had an extensive if purely functional bar. In the ancient white refrigerator frozen meals crammed the frost-caked freezer—all trendy, low-fat entrées with angel hair pasta and the like. I thought of Jerry's curly blond cherub hair and shook my head.

Besides a front-room closet, mostly empty, only one other room opened off the living area. I opened the bedroom door and felt my knees go weak.

The room was wallpapered with women, women frozen in photographic pornography—some the soft-core, soft-focus images seen in shrink-wrapped magazines; most of it vile, sadistic stuff I'd never imagined. Ordinary, innocent snapshots of Jerry's ex-wife, Karen, were tacked up among the raw stuff, and lots of black-and-white photos of the girl I'd seen him arguing with outside Foxy Chix, obviously taken while she was performing. I inched along the photo-papered walls.

Stark black-and-white photos of other real women punctuated the lushly colored and brutal images of anonymous, writhing women: women spread-eagled, women bound, whipped, chained, raped. One small photo of a smiling, pretty young girl had obviously been cut from a high school yearbook. Another subject of a "real" photo, I saw with a shudder, was just a child. I forced myself to study the pornography, the women's faces contorted in pain passing for passion. Then, between the spread thighs of a leather-masked woman, I spotted a small black-and-white photo of myself. Self-recognition was a body blow; my heart pounded, even harder when I realized the photo's source. The employees' club monthly newsletter. I had been cited as a top employee of my department *two* years before. I was a trophy, too, carefully recorded, though a small one.

In the bedroom closet I waded past sadomasochistic props to find boxes of copper-tipped bullets, huge heavy-handled knives, hunting knives, I think. No gun here, but I found lots of the same used, nondescript clothing I wore now, suspended from cheap wire hangers like empty carcasses.

I returned the key and left, wondering if the landlady would bother to tell Rider his mother had called.

I called the police, like a good citizen. Finally referred to a harried-sounding woman detective, I was told that until Jerry did something provable and punishable, nothing in his behavior or his lifestyle was a crime. They could watch him to see if he was involved in a pornography ring if I would give them his name . . . She addressed me as "ma'am" every other sentence. I hung up.

Karen was easy to disguise; just slap some makeup on her whitewashed face and draw her hair back into a sleek ponytail. We bought her a black leather jacket so she would look a little tougher. I wore a blond wig my second daughter had to have when she was eighteen and left behind when she married, and junked up my clothes as best I could.

The taped hard rock music inside Foxy Chix was earsplitting. It made Portnoy's seem like a wake. I identified Jerry's latest girl the moment the stage spotlights hit her long red hair. The show didn't shock me. What these women did was pretty tame, and even playful, compared to the wall of photographs, even though they both fed the same sick needs in a working woman's simple quest to survive . . .

It was easy to talk to Tiffany—after finishing their acts, the women strolled topless among the tables of men. I hooked her attention with a fifty-dollar bill. Maybe lesbians came in here occasionally, but I doubted that. It didn't bother me if anyone thought that's what I was, anyway.

Karen and I took her to an all-night diner nearby, where we huddled in a back booth and everybody had hot fudge sundaes on me.

We told her what Jerry had done to us. She told us what Jerry had done to her, which was worse, much worse. She didn't have to tell us how scared she was. She would leave the planet to escape him, if she could, but she had to work, she had to live somewhere. She could be found. I told her what I'd already told Karen—about Jerry's secret life and how his sanctuary was equipped for bloody murder.

"He's got to be stopped," I said.

Tiffany slurped the last sweet liquid from the bottom of her glass. "Do you mean what I think you do? I don't have the nerve—"

"I'll buy the gun," I said quickly. "I know just where to go. The young man behind the counter said he'd 'walk me through it,' whatever that means. A woman my age, a widow suddenly living alone, logically feels the need for home protection. We should clean out his hole. Mama Rider can do it. The landlady won't care if he never comes back as long as the apartment is empty and clean. The police may ask you two some questions. Have good answers."

"But . . ." Karen's thin face showed hope for the first time. "What about that incident with Jerry on the dance floor? You could be a suspect if something happened to him."

I shook my head to dismiss that objection. I had finally put that sad little episode into the proper proportion.

"Don't worry about that. Like my friends kept telling me, I was making a mountain out of a molehill. Dancing with intent to humiliate is not a killing offense, for heaven's sake. Everybody's forgotten about it. Everybody."

Rule of Law

K. K. Beck

My name is Marius van Houten, and I am a lawyer, just as my father was before me. My grandfather was a lawyer too, so it isn't too surprising that I am able to maintain a businesslike demeanor in the face of any kind of strong emotion. For three generations, we van Houtens have sat quietly across the desk as our clients grew red in the face, made their hands into fists, pounded stacks of papers, swore and shouted. It has been our job to make order out of chaos and conflict, to find legal solutions to human problems. Perhaps it is in our genes, although the line will die out with me.

I was in my office reviewing the will of old Meneer van Dongen. He was a very, very old man, and a very, very rich one. This old pirate had lived in a villa in Aardenhout, and I had handled his business affairs for many years. He had outlived two other lawyers.

He had mentioned, when I first began my association with him, that he had a proper will which left his considerable fortune to one of his nephews.

There were two nephews, he explained. The first emigrated right after the war. "A good lad with the right stuff in him," van Dongen had said, nodding through a cloud of cigar smoke. The other, he had taken reluctantly into business with him, and he had been disappointed.

In fact, he had told me that the second nephew had stolen from him. "I could have gone to the law," he said, "but the little bastard whined and carried on to his mother—my sister. I agreed to drop the matter if he left the country. Last I heard, he was in Australia. A good place for him. All descended from a bunch of criminals anyway."

"I think nowdays they are reasonably law-abiding," I said. "Although they do drive on the wrong side of the road."

This feeble witticism had been met with great glee. Meneer van Dongen, a rough sort who had made his fortune in Indonesia years ago when it was still a Dutch colony, used to tell me that he liked having a dull, boring lawyer handle his affairs. Yet whenever I tried to joke with him a little, he seemed pleased, as if he, somehow, were humanizing me. I had allowed him this pleasure once in a while.

And now van Dongen was dead. A heart attack after a heavy meal. The housekeeper found him in front of the television set the next morning. It was she who had delivered the will I was reading now, and it was just as he had described it.

The fortunate nephew's name and address were

there. He lived in Los Angeles, California, and his name was Nicolaas Octavius Overdijk. He got everything, unless he had predeceased his uncle, in which case everything went to the housekeeper.

Octavius! That ridiculous second name! His mother must have been a very foolish woman. That silly name could seal his fate, because it could only be he. My own Nico Overdijk.

I looked up from the will at Anneke, my secretary. She just smiled. She hadn't noticed any reaction, thank goodness. Anneke so often knows what I am thinking.

The poor girl is in love with me, I thought. She'd been my secretary for seven or eight years at that point, and she was in her forties when she arrived, so I suppose she's no longer a girl. Foolish Anneke. Someday, I thought, I must tell her very delicately how hopeless it is to love an old bachelor like me.

There might have been a time when I could have married and had a normal family life. But that time had passed. It probably ended on the night back in 1943 when I was six years old. It ended with that knock on the door.

"He must come to Holland to settle the estate," I said, rousing myself, handing Anneke the will. "Draft a letter. In English, I think. Enclose a copy of the will."

Some weeks later, we received a reply. Mr. Overdijk didn't want to come to Holland. He wanted me to settle everything. He wished me to communicate with his American lawyer and provide a full inventory of his uncle's assets. He would then send instructions on how to liquidate the estate and wanted to receive some kind of bank draft in U.S. funds.

I wrote his American lawyer. Mr. Overdijk's presence in Holland was essential. The estate was very complex. Dutch law was different from American law, and these differences would make things even more complicated. (Here I threw in some irrelevant facts about Dutch taxation, designed to confuse.) Mr. Overdijk's signature would be required on innumerable documents. In addition, the contents of the house had to be gone through. There were many valuable artifacts there, as well as some good pictures. One of them was thought to be a Frans Hals, though its provenance was murky.

Anneke was suspicious. She knew our work would be much easier without Nicolaas Overdijk. He was willing to let us settle things on our own and to allow us to deal with another lawyer.

"No," I said firmly when she brought all this up in her quiet but insistent way. "I want him here. I want him on Dutch soil."

And then the unquestioning Anneke said something she seldom said to me. "Why?" she said. Her face, pale and pinkish, looked hurt. "Is there something you aren't telling me?"

I sighed and turned around to face the wall for a moment. I might as well tell her. She would find out soon enough in any case. Perhaps it was better that I tell her. Perhaps it would even prevent me from acting impulsively.

"The man is a war criminal," I replied. "I intend to talk to the Ministry of Justice about his case." But until Anneke had said, "Why?" I hadn't intended that at all. I didn't know what my plans were. I didn't know whether they included legal measures. Papa had been a great champion of the rule of law, and what had happened to him? The barbarians came and took him, and Mama too, and all because of that silly pamphlet. "The Rule of Law," it had been called.

I turned around again. Anneke was looking worried, and twisting her hair at the side of her face like a little girl. Suddenly I grew impatient. "Oh, don't look at me like that!" I said irritably. I regretted it at once, but she didn't crumple as I expected. She gave me another look—one I'd never seen before. She tilted her head back with her chin up and her eyes narrowed defiantly. "Very well," she said, leaving the room.

It occurred to me that she might leave. I was horrified. All those peaceful years together. And I needed her now, more than ever.

I went into the outer office after her. She seemed to be sorting papers on her desk furiously. An ominous sign. Was she planning to clear out?

"Anneke, I'm sorry," I said. "Let me take you to lunch. Please."

She stopped sorting the papers and looked at me angrily for a moment. Then she sighed in a sulky way and said, "All right." She opened her handbag and took out a lipstick and a mirror and painted her mouth. I was surprised. Anneke always looked neat and presentable, her rather old-fashioned face always subtly made-up, but she had never allowed me to see her actually do anything that reflected any concern with her appearance. Her applying lipstick like this seemed very intimate and blatantly coquettish.

I took her to a very nice restaurant near the office.

We had a sherry before lunch. The food hadn't even arrived before she bore down on me. "Marius," she said, "tell me." After she had worked for me for three years, I had asked her to call me by my first name. She had assented, but in actual practice still managed to avoid calling me anything for the subsequent years.

I told her. Who else was there to tell?

"In 1943," I said, leaning back in my chair and putting the tips of my fingers together like the pompous old lawyer I had become, "I was six years old. There was a knock at the door. It was late. My parents had actually forgotten to put me to bed. I played with my big wooden train in the hall while they talked behind the closed glass doors of the parlor.

"I couldn't imagine why they had let me stay up so late. I had just learned to tell time, and there was a big grandfather clock in the hall. An old one with a moon and the sun rotating on a separate dial on the face. It was ten o'clock, and they just kept talking in low, worried tones. I tried to be as quiet as possible so they would forget about me and let me stay up.

"When the knock came, my mother rushed out to me. She picked me up, kissed me, and put me in a big old-fashioned wardrobe that stood there, and tucked me in among coats and galoshes.

"Be still," she said. "Whatever happens, be still. Papa and I may go away tonight, but we love you. If we are not here in the morning, then go to Mevrouw Huisinga next door."

I nodded sleepily and she gently closed the two doors that closed in the middle, leaving me just a few centimeters to look out."

Anneke began to cry and I looked down at the tablecloth and straightened the silver.

"The Gestapo came. And they brought with them a local member of the NSB. We all knew who he was. Nico Overdijk. Young, tall, blond. A little swaggering baby collaborator. Mama and Papa left. Forever."

"My God," said Anneke. "And you're sure he's the same one?"

I nodded. "I found out later he had that silly second name—Octavius. He was the one who denounced my father. For a little leaflet about the rule of law."

"And you had no idea that Meneer van Dongen was his uncle?" said Anneke now, taking my handkerchief I offered her and drying her tears.

"No. Ironic, isn't it? I've spent years doing everything I can to make sure van Dongen's estate is in fine shape so it can all be handed over to the man who killed my parents. It makes you wonder about justice."

"I had wondered," said Anneke, "about you."

"Well," I said briskly, "it will take some time, but I want us to make inquiries and see if we can arrange to have the little thug brought to justice."

Later, I cursed myself for telling Anneke. Because I knew that nothing would be done about Nico. I had managed only to get a lot of bureaucratic claptrap from the Justice Ministry. The case was too old. It had been put on some sort of inactive status in 1947. Yes, there was an ancient file on Nico Overdijk, now apparently an American citizen, but the Dutch government had no interest in pursuing the case. The young woman I discussed all of this with had been born long after the war.

"You realize he's coming tomorrow," I said to Anneke. "We're going to hand over a fortune to him and he'll leave again."

"There are the Americans," said Anneke, who had become an expert on the case in a period of weeks. "He could have his citizenship revoked. If he lied on his application to go to America, if he said he had never been a Nazi—"

"So what?" I said. "He'll just come back to Holland and live like a king in that villa in Aardenhout. It's the ones they used to want to send back to the old Soviet empire who once had something to fear."

Anneke and I met Overdijk and his wife at Schiphol airport. "Listen," I said to her harshly as we waited. "Not a word. Not a glance. Nothing to indicate we know who he is. I want you to promise that."

"Marius," she said. "I'm afraid. I've never seen you like this."

"There may still be some remedy, and I want him to feel completely safe. Not a word." I seized her arm and squeezed it until she let out a little cry, and then I apologized.

I don't know what I expected to see. A young blond bully, I suppose. The one I'd glimpsed through that cupboard door. Instead, I saw an old man. A fit old man, to be sure. Dark brown skin from the California sun, in strange contrast to the light blue eyes. Gray hair that had the look of having once been blond. And a big, friendly, open American-looking face.

His wife was younger. About fifty-five maybe. She

looked like an actress from some American television film. Too much bleached blond hair all puffed up around her head. She was dressed very casually, in a jogging outfit and running shoes, but with little bits of gold and diamond jewelry. She too was all smiles in that American way.

"Hi!" she said.

We exchanged greetings and introductions, while they shifted their suitcases around on their airport cart. I suggested we drive to the hotel in nearby Haarlem where we had reserved a room for them.

"Oh no," said Mrs. Overdijk, evidently speaking for both of them out of habit. "We want to stay at your uncle's place, don't we, honey?"

"Well, yes," he said, just a little uncertain.

"I want to see those pictures," she said. "There'll be a ton of stuff to go through. I've been through it all before when my mother died. These old people never throw away a thing. I bet there are some great antiques."

"It is a big house, full of many old things," said Anneke in her shy English.

"Well, maybe you can give me a hand, dear," said Mrs. Overdijk. "Men aren't any good at that kind of thing, and I need someone who knows the territory."

"I sure hope we can get this business cleared up quickly," said Nico to me, in Dutch. "I don't want to spend a lot of time here."

I bet you don't, I thought to myself. I managed to smile. "Perhaps it would be best if we all moved into Meneer van Dongen's house. Well, your house, actually. We can go over everything there much more quickly than if we have to drive or take the train back and forth to my office. It's a little irregular, of course, but it's a very large house, and the housekeeper is still in residence. I assumed you'd want to keep her on until we close things up."

"What's he saying?" said his wife, and I apologized for speaking Dutch in front of her and translated.

"Sounds good to me," she said.

She turned to Anneke. "You too, I hope. You know, you look like one of those Dutch pictures. Those ladies in rooms with the tile floors. You have such pretty skin."

Anneke blushed a little. "Anneke is a Vermeer," I said, smiling at her. I was sorry I'd squeezed her arm tightly. I hoped she could manage not to tip off Nico when we were all under the same roof. I was counting on her feelings for me.

"I just ruined my skin in the California sun," pouted Mrs. Overdijk. "Years and years I spent tanning, and now they say it's terrible for you." She held out her left arm and pushed up her sleeve. "Look. My driving arm is leathery and you get these little white flecks."

I imagined both of them driving the Los Angeles freeways, arms hanging out of the window, sunglasses on, radios blaring, years and years of aimless driving around while I was growing up alone here in Holland.

"Say, look at that," said Overdijk back in Dutch as we passed a kiosk in the airport. "Salt drops. I loved those when I was a kid. I haven't had one since I left this country. I've got to have some."

"What?" said his wife, obviously irritated at his lapse into his native language. He went over and bought a roll of the things.

"Licorice drops with salt instead of sugar," said Anneke. Her English was really very good. I wouldn't have known the word *licorice.* Anneke looked over at me. She seemed worried. I hoped she wouldn't fall apart. I patted her hand and smiled at her.

Van Dongen's villa hadn't changed in years. It was a big gloomy place, full of Oriental carpets and Indonesian bric-a-brac. It smelled of an old-fashioned cleaning agent called *spiritus.* After we went into the parlor and they stood there gawking for a minute, I went back out to the car to help Mevrouw Termeulen, the elderly housekeeper, carry in the luggage.

Overdijk didn't think of giving me a hand. He was wandering around, looking pleased. "Place hasn't changed since I was a boy," he exclaimed, shedding his jacket on the sofa. He was wearing a bright striped knit shirt and slacks. The man looked as if he's just wandered off the golf course, hopped on a plane, and come to pick up several millions. He'd probably had a perfectly delightful life. Did he ever wake up at night and think about the boy he'd been? I doubted it. He still seemed like a boy.

"My God," he said in English to his wife. "Nothing's changed." As far as I could tell, it sounded like he still had a strong Dutch accent in English. I couldn't hear that nasal American quality, and he had never mastered the devilish "th" sound, so "nothing" came out "nuzzing." "Let me show you around," he said to her. "The kitchen is back here. And the dining room." He led her through some old red velvet curtains that separated the parlor from the dining room.

"And the bedrooms are up the stairs here. The one I

used to stay in was right over a big linden tree. I'd climb up and down it when I was supposed to be in bed at night."

"My goodness," said his wife from the hall. "That Oriental runner down the stairs looks real. And look at those brass rods holding it down. They're so shiny. Imagine polishing them. That housekeeper must be a treasure."

"Maybe we should settle some money on her," said Nico.

"Well, maybe," replied his wife. "Was she around in your day?"

"No, but she's done a good job for the old boy over the years."

They went upstairs. Anneke turned to me. "What are you feeling?" she said.

"He's never worried about what he's done. Not for a moment," I said.

"She's very friendly," said Anneke.

"All Americans act like that," I said. "It doesn't mean a thing. She's a greedy woman. Can hardly wait to plow through this house and grab what she can. Mark my words, she'll be counting everything down to the last guilder."

"Marius," she said, "are you sure we should stay here? Is it really a good idea?"

"Why not?" I said. I didn't really have a plan. I just knew that I wanted him to realize that he couldn't get away with what he had done. He had been living on borrowed time for too long.

They came back downstairs, smiling those idiot grins.

"Well," I said. "You must be tired. Perhaps you'd like to rest. The time difference and so forth. Anneke and I will go to our homes and pack and return later this evening. Mrs. Termeulen can make us a meal, then we can all get an early start in the morning."

"Fine," said Overdijk, collapsing into a chair. He pulled his salted licorice drops from his pocket, opened the roll with a childish expression of pleasure, and popped one into his mouth.

"Those horrible salt drops," his wife said. "I have never understood how he can stand them. People are supposed to like sugar, not salt."

"In Holland we like sugar and salt," said Anneke.

"I used to get my hand slapped for poking it into the salt canister in the kitchen," said Overdijk. "Maybe we had poor diets or something."

"During the war we did," I said. "Most of us, anyway."

Overdijk didn't bat an eye. "It was pretty bad," he said to his wife. "The hunger winter, we called it. People ate tulip bulbs."

Mrs. Overdijk shuddered. "How terrible," she said. There were tears in her eyes. "I had no idea."

"I never talk much about the past," said Overdijk as if by way of explanation. "It's as if the past never happened. That's how it is when you emigrate."

Perhaps if I had emigrated, things would have been different. At one time, I thought I would. After the war the Red Cross took charge of me, and there was some talk of having me adopted by a Canadian couple. They even went so far as to send me pictures of their farm, a huge wheat farm somewhere in Alberta—as flat as Holland but not as crowded. Finally, though, they decided I was too old.

After my night in the wardrobe, I had gone to the neighbors as Mama had told me to do. They kept me for a while, then found some of my family. I moved around among some cousins during the war, always mindful that I shouldn't speak about what happened to my parents. I wasn't really sure what had happened to them, and I dreamed, of course, that they would come back and get me after the war.

An old aunt kept my hopes up, promising that when the Germans left, Mama and Papa would come back from the police station. However, most of the people who cared for me as best they could never spoke of my parents. I began to feel that their being taken away was somehow a shameful thing.

And I was always mindful of the fact that I was another mouth to feed. Boys can get so hungry. To this day I grow irrational when I see people waste food. But it was the silence about my parents that I believe had the most profound effect on my character. That sense of shame at the silence became entwined with a sense of shame at having no one who loved me.

If I had believed in psychiatry, I could have spent a fortune sorting it out, but it all seemed rather pointless. And in any case, plenty of people had suffered during the war.

Miraculously, I got through the next day as if I had had a good night's sleep. We went through the papers, Overdijk and I, and he seemed pleased and delighted to learn he was now a millionaire several times over.

In dollars, too. He kept figuring the exchange rate on his pocket calculator.

Anneke followed his wife around the house with a fussy little man from an auction house. At one point, the women bustled into the room where we were working. "You sure there's nothing you want to keep, Nick?" said Mrs. Overdijk.

"We talked about this," he said. "Liquidate it all—strictly cash," he said.

"I know, but those carpets—"

"Forget it." He sounded a little testy. "Take the money and buy new ones in California if you want Oriental rugs."

He stretched out his arms, one brown, one whiter, like his wife's. He reached over with the darker one to the mantelpiece. "I might like this, though. I always loved it when I was a kid." He picked up a curved dagger in a scabbard lying there. "The Moslems used to kill infidels with this back in Indonesia. My uncle said so, anyway. He said they'd slit a man's throat with this and they didn't care if they were caught because they thought they'd go straight to paradise. It scared the hell out of me. Who knows if it's true?" He drew it out of the scabbard. "Still sharp as hell," he said.

I glanced over at Anneke. This was one of the times when she knew just what I was thinking.

After all, I thought. Of what use was I to anyone? Not to poor Anneke, who was, as far as I knew, the only one who really cared. She would find something better to do with her life than follow me around the office. I would actually be doing her a favor.

To my amazement, I felt quite gay and light-headed

at dinner. Mevrouw Termeulen had put on quite a tasty spread. I savored every bite. Maybe it was the wine. We had uncorked a couple of excellent bottles from old van Dongen's cellar. I knew I wasn't thinking clearly from lack of sleep, but I seemed to be running on sheer adrenaline.

Anneke looked drawn but was putting on a good show and making conversation in her excellent English. She and Mrs. Overdijk seemed to have become very chummy. The four of us actually had a rather cozy evening of it. Mrs. Overdijk got a little tipsy and giggled. "Mrs. Termeulen has given us two bedrooms upstairs," she said. "Nick is such a terrible snorer that I take the opportunity to sleep alone whenever I can."

"Should be no problem shortly," I said. Anneke shot me a horrified look and I added, "With your uncle's money you can build a house with separate wings."

"Yes, I have to be honest. It will be fabulous to have all that money," she said, reaching simultaneously for the wine bottle and her husband's hand. Anneke watched them, sitting smugly side by side, their overtanned, veined old hands massaging each other.

"And what about you two? Separate bedrooms for you?" She gave Anneke a vulgar leer.

"I'm afraid so," I said.

Anneke looked me straight in the eye. "Mr. van Houten has always been strictly business," she said.

"Yes, yes, everything by the book. The rule of law and all that," I said, and heard myself laughing rather recklessly. And then I had a wild thought. I had two choices tonight. I could either use this night to seek revenge, or I could turn my back on the past and creep down the corridor to Anneke's room. I imagined her in some kind of white nightdress, waiting for me, warm and soft and pink. Sometimes, in the office, I had stood close enough to her to smell her hair, a nice flowery, springlike smell, and had wanted to reach out and touch it. It was very fine and a golden color, shot through with coarser silver hairs.

Anneke flung down her napkin. "I must speak to you, Marius," she said. "A business matter."

Naturally the Overdijks looked startled.

"Sit down," I said. "It can wait until morning. It's an early night for me." I excused myself and went up to my room.

Later, much later, Anneke knocked on the door. "I've got to talk to you," she whispered urgently through the door.

"Go away," I said firmly.

Finally she did, and I lay in a state of twilight sleep. It was almost dawn and my heart was pounding when I rose. I could hear some birds outside my window, and the sky was a pale purple color.

It was all so easy. I went down to the mantel and picked up the dagger. Then I went back upstairs and let myself into Nico's room. He lay there like a baby, his arms, hands, open defenselessly, lying on the white coverlet. He wasn't snoring now.

I laid the blade on his throat and gave his shoulder a push. He woke up in terror. It took him a second to understand where he was and that it was a blade that touched his throat.

"I'm going to kill you," I said, "but first I will tell you why."

I heard Anneke behind me. "Marius!" she said. She had come into the room, but I couldn't take my eyes off Nico's throat and the blade thay lay against it.

"Don't stop me," I said. "I'm going through with it. It makes no difference what you say. I suppose you're going to tell me not to take the law into my own hands. The rule of law and all that."

Even then, I began to wonder if I could go through with it. I was furious with Anneke. I wanted to turn and look at her, but I was afraid I would lose control of Nico if I did. And I thought of my father and his damned pamphlet. But it felt so right—it was only simple justice.

"Marius, you fool," said Anneke. "That's not Nicolaas."

I looked down into my victim's terrified eyes. He was too frightened to speak.

"Look at his driving arm," she shouted.

I looked down at his arms. The right arm was darker than the left.

"Marius," she screamed. "What side of the road do they drive on in Australia?" she demanded.

"The wrong side," I said. "By our lights. And the steering wheel is on the other side. So the right arm would get more sun."

"But in America," said Anneke, walking slowly toward me, her hand extended, "it's like here. His left arm should be darker. Like hers. The wrong arm is brown. It's the wrong nephew."

By now Mrs. Overdijk had crept into the room.

"Jesus," she said. "Oh my God."

"And the salt drops," said Anneke, standing next to me now and speaking very quickly. "He told us in

86

Dutch that he hadn't had any in years. She didn't understand. Later she said she'd never understood how he could stand them, remember?"

I lifted the blade from his neck and I handed the knife to Anneke. The American woman was screaming, "What is she saying? Speak English."

Anneke went over to her and slapped her. "Shut up," she said. "Don't wake the housekeeper and we can all make it out of here."

That slap was the last thing I remember before I collapsed. I suppose I fainted. Later, Anneke told me I'd been asleep for hours. She was sitting in a chair next to Overdijk's bed where I lay on the coverlet, waiting for me to come around.

"I tried to tell you," she said. "But you wouldn't listen. So I waited in the hall just in case you tried—I fell asleep there—but I heard you leave your room. You wouldn't listen, but I had figured it out when I saw them holding hands.

"They've admitted it. Nico died three years ago. They were his widow and his brother, the one from Australia. They wanted the money, naturally. The brothers looked enough alike to manage the deception. No one in Holland had seen them for years."

I began to tremble. "And I almost killed an innocent man." I sat on the side of the bed.

"That's right," she said. "He won't pursue it, though. I put them in a cab back to the airport. Our silence is as important to them as theirs is to us. We'll keep all those papers he signed with his dead brother's name as evidence, just in case."

"And the housekeeper?"

"Mevrouw Termeulen was delighted to hear she'd

inherited a fortune. Whatever she heard last night will go with her to her grave."

"Anneke," I said. "You kept your head while I was mad. Thank God for that."

"How do you feel now, Marius?" she said. She looked very tired and relieved.

"I feel as if I were back among the living," I said, reaching for her and wrapping my arms around her and burying my face in her sweet-smelling hair.

Put Out the Light; or, The Napoleon of Science

P. M. Carlson

Proper ladies don't frequent low places like Danny Doyle's. But sometimes a girl has reason to lie low for a while, and Danny is known to keep mum when Pinkerton men come asking questions about his clientele. So I was having a bite of Danny's watery Irish stew in a dark corner of his establishment, glumly wondering if my shrunken resources would allow me to leave New York for a short time, since I could not appear onstage even though I'd been hired to play Desdemona. The problem was that the florid gentleman who had taken me to Delmonico's the night before had not been quite as thoroughly inebriated as I'd believed, and was making a silly fuss about the disappearance of his watch and the diamond-studded gold ring he wore on his little finger. He'd posted a Pinkerton man at the stage door, and another was asking questions of all the pawnbrokers and even of my landlady.

"Bridget! Lordy, it's Bridget Mooney!" caroled a happy voice.

I squinted into the smoky dimness and exclaimed, "Mary Ann! What a surprise!"

"Ain't it, though! It must be ten years since I saw you!" She plumped herself down at my table. Mary Ann was even taller than I, with thick hair and sparkling eyes, though her nose was turning rather red from overindulgence in Danny's cheap Irish whiskey, and I could tell from her unfashionable gown that she had not come up in the world as far as I. She said, "My, Bridget, it all comes back! We had good times in those days with Al and his boys, didn't we?"

Well, I'm bound to admit that we had. Al was a most uncommonly bright fellow, of course, and generous-hearted whenever he wasn't short on cash. He loved the theatre and a good lark, and when he and his men built a new dynamo with a pair of four-foot-long upthrust wire-wrapped columns, he'd named it the "Long-legged Mary Ann."

Oh, I know, I know, proper ladies don't know such vulgar terms. But Al Edison was a salty sort, and that dynamo had been crucial to the success of his famous electric light. So don't you think he was doing my tall friend a great honor? Yes indeed. He never named anything after his wives.

Mary Ann was eyeing my visiting dress, striped in rose, green, and brown, and trimmed with black velvet and white guipure lace. She said, "I suppose you're above such things now."

Indeed I was—though if I couldn't think of a way

past the Pinkertons, I might soon be driven to desperate measures. I said, "I'm not in that line of work anymore. But I hear Al's doing well now."

"Oh, yes! He has a grand new place in New Jersey. West Orange. Much bigger than the old lab, and he's hiring heaps of men to work for him."

"Well, he's a clever fellow. Is it true that he has a new wife?"

"Little Mina, yes. And a baby. It makes no matter. You know Al, working all the time. Though I hear he's going to take her to the Paris Exposition, and he bought her a grand new mansion called Glenmont. It's just up the hill from his lab, so he can walk to work. Not that he walks back home often." She winked at me. "He still works night and day."

"He probably always will." That had struck me about Al when I'd become acquainted with him ten years before. He loved his work almost as much as we theatre people love ours, and toiled day and night on his projects. Mary Ann and the rest of us could distract him only briefly. "So Al's rich now?" I asked.

"Oh, yes! Though I do hear he has lots of creditors."

"Most rich people do," I explained. "That's one way to become rich, to tell people you'll do something splendid and then borrow money from them."

We had a nice long gabble about rich people we'd known. But after Mary Ann left me, I found myself thinking again of Al, and of how far West Orange was from where the Pinkerton men were searching. And I reckoned the Paris Exposition was even farther.

But I didn't want to approach him in Mary Ann's line of work, because I needed more than a night's shelter from the Pinkertons.

At the ragpickers I found a shabby black jacket and trousers that fit me, and a man's shirt that had seen better days, being frayed along the edges. I bound up my hair under a cloth cap, tucked my Colt and other special possessions into a knapsack, and boarded the Delaware, Lackawanna and Western Railroad for New Jersey.

Well, of course, the clothes weren't very becoming! But young men get better wages than young ladies. And I'd played Portia, and knew how to wear my dagger with the braver grace, and turn two mincing steps into a manly stride, and speak of frays like a fine bragging youth. And don't you reckon a girl's entitled to a disguise every now and then to slip past the Pinkertons, and to avoid stirring up unpleasant memories—well, unmentionable memories—in the mind of our nation's greatest inventor?

Glenmont was as splendid a place as ever I'd seen, with gables and verandas, stained-glass windows and a conservatory, grand Queen Anne chimneys, and a widow's walk on top. The man who built it had embezzled the money from Arnold Constable Inc. When he went to prison, he'd sold it to Edison. Of course, he was a wicked sinful man, but I'm bound to admit he had a pretty taste. The great house sat on a hill amidst lawns and acres of woods, and far across the valley one could see New York City.

But my business lay in the laboratory. I inquired the way of a gardener working on the grounds of Glenmont. He said, "You don't want to go to that laboratory, sir!"

"Why not?"

He looked around and then bent closer. He was a

small man with a hawk nose and thin unkempt hair. "That place is full of evil spirits," he informed me, jerking his thumb at an enormous brick building at the foot of the hill. "There's flashes and booms, and glimmerings and groanings, and poor dead creatures carried out by night. Evil spirits, or my name isn't Silas Bell!"

I looked at the brick building he'd indicated. "But hang it, everyone knows that Mr. Edison is doing splendid work!"

"They call him the Wizard of Menlo Park," he reminded me, as though that were proof. "Now, Miz Mina, she's a good churchgoing lady. But Mr. Thomas, he's doing Satan's work. Somebody should stop him, they should."

The laboratory was as grand as the house. It was three stories high, with several smaller buildings lined up on the north side and a tall picket fence marching around the whole. It had a water tower on the roof and a watchman who was in the process of ejecting a man from the building.

"How many times do we have to tell you, Boggs? You're to see Mr. Edison's secretary, Mr. Tate," said the watchman.

"I've seen Mr. Tate eight times, and still no money!" The visitor added an oath and shook his fist at the watchman, and I thought it prudent to shrink back against the outside of the picket fence, so as not to be in the gentlemen's way if they required more room. "It's Mr. Edison I have to see!"

"Mr. Tate," repeated the watchman firmly.

The angry visitor was a tall, burly man with worn blunt hands and a cloth cap like mine. He pointed a finger at the great building. "Two years ago, I built that! And still not paid!"

The watchman was even taller and burlier, and carried a staff besides. "Now, Mr. Boggs, we've discussed this before," he said in a reasonable tone, lifting the staff. "You know that Mr. Edison is not to be disturbed at work."

Mr. Boggs fell to cursing in a manner so vulgar that I shan't inflict it upon your ears. The watchman forced him out through the gate at last and he stormed away. I approached respectfully and explained that I was applying for work. "See Mr. Tate," said the watchman, and let me pass.

Inside, a placard informed me that Mr. Edison was so occupied with his work that he was constrained to deny himself to visitors. Well, that's not very hospitable, is it? I ignored the placard and walked in with manly stride. I passed a handsome library with a marquetry floor, Smyrna rugs, and bookshelves in alcoves, all brilliantly lit by electric lights, and approached the laboratory.

And wasn't it grand, far more splendid than Menlo Park! Al was doing well, yes indeed! It was a vast reeking humming space filled with noisy mechanical contraptions and peculiar smells. It was lit by the famous glowing lamps of Al's invention. Men, perhaps fifty of them, worked at the contraptions, alone or in small groups, and occasional bursts of laughter could be heard above the hums and clanks. I saw Al standing near the wall, coughing dreadfully, and after a moment's hesitation I approached him. "Sir, please, I want to work here."

"Work?" He turned toward me.

"Oh, I'm sorry, sir," I corrected myself. Now that he'd moved the handkerchief from his face, I could see that he wasn't Al at all. His height and manner of carrying himself were similar, and in the dimness I'd mistaken his blond hair for Al's gray. But he was much younger than Al, and much more handsome and blue-eyed.

"Who are you, lad?" He smiled in a drowsy way and sat down on a cot.

"I'm Mike O'Rourke, and I need work, sir." I often borrow my uncle Mike's name. He borrowed heaps of things from Aunt Mollie and me.

"And I'm Jesse Cheever." He paused to cough and sniff from a little bottle he held. "And I think if you speak to Tate, you'll find that we need bottle washers. We certainly need them in the chemistry department."

Well, I'm bound to admit I have a weakness for handsome men named Jesse, troublesome though they all turn out to be. This one's drowsy blue eyes were quite fetching, and I began to regret my masculine disguise. I smiled at him. "Pleased to make your acquaintance, Mr. Cheever. Can you tell me where to find Mr. Tate?"

He looked around the huge machine shop, frowned, and elbowed a man sleeping on the cot. "Wake up, Lem Symington."

"What is it, Jesse?"

"Where is—" Jesse Cheever interrupted himself with a fit of coughing.

I asked, "Mr. Cheever, sir, would you like a lozenge for your cough?" Those of us in the theatrical trade always keep a supply of throat remedies to hand.

"Dear me, no, Mike O'Rourke! It's not that sort of cough!" He laughed and coughed again.

Lem Symington had amber eyes as shiny as a cat's and hair that stuck out like a scrub brush from under his hat. He wore a white shirt and dark waistcoat like Jesse's. He sat up on the cot and indicated a closed door nearby. "He's put some of us muckers to work producing chlorine gas," he told me. "It's poison, you know. If it seeps out of its containers, it's very distressing to the lungs."

Jesse Cheever sniffed at his bottle again and explained, "This is chloroform. It's the antidote. But it does make a feller sleepy."

I looked about nervously. "I would think that a famous inventor who can capture electricity in a glass lamp could keep poison gases in their containers."

For some reason Lem Symington frowned ferociously. Jesse Cheever twinkled at me and said, "Hush, O'Rourke, you must never refer to the invention of the electric light in the presence of the inventor of the carbon filament!"

"Oh, don't rag me, Jesse! That was long ago!" Lem Symington said with irritation. "I wish I'd never told you!"

"Well, it wasn't time wasted. He hired you when you told him you'd come up with it independently," Jesse said.

Lem Symington ignored him and looked at me. "Now, what did you want?"

"I want to find Mr. Tate, sir."

"Oh, yes. He wasn't in the office by the library? Well, I don't see him down here in the machine shop, do you, Jesse?" They both stood and looked about. "He's probably with Al up on the third floor, working on the phonograph. Or on that photographic thing of Dickson's."

"The kinetoscope," said my handsome Jesse. "Yes, O'Rourke, try the third floor. There are the stairs."

I gathered up my knapsack and started up, looking about as I did. The first two floors, I saw, were devoted to machinery, except for the west end of the building, which housed the library. When I reached the third floor, I entered a large room over the library. Al Edison sat in a clump of men around a strange little machine. He was stouter than when I'd seen him last, and his brown hair was even grayer, but still fell unkempt over his broad thoughtful brow in a manner that inspired reporters to call him "the Napoleon of science." He ignored the conversation around him, probably because he was deaf. He finished adjusting the machine, started its wax cylinder turning, and shouted at a little disk next to the cylinder, "Mary had a brand-new gown, it was too tight by half! Who gives a damn for Mary's lamb, when he can see her calf!"

The men chuckled, then waited nervously as Al adjusted a little arm on the machine and pushed something. The cylinder turned again and a thin little voice proclaimed, "Mary had a brand-new—" The rest was drowned out by applause and cheers. A couple of the men shouted, "Best yet!"

A great flash of light came from behind me. All the men except Al crowded to the door and peered out. "Just a lamp blowing up," said one.

"Glad it's not another accident," replied another.

Al had ignored the commotion, paying attention only to his machine. He reached into one of the boxes on the floor and pulled out a fresh wax cylinder, and fitted it onto the phonograph. "Who's next?" His eye lit on me. "Ah, come here, my lad! Let's see if our machine can stand up to the onslaught of a new voice!"

"Yes, sir." I laid down my knapsack and approached the machine. Al started the cylinder turning. I scoured my memory for a man's speech, and perhaps inspired by the explosion of the lamp, I declaimed, "Put out the light, and then put out the light:/ If I quench thee, thou flaming minister,/ I can again thy former light restore,/ Should I repent me; but once put out thy light,/ Thou cunning'st pattern of excelling nature,/ I know not where is that Promethean heat/ That can thy light relume."

"Why, bless you, lad!" Al exclaimed, with a puzzled look at me. "What is your name?" He cocked a hand behind his ear.

"Mike O'Rourke, sir. I hope to find work here."

"Ah." He glanced at my worn clothes. "Well, any man who knows his Shakespeare will be given a chance. Tate will see to it by and by. First let's hear your Othello." He adjusted a screw and lowered his ear to the machine.

My voice emerged, the actual words. "Put out the light, and then put out the light." Can you imagine? It was wizardry indeed! I clapped my hands gleefully. "Oh, sir, what an excellent machine!"

Al held up a finger. My words continued until, "but once put out thy—" Then they disappeared amid sputters and buzzes. Al groaned and said a few words almost as vulgar as Mr. Boggs's.

One of the other men squatted by the machine and said, "Wax shavings in the works again!"

Al said, "We need a harder wax, Jonas."

"I have a couple of ideas."

"Well, let's get to work! Ninety-nine percent perspiration, you know!"

They were all ignoring me. I located Mr. Tate, a genial Canadian who served as Al's secretary and business manager. He told me to report to Jonas Aylsworth, the chemist who needed bottles washed. I started for the stairs, glancing back over my shoulder to see Al Edison, lost in thought, pondering his magical machine.

As I started down, a tall, lean gentleman carrying a set of nearly identical photographs of a man with his arms out entered another third-floor room. I was puzzled and addressed a boy who was on the stairs just behind me. "Who is that man?"

"That's Mr. Dickson, the photographer."

"What is he doing?"

"Kinetoscope photographs. They plan to link moving photographs to the phonograph."

"Moving photographs? That's impossible!"

"I've seen them, I have!" said the boy indignantly. "They're little pictures, and they move! Those pictures he's got show Fred Ott waving his arms about."

"What wonderful inventions are coming from this place!"

"That's as may be." He scowled.

"You don't think so?"

He glanced around and beckoned me into a corner by the stairs. "He can be evil, that Mr. Edison."

"Evil? Why, boy— I don't know your name—"

"They call me Kit Herbert."

"My name is Mike O'Rourke. Well, Kit, I'm certain that Mr. Edison isn't evil! He's doing splendid things for all mankind!"

"That's what they all say," said Kit sullenly.

What could the boy mean? I said thoughtfully, "No, not all. I've heard rumors that Mr. Edison is a wizard, doing Satan's work."

"Oh, that old story." Kit sniffed in derision. "Some people don't understand science. They think it's wizardry. But it's just ordinary electricity."

"But, Kit, you just said he was evil!"

"Just ordinary evil. Look!" He drew me across to a door and into a room attached to the main building. It was filled with strange machines, huge shafts and turning wheels and a great boiler puffing steam like a locomotive. Kit pointed at one of the contraptions. "That's a dynamo. It makes electricity."

I squinted at the wire-wrapped columns. "That's a Long-legged Mary Ann?"

Kit burst out laughing. "Don't say that before the ladies! We call it a Long-waisted Mary Ann in public."

"I see."

"And that . . ." He scowled again as he pointed to a thick horizontal sheet of metal. "Well, go stand on that metal plate."

Obediently, I did. Kit, still scowling, said, "If I throw this switch, fourteen hundred volts of electricity will course through you and kill you."

Well, I've seldom been so spry! I leapt about ten feet from the plate and lit out for the other side of the room. "Hang it, Kit, that's not a good joke!" I exclaimed. I remembered the hawk-nosed Silas Bell's dark mutters about poor dead creatures carried out by night.

"It's no joke, you're right!" Kit exclaimed. "They'll do anything for an experiment! They'll put a fellow's dog on that plate and turn on the electricity! They killed fifty dogs and cats, and a calf, and even a horse!"

I felt myself grow clammy. Was Silas Bell right? Was this marvelous laboratory, with its talking machines and moving pictures, in fact a den of Satan? I asked feebly, "Why did they kill your dog?"

"Well, poor old Biff followed me here to work last year. When they had to do an experiment, they'd send out a boy to catch a stray. That boy thought Biff was a stray. I didn't see them bring him in. They pushed him onto that plate, and turned on the electricity. Poor old critter. He did get revenge, though."

"How?" I asked, looking about nervously for ghostly satanic dogs bent on vengeance.

"One of the experimenters tried to nudge him farther onto the plate. But the current was already on and he was shocked too. Wasn't the same for days. At least I know poor old Biff died quickly."

"What is the purpose of these cruel experiments?"

"The state of New York wants a new way to kill people. They want to replace hanging with something more humane. Executioners can turn on death the way we turn on a lamp."

I shuddered. I preferred electricity safely bottled up in the Edison lamps. "But I read somewhere that Mr. Edison was opposed to capital punishment!"

"He is. But he also needs money. He let Mr. Brown take the job, and they invented the electric chair."

I had seen enough of this room. "Kit, I must get to work! I'm happy to have met you, though I'm truly sorry to hear your sad story."

We returned to our respective chores, but I was boiling with curiosity. What splendid and terrible projects Al Edison had! I understood better why he sometimes spent days and nights at the labs, and why scientists like handsome Jesse Cheever were willing to sacrifice their health to be part of the work here.

Along with his chemist Jonas Aylsworth, Jesse Cheever, Lem Symington, Mr. Dickson, Fred Ott, and assorted others, Al Edison was spending twenty-four hours a day here perfecting the phonograph, napping occasionally on the cots where I'd first seen Jesse and Lem. Mina Edison delivered a nice dinner to him every day, but I noticed he seldom ate anything but the pie.

Then the unpleasantness began.

The first problem was when I was called in to receive my week's wages. Tate said, "Well, O'Rourke, I hope it won't be any inconvenience if I wait till next week to pay you. We're short of cash just now."

"Yes, sir, but begging your pardon, I too am short of cash just now."

He frowned. "Well, here's half. That's the best I can do."

I accepted it, but could almost hear that excellent businesswoman Aunt Mollie chiding me because I hadn't insisted on payment in advance. I went straight to Jesse Cheever. "Sir, why is it that a rich man like Mr. Edison can't pay us our wages?"

"Oh, he'll pay us, O'Rourke." Jesse had such a kindly smile! "Al's wealth is tied up in his lighting companies and in this laboratory. But he's selling them to a new company he's forming with some important financiers, Mr. Villard and Mr. J. Pierpont Morgan. They've already incorporated it. Edison General Electric, they'll call it. There's some little problem, so they haven't yet signed all the papers. But as soon as they do, we'll all have plenty of money, and he may send some of us to the Paris Exposition!"

"How splendid!" I exclaimed, quite caught up in Jesse Cheever's enthusiasm. Plenty of money and the Paris Exposition was precisely what I wanted too.

But the missing wages were only the first problem.

The Pinkerton men arrived that afternoon. Mr. Tate took them around the laboratory, denying the presence of any ladies, and Al agreed with him absentmindedly. I washed bottles with great industry, quaking all the while, until they left with a final suspicious glance around the laboratory. I hoped they had paid Mary Ann well for her information.

And then that night the abusive Mr. Boggs succeeded in getting inside the laboratory, and broke some bottles and lamps before the watchman carried him thrashing and screaming out the door. A little later there was a commotion on the third floor. I ran up the stairs and found the men in turmoil, all crowded around the door of the photography room, even Kit bouncing up and down at the edge of the crowd, trying to see. As I pieced the story together,

Mr. Dickson, the photographer, had come back to his darkroom after a brief absence and stumbled over a body. "Help! They've killed Edison!" he'd cried.

You can imagine my consternation, and my relief when I saw Al standing there, hale and hearty. But then came another blow. Lem Symington uttered an oath and his amber eyes widened. "It's Jesse Cheever!" He hid his face in his hands.

I know not where is that Promethean heat, that can thy light relume. My poor Jesse! The handsomest scientist that ever there was, and the second dear Jesse I'd lost!

"There, there, O'Rourke, pull yourself together," said Al, slapping me on the back.

I remembered that boys weren't supposed to cry, and swallowed my sobs, saying gruffly, "I'm all right, sir." I peeked through the crowd at poor Jesse's body. The back of his blond head was crimson from ear to ear. "He was hit from behind," I blurted. "With a large stick."

"No, no," protested Al. "He merely fell and hit his head. Now, come with me to the chemistry room. We'll find something to revive him."

Now, wasn't Al a silly goose to think that? Nothing could revive a man with a horrid wound like Jesse's! His light was quite put out. But men in the inventing trade are dreamers, and love their inventions as though they were children. The electric light, the phonograph, the dynamo, the electric chair, the kinetograph—all were little miracles. His patent medicine, Edison's Polyform, had sold well for years. Perhaps Al truly believed that he could raise the dead.

"Does anyone know who killed him?" I asked after

half an hour of Polyform and other evil-smelling concoctions had failed to revive the corpse.

"No one killed him! Holy Moses, who'd want to kill Jesse Cheever?" Al protested. "He fell and hit his head!"

"But, sir—"

"O'Rourke, you'll find the inventing business is full of dangers. We're on the edge, the cusp between the known and the unknown, so accidents will happen. We must take courage, and continue to work. That's what our fallen comrade would wish."

Everyone nodded in sober agreement. After all, Al was an uncommonly bright fellow, yes indeed. They summoned the undertakers and went back to work.

Well, Al might dismiss Jesse's death as an accident, but I was certain it had nothing to do with the cusp between the known and the unknown. It had to do with someone fetching Jesse a great whack on the head. And I was also certain that the man who struck him thought he was killing Edison. Jesse had paid a high price for his resemblance to the great inventor.

But who might it be? Al Edison's life was full of projects and incidents and huge sums of money. Mr. Villard and Mr. J. Pierpont Morgan, of course, wanted him alive, because the proposed new company would be almost worthless without him. But great financiers have enemies. Did a rival financier, a Jay Gould or perhaps a Vanderbilt, want to stop the company? Would it be difficult to hire one of us to kill the Napoleon of science? Many of us were disgruntled by half wages. Lem Symington bore him a grudge having to do with his long-ago invention. Young Kit blamed Al for the death of a beloved dog. Mr. Boggs was a violent man who believed Al owed him money. Even Silas Bell, the Glenmont gardener, believed that Al was in Satan's thrall and would lead us all to perdition if he wasn't stopped. Would they need much more in the way of incentive?

I seemed to be alone in my conviction that a murderer was stalking the laboratory. Still, I vowed to avenge the death of dear Jesse Cheever. And it was important to save Al Edison, even if he was being leather-headed about the situation. His fruitful mind had so much to offer the future. Besides, I wanted to make sure he survived to pay my wages.

That night I didn't leave the lab but pretended that I had many more bottles to wash. The watchman was alert, walking around the building and through it, and the gate in the picket fence was closed. I told him I wasn't able to sleep because I hadn't finished my work. "Mr. Edison affects people that way," he said, and continued his rounds.

Only a few of the men worked at night, most choosing to be home sleeping with their families. But Al always preferred the night. Night is the time of assignations and of goblins, of secrets and of ghosts. Night is the time when ordinary shapes become grotesque and unfamiliar, the very witching time, when churchyards yawn and hell itself breathes out contagion to this world, and anything is possible. I think Al worked best then, freed of the conventional expectations of the daylight hours. We in the theatre business love night too.

Electric lamps still burned here and there in the vast laboratory, making the shadows of machines and worktables even blacker. Except for the engines in the dynamo room, most of the machinery was silent. A few men were dozing on the cots. I heard Al's voice shouting a song in the phonograph room, "I'll Take You Home Again, Kathleen!" I washed bottles until the watchman passed, then crept to the bottom of the stairs and hid in a black shadow.

A tiny voice was now singing, "I'll take you home again, Kathleen!" Truly, the phonograph was an amazing invention! Silas Bell could well believe it was the work of the devil, yes indeed. But once again, I heard the song disintegrate into sputters.

"Well, let's try Jonas's new concoction," Al said cheerfully. "It should be melted by now."

"Jonas is asleep," someone answered.

"I'll get it while you clean out the works."

Al emerged from the phonograph room and bounced down the stairs. He'd never been very well coordinated and I hoped he wouldn't fall. Still, despite the lateness of the hour, or perhaps because of it, he seemed frisky as young Kit Herbert. And twice as foolish. Someone was trying to kill him, but he wouldn't believe it, and he was walking through the enormous half-abandoned lab as though angels watched over him.

But there were no angels in evidence, not even the watchman, so I left my hiding place and followed him across the building.

He entered the chemistry room, the long room full of bottles and beakers where dear Jesse Cheever had once worked. I recognized Jonas Aylsworth, the chemist, snoring near the door. Al hurried into the room and over to a crucible where something was bubbling over a gas flame. He began to hum the song and picked up a ladle.

Behind him, another table was laden with the apparatus for other experiments. It was lit from above by an Edison lamp. A bit of shadow holding a staff detached itself from the blackness beneath the table and stretched high. I grabbed for the Colt I usually kept in my bustle and then realized I was not wearing my maiden's attire. I could only hurl myself at the shadow's knees and hope that the great staff would miss Al's gray head when it came crashing down. In fact, it hit the crucible and some of the molten contents splashed onto Al's clothing, and onto my jacket and trousers as well. "Stop! Stop!" I cried indignantly. But the shadow lurched to his feet and bounded out the window.

Al sat up and looked at the wax still sizzling on the floor. "Holy Moses! What a clumsy oaf that was!"

"Yes, sir."

"It would have gone ill with me if you hadn't bumped me, Mike O'Rourke. Thank you."

"Yes, sir."

"Who was it?" He cocked a hand behind his ear.

"I'm sorry, sir. He was muffled in a black scarf, and very quick out the window."

"Some thief, I suppose. I must speak sternly to the watchman, and—"

Well, isn't that enough to make you despair? Inventors are such impractical men, unable to see what's as clear as day. I cleared my throat and shouted, "Sir?"

"Yes, my boy?"

"Begging your pardon, sir, but I think he was trying

to kill you. I think he thought Jesse Cheever was you, and—"

"Hush, O'Rourke!" Al beckoned me nearer. "You must say nothing of your suspicions. Do you understand? Nothing!"

"But, sir, why not?" I spoke into his ear. "A murderer is loose! Your life is in danger!"

"O'Rourke, I am engaged in a very delicate business transaction. News that someone is trying to attack me could endanger years of work. Even the loss of Jonas's new wax in that crucible is a setback."

Well, he was right, of course. Mr. Villard and Mr. J. Pierpont Morgan would be unlikely to give lots of money to Al if they thought he might be killed at any moment. They'd be reluctant too if they thought someone was sabotaging his new inventions. I said into his ear, "Sir, I understand that this news could dim the luster of your proposed new company. But suppose you claim this was merely an accident, and that you are working despite it all—"

Al thought about it and chuckled. "Then Villard and Pierpont Morgan may be more eager to sign! And furthermore, we may be able to trap the villain! Here, O'Rourke, you're the only one who's proven trustworthy. We shall make a plan!"

Jonas Aylsworth had awakened at last and was shuffling toward us, blinking sleepily. "What's happened?"

Al began to yowl. "I'm burnt! The crucible exploded! Ow, ow!" He sounded like a fenceful of alley cats. The men who were not too deeply asleep to hear the ruckus hurried in and crowded around him. They carried him up to Glenmont, where Mina Edison fluttered about exclaiming, "Oh, poor Thomas! Poor dearie! Now, just let me put this bandage on!"

Of course, he couldn't stand much of that kind of treatment, and soon he was back in the lab, his head bundled up in bandages so he looked like a Turk. He called the reporters in. "Edison Burned but Busy," said the headlines. And he was busy. Stubborn as ever, he was still trying to perfect the phonograph.

And foolhardy as ever, he wandered about the lab the next night, bandages and all, an easy target. I stayed at the lab again to watch over him.

It grew later and later. One by one, the people working with Al—Lem Symington, Dickson the photographer, Jonas Aylsworth, even vigorous young Kit —stumbled off to take naps. The watchman was yawning. I too dozed on one of the cots, dimly aware of Al singing "I'll Take You Home Again, Kathleen," when I felt a cool breeze on my cheek. I sat up, alert, and realized that a window was open somewhere, letting in the April air. It was the witching time, yes indeed. But all was quiet, except for Al and the phonograph on the third floor, and the clanking and humming of the huge machines in the dynamo room, and the snores of the men who were catching their forty winks.

It was time to take action.

I tucked my gun into my belt and slipped through the shadows to the dynamo room. No one was there. Quickly I tiptoed out and threw a lever, then scurried back to the shadows behind the door.

Half the lights in the main building had gone out when I threw the lever. Though the snores did not abate, there was faraway cursing from the third floor. I heard Al descending the stairs. In a moment he was in the dynamo room, his head turbaned in bandages. He began to examine the contraption that had stopped.

And, as I'd hoped and dreaded, a muffled figure slipped through the door and closed it behind him. He held a great staff in his hand. As he approached Al from behind, he raised the staff.

I stepped from behind the door and cried, "Hold, sir! I have a gun!"

The muffled figure spun to look at me and my Colt. Ten feet farther on, so did Al. Al shouted, "Holy Moses, don't shoot! A bullet could ricochet and damage the machines!"

Hang it, inventors are so impractical! They've got no more common sense than a pup. I sighed and explained, "Just getting his attention, sir. I don't need to shoot, because if he moves at all, I throw this switch."

The muffled figure looked down at his feet and gasped. He lifted one foot from the electrified plate and I made a show of grasping the switch. "No, O'Rourke, no!" he whimpered, holding himself very still.

"Lem Symington!" I cried, recognizing his voice and scrub-brush hair. "What in the world are you doing here?"

Al looked just as confounded as I was. "Lem Symington? You're the one who's been trying to kill me?"

"No, no, I—"

"Don't move!" I reminded him. Lem froze again.

"Don't deny it," Al said. "I've seen you trying to strike me twice, and now I recognize you."

I asked, "But, Mr. Symington, why did you kill Jesse Cheever? He was your friend!"

Lem bowed his head but didn't answer.

I said, "You mistook him for Mr. Edison, didn't you?"

He still didn't answer.

I said, "I don't understand why you used that wooden staff! You're an inventor. You could have found a clever scientific way to kill Mr. Edison. Electrocution, or poison gas—there are so many ways to die in this laboratory! Why would a clever scientist use an old-fashioned stick? Why, I thought the killer would turn out to be a crude day laborer, a mason or a gardener or even a watchman!"

A crafty look came into Lem's amber eyes, and I exclaimed, "That's the reason! That's what he wanted us to think!"

Al had been frowning throughout this discussion. Now he said, "Lem, I don't understand why you did it. I've been good to you! There's no better job anywhere for a man of science!"

Lem burst out, "And why would you hire your rival, except from guilt?"

"Rival?" asked Al. "Guilt? What guilt?"

I explained, "He's jealous, Mr. Edison, because he invented some sort of filament, and you became rich and famous from it."

Al looked puzzled. "Many people claimed to invent the electric light. But I invented it first!"

"No you didn't!" Lem shouted. "I did! You heard about it somehow and stole it!"

"I did not!" Al stepped toward him.

"Al, don't go any closer!" I called.

Lem glanced at my hand on the switch but went on shouting at Al. "You stole it! I invented it first!"

"Balderdash! I invented it!"

"Al!" I called again.

But it was too late. Immersed in this silly schoolboy quarrel, the Napoleon of science stepped close, shaking his fist. Lem seized his wrist and looked at me triumphantly.

"Al, you idiot!" I stamped my foot in vexation. "I've a notion to throw this switch!"

The horror of his situation finally penetrated. Al looked at Lem's feet on the electrified plate, then at Lem's hand around his wrist, and finally at the switch I held in my hand. He mentioned a few of Mr. Bogg's favorite words as a look of pure terror invaded his features.

Lem, knowing I couldn't electrocute him without killing Al too, smirked and stepped off the plate, shoving Al to the floor as he did. He lifted the great staff. Al cringed, certain that he'd breathed his last.

Isn't that just like inventors, to forget the practical side of things? I shot Lem in the knee and he crumpled screaming to the floor. Al and I tied him up with electric wire.

"I truly did think of that filament first," Al assured me.

"Of course you did, Mr. Edison. But this yowling fellow loves his invention as much as you love yours."

Al seemed to understand. "Inventions are like sweethearts, or like children," he agreed.

"He loved not wisely, but too well."

"That's true." We started out to find the watchman. "Your marksmanship is excellent. How can I ever thank you?"

"Well, sir, seeing as how you're going anyway, I would very much appreciate a trip to Paris."

He grinned. "Fleeing the Pinkertons, eh? I'm sure a trip to Paris can be arranged, Bridget."

"You know I'm Bridget?" I asked, astounded.

"You looked familiar," he explained. "And the Pinkerton men were asking about you. And just now you called me Al, as in those dear old days at Menlo Park."

"I see."

"Besides, few lads can recite Othello as well as you."

You see? Didn't I tell you that Al Edison was a most uncommonly bright fellow?

Killer Fudge

Kathy Hogan Trocheck

I was busy touching up my mental image of the new
Callahan Garrity: long sleek legs, nonexistent thighs,
flat belly, firm shapely arms. My stomach growled
angrily. I love the first day of a diet. The happy feeling
of starvation, the power you feel over your gnawing
appetite.

A shadow fell over the lawn chair where I was
stretched out.

I opened one eye. A generously built black woman
with a sad expression stood beside me, blocking out
the sun that was to tone me, bake me, turn me into
something out of a Coppertone ad.

"Callahan," she said tentatively. "Edna told me to
come talk to you."

"Hello, Ruby," I said, with little enthusiasm. "If it's
about that extra day you want to work, take it up with

Edna. It's her day on the books. I'm taking the afternoon off for self-improvement."

Edna, my mother and business partner, was supposed to be handling the office while I recharged my batteries. It had been an awful week.

"No'm, it's not about work," Ruby said. "Well, it sort of is, but it's really about Darius."

"Darius," I said. "Is he one of your nephews?" Ruby has so many nieces and nephews, grandchildren and great-grandchildren, that I can never keep track of them all.

"Foster grandson," she prompted. "My Darius is in trouble, Callahan. I need you to see about it."

Seeing about other people's troubles is what I do in my nonexistent spare time. I bought The House Mouse shortly after quitting my job as a detective for the Atlanta Police Department. Some women take up tennis. I dabble in private investigation. Doesn't burn up near the calories, unfortunately.

I sat up slowly and looked down at my belly, slightly pink and flabby and oily from the suntan lotion. Not flat and brown. Oh well.

Ruby is a rock usually, one of those imperturbable women whose expressions stay calm in the face of untold troubles. She's a mainstay of The House Mouse, the cleaning business Edna and I run out of my house here in Atlanta. But today her lower lip was trembling, and she dabbed continually at her eyes with a crumpled hankie.

She perched at the edge of my lawn chair, smoothing her white cleaning smock down over her knees.

"You know Mr. Ragan, my Thursday morning job?

Old gentleman lives alone over there off Hooper Avenue?"

I remembered the name.

"Mr. Ragan's dead," Ruby said. Tears spilled down her smooth round cheeks. "Murdered. And the police think my Darius did it. They come to the house this morning and took him away. Handcuffed him like you see on the TV news."

"Why would they suspect Darius?" I asked. "Does he even know Merritt Ragan?"

She nodded. "Darius been doing Mr. Ragan's yard work for a year. He liked that old man a lot. And Mr. Ragan liked him too. Paid Darius twenty-five dollars to keep the yard nice. Darius wouldn't hurt that old man. He's a good boy. A good worker. So I want to know can you see about it? I'll pay. You can take the money out of my check every week."

She reached in her smock pocket and pulled out a crisp hundred-dollar bill and held it toward me. "This here's the down payment. Is that right?"

I stood up and pulled on the shorts I'd left on the ground, then straightened up to zip. They were definitely looser. "Keep the money, Ruby. Employees get a fifty percent discount on private investigation work."

Edna looked up from the bank deposit she'd been preparing, and frowned. A stack of checks sat on the table next to a smaller stack of twenties. She took a deep drag on the extra-long filtered cigarette and exhaled slowly, letting the smoke halo her carefully coiffed white hair.

"You gonna help Ruby?"

"Yeah," I sighed. "Of course I'll help her. The woman's a saint. But that doesn't mean little Darius is. I guess I'll head down to homicide to see what the deal is with the charges. Can you hold the fort here?"

She glanced at the kitchen clock. "It's four now. The girls are done for the day. I'll put the answering machine on and come with you."

The last thing I needed was my mother along for the ride. "I may need you to do some phone work for me," I said tactfully. "Stay here and I'll call you after I know if they intend to keep him."

She pooched out her lower lip, took another drag on her cigarette, and regarded me through narrowed eyes. "I know a brush-off when I hear one."

As luck would have it, the only soul occupying the homicide detective's office was a friendly face, Bucky Deavers, an old friend from my days as a burglary detective.

We traded good-natured insults, then I got down to business.

"I'm looking for information on the Merritt Ragan homicide. I'm working for the kid you picked up and charged this morning."

Bucky leafed through some papers in a box of reports on his desk. "Oh yea. Merritt Ragan. He's the old dude over off of Hooper Avenue. Kid came in the house, saw all this money, bopped him on the head, took the money, and split."

I reached over and plucked the report from his hands. "I doubt the report says that."

He leaned back in the chair and folded his hands

behind his neck. "Read it and weep," he said. "The kid did it, Callahan. His fingerprints are all over the kitchen, and the murder weapon. Which was one of those heavy old-fashioned irons, by the way."

"He worked there," I said. "Yard man. And Ragan invited him in all the time. He probably saw the iron some other time and picked it up to ask about it."

"He's got a sheet," Bucky said. "Did time at the Youth Detention Center up in Alto for burglary and assault."

"Misspent youth," I said, scanning the report. "He's lived with his grandma for a year, cleaned up his act, works all the time, goes to church regular. He's a new kid."

"He's a rotten little killer," Bucky said. "We found the cash on him, two hundred bucks. Had it stashed in his Air Jordans. He admitted he took it from Ragan."

"What?" I said, startled. "His grandmother doesn't know about any confession."

"Grannies don't know a lot of stuff," Bucky said, a touch too smugly. "Your friend Darius says he went to the house yesterday afternoon to see about getting paid early. He says he went in, saw a bunch of money laying around by the front door, and left."

"But he doesn't admit he killed the old man."

"Not yet," Bucky said. "But we know he did it and he knows it too. Homicide in commission of another felony. Robbery. He's seventeen now, eighteen next month. We can try him as an adult. The DA's looking at the death penalty."

I sat up straight at the mention of Old Sparky, which is what they call Georgia's electric chair, the one they keep warmed up down at the state prison at Jackson. "Jesus, the kid's grandmother works for me. She swears he's been rehabilitated."

He was suddenly busy tidying things on his desktop. "I saw the grandmother this morning when we picked the kid up. Nice lady. She's lucky Darius didn't turn on her."

I stood up to leave. "She knows the kid and she says he didn't do it. That's enough for me. Can you get me in to see him?"

Darius Greene wasn't overjoyed to see me. He was slumped over in a chair when the guard escorted me into the visiting area. Long, blue-clad legs stretched out in front of him. He had one of those trick haircuts the kids were into lately, with the hair shaved to the scalp in the back, moderating to a wedge shape that angled sharply to the left.

"Darius, I'm Callahan. Your grandmother works for me. She thinks I can help you."

He cocked his head to the side and ran a practiced eye over me, then turned his attention back to the floor.

"You're the one who keep Grandmama washing toilets," he said tonelessly. "How're you gonna help me? Gimme some toilets to scrub?"

I felt my face flush hot with guilt. And then I got mad. "I'm the one who takes your grandmama to the hospital when her blood pressure goes up. I'm the one sees she gets paid a decent wage for her work, so she can buy fancy basketball shoes for some snot-nosed kid she loves. And I'm also a former cop and a private detective. I can help you if you let me. Did you know the DA is thinking of asking for the death penalty for Merritt Ragan's murder?"

"I heard," he mumbled. He didn't look worried.

I was losing patience. "Look, Darius. I've seen the police reports. This does not look good. Can you tell me anything at all about yesterday? Could anyone else have been in that house before you got there? Did you see Mr. Ragan when you went into the house? Had the door been forced?"

No answer.

"Did you kill him, Darius? Did you? Ruby says you're a good boy. What happened? Why'd you take the money and kill him? He was a helpless old man. Is that what you'd like to have happen to Ruby?"

He continued to stare at the floor. "Ain't tellin' you nothin'. I'm gettin' me a lawyer."

On the other side of the screened door, Caroline Ragan's lips set in a tight disapproving line when I told her who I was and what I wanted.

Somebody had told her that old-maid schoolteachers were supposed to be thin and humorless, and she'd taken their advice to heart. She had mouse-colored hair and close-set brown eyes, which she blinked continually.

"I'm sorry for Ruby's troubles. She kept this house immaculate. I guess it wouldn't hurt to let you come in and look around. The police said I could start cleaning things up today."

Merritt Ragan's gray saltbox house could have been an antiques shop. Shelves lined the walls of every room, and each held a different collection. There were silver candlesticks, Steiff teddy bears, majolica, miniature snuffboxes, and blue and white porcelains. The wooden floor was dotted with jewel-toned Oriental rugs. The furniture was old too, and the mellow wood glowed in the late afternoon sunlight that poured through the windows.

"The kitchen's in there," Caroline said as we neared the back of the house. "That's where they found Daddy. Go ahead in. I . . . don't like to be there. Because of Daddy and all. The new cleaning service is supposed to take care of it tomorrow." She glared at me when she mentioned the new cleaning service.

Merritt Ragan's kitchen was one of the cheeriest murder scenes I've ever examined. White-painted cabinets lined the room, and a fruit-motif wallpaper covered the walls. Crisply ruffled white curtains hung at the windows. The floor was gleaming yellow vinyl. Spotless. I walked over to the back door and took a look. Fingerprint powder stained the wall and the woodwork of the door. About the door. The lock didn't look like it had been tampered with.

"The police cleaned up the blood," she said.

I turned around. Caroline stood in the doorway, her matchstick arms crossed over her chest, as though she were chilled.

"Daddy must have let him in," she added. "I begged him to get a lawn service. But he wouldn't hear of it. He was fascinated with that Darius."

I got up and walked slowly around the room. The countertops were those of a man who lived alone and liked things orderly. A toaster, coffee maker, and cordless phone were lined up in military fashion. The stove held a copper teakettle and a small wooden file box. Idly I flipped up the lid. A grease-spotted index card had a recipe for tomato aspic written in purple ink in a tiny crabbed handwriting. I closed the box.

"Your father got on with Darius?"

"They were thick as thieves," she said, then laughed bitterly. "Literally, one might say."

"The police say they found quite a bit of cash on Darius. Two hundred dollars. Cash he admitted taking from the house. Was your father in the habit of keeping that much cash around?"

She pulled nervously at the collar of her blouse.

"Cash? Daddy? I suppose he could have had that much around the house. Usually he liked to pay for things by check or credit card. It helped him with his record keeping."

I roamed the small room again, looking for something the police might have missed. On a wooden chair pushed up to a small built-in desk I spotted a cardboard box. The contents were a jumble of odds and ends. A small blue and white platter. A sugar bowl with an unusual hand-painted pattern of bluebirds and butterflies, a green Depression glass cake plate, and a pink tulip-shaped flower vase. McCoy, probably.

"What's all this?" I asked.

She came over to look, and when she saw what was in the box, gave a small indignant snort.

"More of Daddy's trash. He went to estate sales every week and bought a lot of broken old junk. The good stuff he took to a flea market down by the airport and sold. It's so humiliating, having your own father paw through dead people's belongings. And actually selling them." She shuddered. "It's not as though he needed the money. Dad was retired from IBM."

I looked closer at Caroline Ragan. Her blouse was real silk and the slacks she wore were well tailored. She wore a square-cut amethyst ring on her right hand, and a gold chain around her neck held a teardrop-shaped diamond pendant. Nice stuff for an old-maid schoolmarm.

"Are you the only heir?"

She stiffened. "I suppose. Stephen certainly couldn't inherit."

"Stephen?"

"My brother."

"Why not?"

She was annoyed with me. It happens. "He's institutionalized. At Atlanta Regional Hospital. He's been there for fifteen years. Since Mama died. They say he's schizophrenic."

"Was your brother violent?"

I saw a small muscle twitch in her cheek. "Not at all. He's very calm as long as he takes his medication."

I looked again at the back door. "That lock wasn't forced," I pointed out. "I looked at the front door briefly when you let me in. It didn't look tampered with either. That means your father probably let his murderer in here. Is there any chance Stephen could have gotten out of the hospital and come here?"

Her face flushed an ugly pink.

"That's impossible. I'd like you to leave now.

Darius Greene killed my father. He's dangerous. An animal. My father's skull was crushed. Did you know that?"

I let myself out the back door because it was easier than walking past the wrathful Caroline Ragan.

The backyard was like the rest of the house: well groomed. The scent of new-mown grass hung in the warm afternoon air, and there were lawn mower tracks in the grass. Darius Greene had definitely been here.

A late-model white Buick was parked in the small detached garage. I had a sudden urge to snoop. After glancing around to see if Caroline was still glaring at me, I walked briskly up to the car and peeked in the passenger-side window.

Clean as a whistle. No Big Mac wrappers, Diet Coke cans, or spare pairs of sneakers. Not nothing. I looked around the garage. Hand tools were hung on pegs over a workbench. Rakes, shovels, and hedge clippers hung from nails along the rafters. I ran my fingers along the clipper blades. A couple of still green leaves clung to my fingertips.

It wasn't going to be easy to tell Ruby that her precious grandson might be a murderer.

As I left the garage I glanced again at Ragan's car. This time my eye caught a flash of something sticking out from under the passenger's seat.

Quickly I opened the door and peered under the seat. It was a newspaper page, folded in precise quarters. It was the classified ad page from Thursday's newspaper. Thursday. The day Merritt Ragan had been killed. Four ads were circled in red ink. They were all for garage sales or estate sales. I dug in my purse, got out paper and pen, and copied down the addresses. Then I put the paper back where I'd found it.

I found a pay phone down the street from Ragan's house. Edna answered on the first ring. "House Mouse." She sounded bored.

"Mom? Call Atlanta Regional Hospital and ask about a patient named Stephen Ragan. Find out if there's any way he could have gotten out of there Thursday. Call me back at this number."

I'd pulled the van up close to the phone booth, so I got back in and studied the addresses I'd copied from Merritt Ragan's newspaper while I waited. The inside of the van was hot and stuffy. I got out and walked briskly several times up and down the block, keeping within earshot of the phone. The exercise was part of my new program.

After thirty minutes of pacing, my blouse was sweat-soaked and plastered to my back. A kid sat on the porch of a weather-beaten wooden house across the street. He was staring at me. I stared back. He pulled out a giant Snickers bar, tore off the wrapper, and began licking it, slowly and deliberately, like a cat with a dead mouse. He had chocolate smeared all over his face and hands. It was in his hair, between his toes probably. I could hear my own breathing go shallow. Feel the salivary juices trickling through my chocolate-deprived digestive tract. I wanted to vault across the street, snatch the Snickers from the kid, and inhale it all in one gooey chocolate-caramel-peanut-covered nanosecond. It took every ounce of moral fiber I possess to go back to the phone booth and call the house again.

This time it was Ruby who answered the phone. "Edna had to, uh, go to the, uh, store," she stammered.

"Where is she really, Ruby?" I demanded. She was too saintly to be an effective liar. "Tell me."

"Lord have mercy, I don't know where she went," Ruby wailed. "I was sitting here when you called the last time. She got off the phone, looked up an address in the phone book, and took off out of here like a scalded dog."

"Never mind," I said. "I'll deal with her later."

"Callahan, wait," she said. "Did you talk to Darius?"

"I talked to him, but he wouldn't talk to me."

Silence.

"There's goodness in that boy. But don't nobody but me seem to know it. Can you do anything?"

I looked down at the scrap of paper with the estate sale addresses. "Maybe. What did Merritt Ragan look like? I only ever talked to him on the phone."

"Skinny little old fella. Reminded me of one of them bantam roosters. Had a full head of white hair. Little round bifocal glasses and one of them pointy little chin beards. What was the name of that man in the children's book? The man that made the princess spin gold all night till he guessed her name? He reminded me of him. Can't think of the name myself."

"Rumpelstiltskin?"

"That's the one," she said. "Mr. Ragan looked just that way."

My scrap of paper was looking like Darius Greene's last hope. "Go see him, Ruby," I urged. "Maybe he'll talk to you. Ask him where that money came from. And get him to tell the truth. It's the only thing that might save him."

"I'll see what I can do," she said wearily.

At the first house I had to elbow my way past a throng of people picking through stacks of old *National Geographic* magazines to get into the house. Right inside the front door I tripped over a metal and plastic contraption and nearly impaled myself on a set of brass fireplace tongs.

"That's why I'm selling the darned thing," said the woman who helped me to my feet. "The commercials make it look great; ski your way to a thinner you. They don't tell you it takes up a whole room in your house and you feel like throwing up after five minutes on it."

She'd said the magic word: thinner. I looked at the contraption with renewed interest. "Oh. A Nordic Ski-Track. How much? Does it work?"

"Twenty-five bucks," she said quickly. "I'll get my son to load it in the car for you."

I looked closer at the woman. She was two inches shorter and thirty pounds heavier than me. "I'll pass," I said. I described Merritt Ragan and asked her if she'd seen him.

"Oh, him," she said. "Cheapskate. He was here, talked me out of my grandmother's cake plate for two bucks."

An older woman wearing a large cotton duster over

her dress was packing up boxes at the second address. "Oh yeah, I know Merritt," she said. "He comes to our sales all the time."

"I do this professionally," she said, before I could ask. "Run estate sales, that is. Merritt came by about ten Thursday. We had lots of books and coins and record albums. Nothing he buys. We chatted and he left."

She didn't seem curious about why I was asking, and I hated to tell her anyway.

The third house was in an older neighborhood of brick bungalows. An older man, maybe in his late sixties, said he'd been too busy to notice who'd been at his sale Thursday. He agreed to look through his cash box, but there was no check from Merritt Ragan.

Depressed, I nearly skipped the fourth house entirely after pulling up to the curb. Two young mothers had piled a load of playpens, baby strollers, toys, and other kid paraphernalia in the driveway. It was the exercise bike that caught my eye.

I got out of the van and circled it warily. Kicked the tire. Checked the odometer. It had twelve miles on it. One of the women noticed my interest.

"My husband gave me that last year for an anniversary gift," she said. "I kicked the bum out a week later. Let you have the bike for thirty dollars, and I'll throw in the Thigh Master for nothing."

"Don't think so," I said. It turned out that she hadn't seen anybody who looked like Rumpelstiltskin the day before.

A convenience store a couple blocks away looked like a good place to get a cold drink and use the phone.

I left the drink cooler door open while I decided between Slim Fast and Ultra Slim Fast. I went with the Ultra. Then I called home again.

"House Mouse." My prodigal mother had returned.

"Where the hell were you?"

"You're dieting again, aren't you?" she snapped. "God help us all. If you must know, those old prunes over at the hospital wouldn't tell me diddly over the phone, so I went for a visit."

"You didn't," I said, knowing she had.

"Stephen Ragan hasn't been anywhere since Wednesday," she said. "He burned his hands in a craft class. Second-degree burns. He's in the infirmary and he's heavily sedated. I saw him with my own eyes."

I sighed. "Good work. I don't want to know how you got that information."

"I told 'em I was Sergeant Edna Bentley of the Atlanta PD," she said proudly.

When I pointed out that she'd committed a felony, impersonating a police officer, she made a rude noise. "Don't be late for supper," she said nastily. "It's fried chicken, buttermilk biscuits, and peach cobbler. Don't worry, though; since you're counting calories, I'll make unsweetened iced tea."

I hung up the phone and groaned.

That's when I noticed the cardboard sign tacked to a utility pole across the street. "Estate Sale. Thurs. Fri.," it said. There was an address and an arrow pointing down the nearest cross street.

The house was a two-story white frame affair. The lot was weedy, and the paint was peeling. I knocked at the screen door. When there was no answer, I poked my head in and hollered, "Anybody home?"

The woman who came bustling up the hall was in her early fifties probably. She was short, maybe five two, with gray hair cut in a Dutch boy, and her china blue eyes regarded me warily.

"Most everything's already sold," she said, wiping her hands on the rickrack-trimmed apron tied around her thick middle. "Just a few things left. Come in if you want. I'll be in the kitchen."

She hurried away down the hall. The house smelled of mothballs. She was right, there wasn't much left at all. The living room floors were stripped bare and my footsteps echoed loudly in the high-ceilinged room. All that was left here was a lumpy brown armchair that faced an old rounded-edge television with aluminum-foil-wrapped antennas.

A large mahogany china cabinet looked forlorn in the dining room. There were light rectangles on the painted walls, where pictures had once hung. I peered inside the cabinet. There were some chipped crystal goblets and two solitary rose-patterned dinner plates. And a cracked cream pitcher with a familiar-looking design of bluebirds and butterflies. I picked it up. The handle had been broken and clumsily glued back together.

I wandered down the hallway toward the back of the house. The kitchen was an old-fashioned room, with worn green and white checkerboard linoleum, scarred wooden cabinets, and an immense old stove.

The room was thick with heat and a good, sugary smell. The woman was humming as she poured something chocolate into a square metal pan. She reached into a small white bowl and scattered nuts across the top, then moved to an ancient white Norge. She pulled the door open, put the pan inside, and pulled out another pan, setting it on a white-painted kitchen table.

"If you see anything you can't live without, make the check out to Barbara Jane Booker," she said. "That's me."

My stomach growled loudly. Embarrassed, I patted my tummy. "I'm dieting," I said apologetically.

"What a shame," she said. "I was going to offer you a piece of fudge. It's a new recipe I'm testing."

I held out the pitcher then. "Pretty, isn't it? And unusual too. It matches a sugar bowl I found at a dead man's house earlier today. It's cracked, see? I guess that's why he didn't buy it."

"I wouldn't know," she said. But she'd wrapped her hands in the apron and was nervously rolling and unrolling it.

"The man I'm referring to was murdered," I said, keeping my tone conversational. "Bludgeoned to death with an iron. The police think a seventeen-year-old kid did it."

While I was talking I was strolling around the kitchen. I stopped in front of the stove. It was still hot. She'd left the burner on. When I reached to turn it off, my hand brushed a small white card written on in purple ink. The card fluttered to the floor. I bent down to pick it up, and the last thing I remember was the sensation of cold metal meeting the side of my skull.

When I came to, I had a splitting headache. Something warm was oozing down the side of my face. I reached up gingerly to see how much blood there was. My fingers came back coated with chocolate and pecans.

"The fudge needed to set longer," Barbara Jane Booker said apologetically. "I guess I was too impatient to test it." She was kneeling over me with a roll of silver duct tape, which she was busily wrapping around my ankles. "When I get back from our little trip, I'll make a note to let it sit for at least four hours."

"Trip?" I said, wincing. My head hurt like hell.

"I can't leave you here," she said. "The house has been sold. We close tomorrow. Maybe six hours would be better. I hate runny fudge, don't you?"

"Uh-huh."

"So I thought, what about that big aluminum recycling bin over behind the high school? I've got bags and bags of cans in the trunk of my car that I was going to drop off anyway. I'm a firm believer in recycling. Aren't you? I'll just pop over there in your car, put you in, then dump the cans on top. To cover you up, you see. Monday is pickup day. I'm afraid I'll have to vandalize your car. To make it look like it was stolen by some of these teenage hoodlums who terrorize decent folks like me."

She was chattering away a mile a minute, wrapping that tape around and around my ankles.

"Mrs. Booker?"

She looked up. "I'm sorry. I didn't catch your name."

"Callahan. Callahan Garrity. I was just wondering how you were planning to dump me in one of those bins. I'm lots bigger than you, you know."

She smiled and flashed a dimple, then reached in the pocket of her apron and brought out a big rusty black revolver. "I thought this would persuade you to climb into the bin by yourself. I've got a touch of lumbago in my lower back. The doctor says absolutely no heavy lifting."

The gun was so big, she had to use both hands to hold it up. I folded my knees up against my chest, swiveled, and kicked her square in the chest, as hard as I could.

She fell backwards, ass over teakettle, and the gun went clattering across that checkerboard floor. I scooted across the linoleum on my own butt, propelling myself forward with my bound ankles.

When I had the revolver, I trained it on her and managed, with difficulty, to stand up. Mrs. Booker, on the other hand, was howling with pain, screaming about her lumbago.

I cut myself free of the tape with a kitchen knife, and held the gun on her with one hand while I dialed homicide with the other. While we waited for the cops to arrive, she told me what had happened. I fixed us both a glass of iced tea. Assault and battery is thirsty work.

"He got here around noon. I'd gone to get us some lunch. My husband sold him that box of recipes. You can imagine how I felt when I got back. Aunt Velma's recipes. Gone. I liked to have died. Aunt Velma's fudge recipe was in there. That was mine. Aunt Velma promised. My sisters and I are splitting the money from the house and the rest of the junk in here, but the fudge recipe was mine. Jerry, my husband, couldn't remember who'd bought what. Just like a man. But he did remember he'd taken mostly checks. I took the checks and drove to every address."

"And you ended up at a gray house off Hooper," I suggested.

"Nasty old bastard," she spat out. "He laughed when I asked for the recipe back. Said the box was full of money. No way would he give it back."

"Money?"

"Aunt Velma," she said, shaking her head fondly. "We found near fifteen hundred dollars just in the kitchen. All tens and twenties. She grew up in the Depression, you know, and she never trusted banks. We found bills tucked under the shelf paper, in the pages of books, sewn into the hem of coats."

"And in the recipe box."

"I told him he could have the money," she said. "He laughed at me. So I pushed right past him. He was a runty little old thing. Came nipping and yapping at my heels, like one of those little lap dogs.

" 'Get out or I'll call the police,' he was yelling. I just kept looking. Then I saw the box on the stove, with all the money in a pile around it. I offered him twenty dollars for the fudge recipe card, but he wouldn't take it. 'This was the deal of the year,' he said. 'It's mine now. Get out.'

"When he tried to grab the box away, he hurt me. Broke one of my nails." She held up a plump pink digit to show me. The nail was ripped jaggedly. "I was so mad, I grabbed the nearest thing to hand. One of those old-timey sad irons."

She paused then, and took a long sip of tea. "I grabbed that iron and hit him on the head as hard as I could. He dropped like a rock. I took the fudge recipe and left. I didn't care about any of the others. Aunt

Velma wasn't really all that good of a cook. Except for fudge. I was going to take the money, but on the way out, I dropped it by the front door. It didn't seem right to take it with him dead and all."

Barbara Jane put down the tea glass then, and leaned forward to tell me something in confidence, I thought. Instead, she reached out, ran a finger across my fudge-encrusted cheek, and licked it delicately.

"Mayonnaise," she said softly. "That was Aunt Velma's secret ingredient. Good old Blue Plate mayonnaise. I'd never have guessed in a million years."

Ashes to Ashes

Linda Grant

People were acting weird, even by Berkeley standards. Joe and Charlie could agree on that much as they sat behind their display of crystals, sizing up potential customers. A few yards away, the hate man and the preacher were screaming at each other over some fine point of theology while curious students clustered around and nervous tourists edged by the growing crowd.

To the man from Duluth there to check out the UC campus with his son, Telegraph Avenue, and all of Berkeley for that matter, looked weird. He eyed the two guys in faded tie-dye shirts who sat behind a table covered with rocks and crystals, and wondered why they couldn't find decent clothes and real jobs.

The tie-dyed were too busy exploring the state of the universe to pay much attention to a tourist who was clearly not a potential customer. Charlie, the skinny

137

one with the acne scars, wondered idly how anyone could stand to encase himself in a suit on a warm October day. The ways of the straight always confounded him.

Joe was too concerned with the feel of the day to notice the tourist. He decided that the problem was the weather. Too hot and too still. "Earthquake weather," he said ominously.

"Oh, man, you're still spooked from the quake. We're just past the two-year point, the vibes are still around. That's all," Charlie said.

"No," Joe insisted. "This is different. There's something coming, man. I can feel it."

Later Joe would say it was like being in two dimensions at once; there was an eerie stillness, but there was also the wind. A malevolent wind. You could feel the evil in it. An itchy wind that pricked at your skin. It didn't come from anyplace. It was just there.

Up in the Berkeley hills, the million-dollar view from Clarence Hardy's house didn't include the Avenue. It did offer three bridges and the silhouette of San Francisco, shimmering in the haze. Clarence Hardy would have noticed the weather. He noticed everything, weighed it and put a dollar value on it. If he couldn't assign it a figure, it wasn't worth his time.

But Clarence wasn't weighing anything anymore. He'd keeled over from a massive coronary just one year before and was now enriching the soil in the Mountain View Cemetery.

He'd left behind a wife who hardly missed him because he'd so rarely been around, two middle-aged sons who'd inherited their father's preoccupation with wealth and power, and four grandchildren. On this, the first anniversary of his passing, his widow had invited her sons and their wives to Sunday brunch.

If Louise Hardy noticed that there was something strange in the day, she dismissed it as the product of nerves and anticipation of the difficult morning that lay before her. She'd invited the children only partly because she didn't want to be alone. With Clarence gone for a year, it was time to settle a matter that had been ignored for entirely too long.

She was not interested in presiding over another happy-family charade. When they all behaved themselves very well, they managed to *look* like a happy family. But the Hardy clan had not been a real family for many years. It was Clarence's fault. He'd pitted his sons against each other from the time they were little. Wanted to see what they were made of, he said. Small wonder they'd ended up as they had.

But the next generation, there was hope for them, she thought. Maybe that was why she'd hatched this crazy scheme to try to undo some of the evil Clarence had wrought. She loved her sons. She did not like them much. But she was genuinely fond of her grandchildren. And for their sakes, she was prepared to risk the opening of old wounds.

Damion, Louise's younger son, dreaded the brunch. He'd have bowed out if his wife had let him. But Sarah believed in family, and she wasn't about to leave her mother-in-law alone on the first anniversary of her husband's death. So she'd bullied and pleaded, and as always, she'd gotten her way.

"I don't see why she has to get *all* of us together,"

Damion grouched as he backed the white BMW down the driveway. "We could have had her over here for the day. It's not like Chuck would mind not seeing her."

"She wants the family to be together," Sarah said quietly. She was a small-boned woman with finely drawn facial features. The soft wrinkles around her eyes and mouth had become more firmly etched as she passed fifty, but there was still a youthful quality to her face.

Damion looked older than his fifty-five years. The skin under his eyes had drooped into pouches, and what was left of his hair was a peppery gray. Today he was angry, and his mouth was set in a line so tight and narrow that his lips had almost disappeared. It was a look he wore more often as he got older, Sarah thought sadly.

He'd been tense for the past three weeks, snappish and impatient. She assumed it must have to do with the coming anniversary of his father's death, but she was wrong. Damion was in financial trouble, serious trouble, lose-the-business-and-mortgage-the-house-type trouble.

His chain of office supply stores had been doing okay but not great when he hatched the idea of expanding and adding five new outlets. The economic recovery promised by supply-siders in Washington turned into a near depression in California, and the stores never got into the black. Now the banks wanted their money, and he was in deep doodoo along with his favorite president.

It was a short drive from their Upper Rockridge home to his mother's house, fifteen minutes max. Not nearly long enough as far as Damion was concerned. It always galled him to visit the family home; he still thought of it as his father's house, and he never pulled up in front of the Greek Revival facade without a gnawing pain in his gut. Even dead, the old man still got to him.

Chuck Hardy wasn't any happier about the brunch invitation than his brother. He had a golf date at two with the CEO of American Chemical. They were doing the merger dance, and he couldn't afford to take time out to indulge his mother's maudlin whims. But he couldn't afford to cross the old lady either. She still held the majority share of Hardy stock and voting power on the board of directors. He'd need her support when the merger went through.

Damion would be there, of course. That was always a major irritant. His younger brother had never forgiven him for being smarter and more successful. No family gathering was allowed to go by without at least one whiny reference to how Chuck had done him out of his half of the family business. As if business were like playing croquet where you wore white and made polite conversation.

Chuck glanced at his watch and called upstairs to Norma. "Come on, we're going to be late."

She didn't want to go either, he knew. Second wives were rarely popular with the family, especially younger, prettier second wives. While Mother might be gracious and polite, in her eyes Norma would always be an outsider. He was glad the kids wouldn't be there. It still irritated him that for the first year of his marriage, they had referred to Norma as "the bimbo."

He watched with pride and pleasure as she came down the wide staircase toward him. She was wearing stylish tan pants with a burnt orange silk blouse and an Armani scarf. He put his arm around her, and sneaked a look in the hall mirror as they headed for the door. They were a damn fine-looking couple.

Outside the hot wind washed over them, searing their skin and teasing at Norma's carefully combed hair. Chuck walked faster to the car and felt his irritation grow.

Chuck drove his usual ten miles over the limit and pushed a couple of lights. If he hadn't had to use Tunnel Road, he'd have made it on time. It always infuriated him the way that Berkeley refused to come to grips with the reality of the automobile. Tunnel Road should have been a main artery. Instead the Berkeley geniuses took traffic from two major freeways, mixed it with everything that came down the web of streets in the hills, and dumped it on a two-lane street where it backed up and sat.

He turned at his mother's street and partway up the hill had to pull over for a red Mazda coming toward him. These damn hill streets were too narrow for two cars; they ought to be widened, but the residents weren't about to give up the huge trees that lined the street. Berkeley people loved their trees, even the trashy eucalyptus that dropped leaves and bark all year and went up like torches in a fire.

Chuck checked his watch as they walked up to the door. They were only ten minutes late, right on time by Berkeley standards. He greeted his mother perfunctorily and with little warmth. Louise wondered idly how the boisterous little boy with the broad grin and generous hugs had turned into the coolly formal adult who always seemed to find her presence an imposition. He had never forgiven her for trying to upset his plans to force Damion out of the family business. In truth, it had taken her more than a few years to forgive his shameful behavior.

But their estrangement went back much further, to the beginning of adolescence when Clarence had convinced them all that it was unhealthy for sons to be too close to their mothers. He'd teased and bullied the boys whenever they turned to her for help or support. And, as had become the pattern in their marriage, she'd let him have his way.

Damion arrived fifteen minutes later, no warmer in his greeting than Chuck had been. She suspected that he'd never forgiven her for not saving him from Chuck's takeover. It struck her as ironic that she'd managed to alienate both sons without accomplishing a single thing.

Chuck was pouring his second Bloody Mary by the time that Damion got there. Damion mixed himself a screwdriver that was mostly gin and wandered out onto the deck. He was back almost immediately, complaining of the hot winds. "This whole damn state's going to dry up and blow away at his rate," he said.

Damion's wife, Sarah, was the only person who seemed genuinely glad to be there. She chatted with Louise, trying in her own way to make up for her husband's hostility. Chuck's second wife, the lovely Norma, stood apart as she always did, like an expensive piece of art on display.

Louise made a couple of unsuccessful efforts to get everyone to talk, then headed for the kitchen to ask the maid to serve the meal. Better to get some food into the boys before one of them got drunk and caused an ugly scene. This morning was going to be difficult enough without that.

She called them to eat and forced herself to keep still when both sons headed for the bar instead. It was looking like a long morning.

Back on the Avenue, the sun was hot and the wind was blowing steadily now. Tempers were short; there'd already been a couple of near fights on Charlie's corner.

"Man, look at that," Joe said, pointing to a column of black smoke that rose straight up from someplace in the hills to the southeast.

"Whoa," Charlie said. "That don't look good, man. That's fire."

Joe looked over at the dead leaves skittering down Haste Street like giant brown insects. They were headed west. "That's what's so weird. The wind," Joe said. "It's blowing west, from the valley."

West from the valley, not east from the ocean, the way it did most of the year. A west wind, a dry wind, heated in the oven of the San Joaquin Valley before it swept seaward over the already parched hills, scorching them to tinder-dryness. Down South they'd call it a Santa Ana. Down South it meant fires that could burn to the sea.

Joe muttered a heartfelt "Shit." Now he understood what he'd been feeling that morning. No wonder there were major bad vibes.

Charlie and just about everyone else was busy watching the black column. The itchy twitchy feeling of the day picked at them; voices sounded both strained and excited, some querulous, others whiny. The philosopher appeared about then, wrapped in his dirty, once orange blanket. "Bad day," he pronounced morosely, gave Joe a meaningful nod, and shuffled on.

"He's right for once," Charlie said. "Those hills are dry as dust; they'd burn in a minute."

Joe nodded. "It's the wind, man, that's the deal. It's a death wind."

The Hardys were just finishing a strained but polite meal. Alice, the maid, cleared away the dishes and poured more coffee.

"Please put the dishes in the dishwasher, Alice. When you're finished cleaning up, you can go," Louise said. "I know you're anxious to see your new granddaughter."

Alice smiled broadly. "You sure you won't need me?" she asked.

"No," Louise said, "I'll be fine." She'd have liked to ask Alice to stay, not to do any work, but just to be there. She was more a companion than a servant, but today's work was something Louise had to do alone.

Once Alice had left the room and before either son could make another trip to the liquor cabinet, Louise cleared her throat. "I have something to say to you," she began. "In going through your father's papers, I came across something bearing on an incident that we need to discuss." The room was suddenly very quiet.

"You know that I never approved of the way your father set you against each other over Hardy Enterprises. He was convinced that the company should be under the control of one person, so he forced you to compete to demonstrate which was the better businessman." Chuck smiled up at her, a smug look on his face. Damion studied his plate. Her heart went out to her youngest; he'd never recovered from the humiliation of losing his father's insane contest.

"Well, I now find that the competition was far from honest." She gave Chuck a hard look. "The new generation of office equipment on which Damion based his expansion plans and for which he borrowed so heavily never existed, did it, Chuck?"

Chuck was no longer smiling. He had that cagey look he used to get as a kid when he knew he was in trouble. Damion's mouth hung slightly open as he tried to take it all in.

"You fabricated the whole thing, Chuck." Before he could deny it, she added, "It's all in a report from a private investigator your father hired."

"You set me up?" Damion asked, still not quite believing it.

"You set yourself up," Chuck said. "I offered the bait, but you're the one who jumped up and grabbed it."

Damion leaped to his feet, knocking his chair over. "You son of a bitch. You were behind the whole thing."

Chuck actually smiled. He was enjoying this, she realized. "Hey, Damie," he said, using the nickname with which he'd taunted his brother since they were small, "that's how it is in the big bad world. Dad knew that. That's why he gave me the company."

"Sit down, Damion," Louise said sternly. Damion

hesitated, glaring at his brother, but finally righted his chair and sat down. "Exactly what *did* your father know, Chuck?" Louise asked. "And when?" The cover sheet had been missing from the report, so she had no way of knowing when Clarence had discovered Chuck's treachery.

"You read the report," Chuck said. "He had that done when Damion's division fell apart. He knew the whole thing, but he preferred a cheater to a fool, so he gave the business to me."

Louise felt a bit sick. She'd hoped that Clarence hadn't learned of the fraud until years after when he might reasonably have decided not to act on it. She'd always known he was a hard man, but she hadn't realized he was cruel as well.

"Not quite," Louise said. "He made you his successor. I own the business."

"Well, of course," Chuck said smoothly. His voice had a tight, controlled quality, and a healthy hit of paternalism. He wished to hell that the old man had listened to him and gotten a will drawn up. "But you know that dad intended me to have it eventually."

When I die, Louise thought.

"After all," Chuck added, "Damion's got his trust fund, and Dad set him up in the retail supply business."

"Which was never worth anything like Hardy Industries," Damion charged.

"It was Dad's business to do with as he wished," Chuck shot back. Without even realizing it, both men had risen and were shouting at each other across the table.

"Sit down," Louise ordered in exactly the tone

she'd used with them as preschoolers. She was tired of them both, and more than that, she was tired of the whole stupid argument. "Charles, your father taught you more about business than about decency. It's time you thought a little about what's right rather than what's profitable."

"Now, look, Mother," Chuck began. He was using his oily salesman voice.

"No, you look," she interrupted. "I want you to sit down and figure out the compensation you owe Damion for sabotaging his division. It doesn't have to be half the company, but it has to be a fair settlement. And I want it by the end of next week."

"You expect *him* to be fair?" Damion protested.

She didn't, of course. Not if he could figure a way out of it. But, ironically, she was doing this as much for Chuck as for Damion. He'd kick and scream for a while, but she hoped that in the end he'd learn something, maybe even see that this was better.

"I can't do that, Mother. I won't," Chuck said. "I didn't break any laws. You can't blackmail me."

She rose and walked to the sideboard, pulled a sheet of paper from the drawer, and brought it to the table. "This is a holographic will," she said. "It leaves seventy-five percent of the business to Damion. The rest of the estate is divided among the grandchildren. You have seven days, Chuck. Then I take this to Arthur Grand, my lawyer, and have him put all this into fancy legal language."

Chuck stared at the piece of paper. Holy shit, he thought, she's even signed it. Aloud, he said, "You can't be serious."

The look Louise gave him was as stony as the old

man's. "I am old, Charles, but I am not infirm, and I am not a fool. You have seven days."

Chuck rose stiffly from the table. His internal temperature was well above 212, but experience had taught him never to speak when he felt like this. "We'll be going now," he said, already heading for the front door, leaving Norma to scramble along behind.

Chuck didn't notice that the temperature outside had risen since he'd arrived or that the wind had intensified. But when he reached Tunnel Road, he couldn't miss the wall of thick dark smoke that poured down the valley from the direction of the Caldicott Tunnel.

He was too busy thinking about his mother's crazy scheme to be very curious about the smoke. Norma wondered aloud what was up and immediately turned on the radio. Chuck ignored them both.

Traffic, never good on Tunnel Road, was even heavier than usual. Chuck was sure he could talk the old lady out of this foolishness eventually, but in the short run, she could really screw up the merger arrangements. He needed this merger, and he needed it to happen soon.

"Chuck," Norma said in the tone she used when he'd ignored her efforts to get his attention. "Maybe we should go back. They say the fire could get into Berkeley."

"Damion's there," he said. "He can take care of her. I've got other things to worry about."

Damion was there, all right, but Louise was beginning to wish he'd just go home. He was like a whiny two-year-old. He wanted to know exactly what was in the investigator's report, wanted to see it, wanted to rehash every slight and wrong he'd ever experienced.

He started out being furious at Chuck, moved to resenting his father's complicity, and ended up blaming his mother for not standing up for him sooner. He was on his second chorus of "Daddy always loved him best" when Louise suggested it was time to go.

Damion exploded. "You say you want to make it fair, but you're going to let Chuck tell you how. All he's gonna tell you is how to screw me again. Don't you see that?"

"Damion, stop whining," she ordered. "Try to act like an adult." She regretted the words as soon as they were out of her mouth. It was too close to the taunts Clarence had leveled at their son. The high cost of that kind of cruelty stood before her.

"You're on his side. You don't really want to help me at all," he said.

His face was almost purple. Louise was repulsed by him. There was no point in trying to explain anything when he was like this. "I think we should discuss it later," she said as calmly as she could.

Damion wasn't about to let it go at that, but Sarah stepped in. She, too, knew the futility of trying to reason with him, and announced, "Damion, I need to go home. I'm not feeling well."

It took a second request, this time in a firmer tone, to get him moving, and when he did move, he was still whining and grumbling. Louise closed the door behind him with relief.

She was too involved in her own thoughts to notice the strange shift in the light. A dusky yellow softened the colors, making the street look like a scene from a poorly photographed movie. If she'd looked to the south, she might have seen the gray-black smoke sweeping westward on gusting wind. But her eyesight was so poor that even if she'd seen it, she wouldn't have understood what it was.

Back in the house, she collapsed into a soft leather armchair and felt exhaustion and sadness sweep over her. It didn't surprise her that Chuck had responded as he had; she'd expected no different. But Damion's outburst stung her. She'd thought he'd be . . . what? Pleased? Grateful? Instead, he was the same whiny, resentful child she'd tried so hard to placate since he was a toddler.

It shouldn't surprise her, she thought. We write the scripts for family dramas early, and they rarely get revised. Decades ago, when he was still a boy, Damion had written his script, casting himself as the unjustly abused victim, his father as the tyrant, his older brother as the pampered favorite. He'd cast her as his father's accomplice, she supposed. And having assigned her that role, he wasn't about to let her assume a new one.

She'd always thought of Damion as the soft one, still accessible, but she'd been wrong. Chuck had wrapped himself in his success, Damion in his failure, and both cloaks were as hard as the walls of a vault.

It was all so terribly sad, and futile, really. She could exact some restitution from Chuck, but she couldn't make him a morally responsible person, and she could redress some of Damion's grievances, but she couldn't make him strong or happy.

She stood up, but it took enormous effort. The

weight of depression was as tangible as a forty-pound backpack. She'd worn a real pack only once, but she'd shouldered its emotional equivalent many times. Only a year ago, when it'd threatened to crush her after Clarence's death, she'd discovered that there was a chemical solution. Days after she started taking the small white pills, the weight lifted and she could breathe again. Thank God there were still some left.

She took three instead of two in hopes that she could shorten the time it took them to take effect. Then she gave in to the overwhelming desire to lie down and sleep.

She was just drifting off when the shrill ring of the phone dragged her back to consciousness. It took all her energy to answer it.

"Louise, it's Jean, up the street." It took Louise a moment to connect the high, excited voice to the image of her stout, rather dour neighbor up the block. "Have you heard about the fire?" the shrill voice asked.

She hadn't. "It's a big one," Jean informed her. "They say it started near the tunnel and it's already burned up to Hiller Highlands. They think it might come our way."

Beneath the deadness of depression, Louise felt the stirrings of fear.

"We may have to evacuate. Better be ready. I'm putting my treasures in boxes right now. I can pick you up if you need a ride."

It was a short conversation, no time for chat. As she hung up, Louise tried to think of what she should take. There'd only be room for a box or two. She looked around the room, weighing the relative value of a lifetime's possessions. Which memories to save, which to discard?

She should probably get the papers from the safe, she decided. It took her three tries to open the cranky lock, then as she studied the thick metal walls, she decided the papers were safe where they were.

There was still some space inside the safe, so she stuffed in other papers that ought to be protected. Remembering the holographic will, she got it from the sideboard and stuck it in too, then closed the door and spun the dial so it locked. That was one set of things taken care of.

The rest was harder. The first burst of energy she'd felt when the warning came had evaporated, replaced by the old exhaustion that made even simple decisions difficult.

Sarah wasn't having any trouble making decisions. By the time they'd reached home, she was convinced that Damion had to go back for his mother. She'd realized something was wrong as soon as they hit Tunnel Road. It looked like five o'clock on an especially bad commute day.

To get home, they'd driven under a cloud of smoke so thick it was like twilight beneath it. Ash sifted down onto the windshield, and choruses of sirens filled the air. Looking back toward the hills, Sarah could see explosions of orange as houses burst into flames. The thick smoke was black in some places, red-orange in others. The colors were too bright, almost garish. It felt unreal, like a movie.

As they drove up the block to their house, it was clear that they too were in danger. Neighbors were already on their roofs with garden hoses.

Damion hadn't spoken a word during the tense drive home. She assumed he was angry with her for making him leave his mother's. As she began to comprehend the scope of the fire, she regretted their hasty departure. "I know you're worried," she said, as they pulled up in front of the house. "You go on back for your mother. I'll take care of things here."

The urgency in her voice startled him. Jolted him out of his own thoughts and forced him to awareness of the scene around him. He'd seen the smoke and ash, negotiated the narrow roads crowded with cars full of their owners' pets and possessions, but his thoughts had been so focused on the scene with his mother and Chuck that none of it had sunk in.

All he could think about was Chuck's and his father's treachery. His whole adult life he'd struggled with his damn office supply business, always on the edge, never having quite enough. And every year, he'd watched Chuck get richer running the family business, the business he'd cheated Damion out of.

"Go on," he heard Sarah say as she got out of the car. "I'll be fine."

He didn't want to go; there was stuff here he needed to get to safety. There was his computer system and the new fax machine, and a couple of paintings Sarah'd talked him into buying as an investment. He saw her worried face and knew he'd have to go. He rattled off a list of things for her to get before he started the car and headed back down the hill.

He focused on figuring out the fastest way to get

back, not just because the streets were becoming increasingly crowded but because it kept his mind from other things. He shoved away fears for his mother and reminded himself that she had the power to make things right and was going to leave it up to Chuck. She could give him a new start, but she wasn't going to do it.

By the time Damion got to his mother's, the sky was black and the air stank of smoke. People all along the street were throwing belongings into their cars and shouting anxiously to each other. A couple of houses up the street a guy his age was on the roof with a garden hose while his family pleaded with him to give it up and come down.

It seemed to take forever for his mother to get to the door. He rang the bell and pounded on the wood. For a minute he thought she might already have left.

She looked tired and a bit confused. Another day he'd have noticed how the last year had deepened the lines in her face, drawn the edges of her mouth downward more prominently. But today all he saw was the woman who had never once really defended him from his brother, who had colluded in his father's favoritism.

"You've got to get out of here," he told her.

"I've been putting my things together," she said. "There's just a bit more." She walked away from him, back toward her bedroom.

"Mother," he shouted. "There isn't time." He damn sure wasn't going to stand around her house while she packed boxes of worthless mementos. He had stuff to take care of at his own house.

He went to the bedroom to get her. There were two

boxes on the bed and a pile of photos. "Put those in the box for me, please," she said, then turned and went back to the living room.

The doorbell rang. He could hear a shrill-voiced woman ask if his mother needed a ride. "I'm fine. My son is here," she responded. The door closed.

"Take the boxes to the car," she called to him. "I'm just getting a few more things."

Damion reached for the first box. It was full of albums and photos. On top, staring mockingly up at him, was one of his father with his arm around Chuck. They were wearing tennis whites and looking pleased as hell with themselves. They'd probably just won some stupid tournament at the club.

Damion felt the pressure growing inside him. He wanted to throw the whole damn box on the floor. It was probably full of pictures like that. It was always like this, no matter how she tried to pretend otherwise. In the crunch, it was Chuck she cared about. He'd left his own stuff at home to save the old lady, and she was running around collecting pictures of darling Chuck.

She might talk about justice, but he knew she'd let Chuck have his way. Oh, there'd be some token settlement, something to testify to Chuck's moral superiority, but it wouldn't be half the business.

He left the box, rushed to the sideboard, and pulled open the drawer, searching for the will. Just then Louise came back into the room with a hamper full of stuff.

"Where's the will?" Damion demanded.

"I put it in the safe. It'll be fine there."

"Get it," Damion ordered.

"The safe was built to withstand fire," she told him. "Besides, it's hard to open. We don't have time."

"I want that will," he said.

"Damion," she said sharply, "stop it. We don't have time for this nonsense."

"It wasn't nonsense when Chuck cheated me out of the business," he screamed. "You said you wanted things to be fair, but they're never fair when Chuck's involved. If you loved me, you'd make that will final. You'd give me what's rightly mine."

"Oh, Damion," she said almost wistfully.

"No," he shouted. "I'm not backing down this time. You want me to act like a man. I'm acting a man. I want that goddamn will."

"There isn't time," she said, trying to keep the anger out of her voice.

"I want that will," he shouted. "I want it now."

Louise stared at the angry, contorted features of her younger son and saw not a fifty-five-year-old man but a stubborn, spoiled four-year-old, demanding his way. "Get out," she said. "Just get out."

"I want the will," he screamed.

"Well, you're not going to get it. Now, get out of here or that fire you're so afraid of will get you."

Damion took one last desperate look around. He could smell the fire inside now. It was too close.

He turned and raced toward the door, his eyes already stinging from the smoke. "Then you can stay here and burn, you old witch," he shouted, and he ran from the house, leaving the door open behind him.

Louise walked to it and saw his car pull away. It was

like deep twilight beneath the smoke and she could hear the fire roar in the trees up the hill. The loudness of it startled her. Her eyes stung and the acrid smell burned her nostrils. She closed the door.

She could have left then. She still walked in these hills; she could probably make it down to safety. Even with her poor eyesight, she knew the way. But she was too tired. Tired of her two angry sons, tired of the years of struggle with three men who placed strength above love.

She looked around at the house. Her house. Her refuge. No, she wouldn't leave. There was no point.

"What about Grandma?" Chuck could hear the desperation in his daughter's voice, even over the phone. "Is she in the fire area? The reports are all so confusing."

"We don't know for sure," Chuck said, though having watched the hills burn from lower Broadway, he did know. He just didn't want to admit it to himself, and he didn't want to discuss it with Laura. He'd miscalculated big time, hadn't realized how serious the danger was until too late. Left Damion the role of protector and savior.

It was rotten luck. His mother might be so grateful that she'd leave the whole business to Damion. The burning pain in his gut kicked up a notch at that thought. And what if Damion screwed up and didn't get her out? Chuck didn't like to think of that possibility, though, of course, it would solve his problem. He pushed the guilty thought from his mind.

"I couldn't get up there," he said defensively. "They wouldn't let me."

"Oh, Daddy," she said. "How awful. What can I do?"

"Nothing," he said. "There's nothing any of us can do. We better not tie up the phone lines now." He put the receiver down before she could protest.

At Damion and Sarah's, their son, Jules, loaded the family albums in the car, keeping an eye on the hills behind the house. The smoke was getting thicker, driven relentlessly by the searing wind. Thirty minutes ago, the light had been an eerie orange, and the sun, when you could see it through the smoke, was bloodred. Now orange flames shot up out of the smoke along the top of the hill. He could see the skeletons of houses as they burned.

There was a loud explosion, like a bomb. He'd been hearing them for the last hour. Probably the gas tanks of cars exploding. And there was the constant din of the helicopters. It was like a war movie, he thought. Not quite real. But the chunks of burning wood and the embers that fell like rain on his mother's block were all too real.

There was only one family left on the street, and they were climbing into their car. "We have to go, Mother," he called as he raced up the steps.

She ran out, clutching something he didn't recognize. As she dashed down to him, he realized it was a squirming orange cat. "It's the Hills' kitty. I found her hiding by the porch. It's a miracle she let me catch her."

His mother seemed unaware of the bleeding scratches on her arm, triumphant in her ability to save one small life from the inferno that bore down on them. They jumped in the car and headed down. *Please God,* Jules thought, *let me get her out of here.*

Down at the evacuation center at Tech High, the original chaos had settled into some form of organization as volunteers figured out what needed to be done and took charge. Cars drove up with boxes of food; one woman walked in with a sheet cake.

Joe and Charlie, who'd done everything from medic assist to trash patrol at various mob scenes of the sixties, felt right at home in the friendly anarchy. Joe'd started sorting the boxes of food and blankets dropped off by people looking for a way to help, but his back had begun to bother him, so he'd swapped jobs and was now pouring cups of soft drinks for dazed-looking people and frightened children who wandered in.

Charlie was helping with the message board, taking information and posting it. They'd started a list of everyone who'd checked in, and it was a terrific moment when he could tell someone, "Yeah, they're okay. They checked in an hour ago."

He'd expected everyone to be bummed out, crying or just sitting silent, and some were. But there were also people hugging each other; and some of the tears were from joy.

"Man, it's like teatime on the manic-depressive ward," Joe said.

"Hey, have a little sensitivity, man," Charlie snapped. "Some of these people just lost everything they own. Others don't know if their friends and families are safe."

"It's all illusion, man. It's just stuff. We're all just passing through."

Charlie groaned. He wasn't in the mood for Joe's philosophic bullshit, not when there was so much very real misery around. And he knew damn good and well that Joe'd be singing a different tune if it were his stuff that had just gone up in smoke or if Ramos, the dog, were up there in the smoke or flames.

That was what really got to him—the animals. All the dogs and cats and squirrels caught in that inferno. They'd be so scared, just terrified, and they wouldn't understand. He swallowed hard.

A small woman in her fifties asked again if there was any word of Damion or Louise Hardy. He shook his head, and he could see her lip quiver. A kid in his early twenties who was doing his best imitation of a grown-up put his arm around the woman and led her away.

Someone brought the latest list of hospital admits, and Charlie scanned it anxiously, hoping to find the Hardys. They weren't there.

Word was out about the update and people surged forward, all hoping for news. "They're probably at another center," he'd said dozens of times. And dozens of times, tired-eyed people had nodded, wanting to believe.

Damion Hardy arrived around four. Charlie was almost as happy to see him as his family was. Then they all realized that Louise Hardy was not with him. The small woman he'd come to know as Mrs. Hardy hugged her husband and buried her head against his chest sobbing. The old guy just stood there. He was obviously in shock.

Charlie got him some coffee. "Can I do anything to help?" he asked, then felt like a fool. How can you help someone who's just lost his mother?

The old guy shook his head. His son put an arm around his stiff shoulders. "Maybe someone else got to her," he said. "Maybe Uncle Chuck, or the woman who works for her."

The old guy just shook his head.

Sarah was grateful for the strange bearded man who wanted so desperately to comfort them. This morning she'd have passed him on the street and thought only that he needed a haircut. Now he was an old friend.

Around her groups of people clustered together, taking comfort of each other's presence. She wanted to hold Jules to her, hug him as she'd done when he was small. But he was a man now, or thought he was. It wouldn't be proper.

She wondered for the thousandth time about Louise, alone up on the hill. Hoped that someone, somehow, reached her and carried her to safety. Knew that the chances diminished with each hour that they received no word.

She watched Damion, his face closed tight like a fist, staring at the floor or jumping up and pacing. She knew that he had already given up hope. She could sense it. She knew too that he was shutting her out as he had so often in the past when his own emotions became too much for him to bear and he turned himself to stone in order to survive them.

She longed to hold and comfort him, but stone men

take no comfort. And what words could she speak that could conceivably help? It was the worst possible kind of loss—guilt mixed with impotence. He'd never get a chance to take back the ugly words he'd spoken that morning, to tell his mother he loved her, to say good-bye. That scene, which should have been just an unpleasant incident to be forgotten and put behind them, had become the defining moment of their relationship.

The sky blazed red over the hills that night. The wind had dropped, giving the exhausted firefighters some hope that they might contain the inferno. Like generals on a battlefield, they drew lines at strategic points and dug in.

Joe and Charlie spent the night at the evacuation center. Someone had brought in a portable television, and everyone crowded around to watch the grim-faced reporters interview even grimmer firefighters. Everyone wanted specifics—what was gone, what remained—but there were no specifics in the chaos. Just nightmare images of the horror from which they'd fled.

Joe wondered why they watched, how they could stand to rerun the trauma. Maybe it helped. On the TV the whole scene was reduced to a manageable size. Maybe that put it at a safe distance. Still, it felt weird to be watching a disaster you were right in the middle of like it was a TV movie.

No one slept very well that night. Joe and Charlie were up almost as soon as it was light. They hurried outside to see what was left of the hills now that the thick smoke had dissipated. To the north in the distance the hills were blackened, but around them things seemed remarkably unchanged.

"Weird, man," Joe said. "Too weird."

"They'll need help up in those hills today," Charlie said. "Think I'll volunteer."

Damion was up at dawn, too. He and Sarah had spent the night at a hotel down by the Bay, far from the burning hills and close to the water. It was full of fire victims. Some seemed almost frozen, their faces blank with shock; others were manic, talking nonstop, in constant motion.

Sarah was quiet. He'd feared that she'd question him about his trip to his mother's, but she treated him with great gentleness, allowing him his silence. At first he appreciated her delicacy, but after a couple of hours it irritated him to be treated as if he were so fragile he might break.

He knew she must believe he was mourning for his mother. And of course, he was. It was an awful thing she'd done, choosing to stay and die in the fire. He'd have saved her if she'd let him. But she'd preferred staying in a burning house to helping him get justice from Chuck.

It saddened him that in the end, his mother had sided with Chuck. But there might be some consolation. Because if that damn safe really was fireproof and she'd told the truth about putting the will in it, he'd outsmarted them all. He'd have seventy-five percent of the business, and Chuck could find out what it was like to start from scratch.

From the parking lot of the hotel, he could see the still-smoldering hills. Thin wisps of smoke rose like steam from the charred earth. He had to get back up there.

Sarah slept in, or pretended she did. She'd probably have stayed in bed all day if he hadn't finally demanded that she get up for breakfast.

She tried to argue him out of it when he announced he was going to check on his mother's house. The news was full of warnings not to go back into the fire area.

"They won't let you in," she told him. "They've said so on the television."

"They can't keep me out," he said.

He had to know what had happened. If the house had burned. And he had to know if the safe was still there. The pictures on the television this morning had shown houses burned to their foundations, nothing left but a pile of rubble and sometimes a chimney rising above it like a tombstone.

His mother's body would be in the house somewhere, he realized. He didn't like to think that he might find it. There couldn't be much left. How could flesh withstand the heat that had reduced whole houses to a pile of charred debris?

He pushed his mother from his thoughts. She hadn't thought much about him. She probably spent her last moments worrying about Chuck.

Chuck was one of the reasons he was in such a hurry. Chuck would be worried about the will, might figure it was in the safe, and just might remember, as Damion had, the Thanksgiving night fifteen years ago when the old man had told them the combination.

It was completely out of character for him to part

with that information, but he was in high spirits and had had a good deal to drink both before and during dinner. Afterwards, they'd sat out on the deck and smoked cigars and the old man had made a joke about how his new safe was like a beautiful woman. "Forty, twenty, thirty-five," he said, as his hands framed two curves. "Always a pleasure to open her." With that, the old man had turned to Chuck and given him a big wink, then the two of them had shared a lecherous laugh.

The police had checkpoints on Tunnel Road; no one was allowed up his mother's street. A police cruiser blocked the street and two cops stood beside it. Anxious people clustered around them. One cop, a tall, rangy guy with dark hair, held several sheets of paper. A young woman with a baby in a pack gave him an address on Grandview.

The cop consulted his list. "Sorry, ma'am, that whole street's gone."

She nodded dully. Her expression said she'd expected it. Others stepped up with their addresses or addresses of friends. Most often the answer was "We don't know yet. I'll have more information in a few hours."

When Damion's turn came, he got the same answer. He explained why he had to go himself, that his mother was missing. They listened with sympathy and made note of the address so they could search, but they still wouldn't let him up the street. "Maybe tomorrow," the cop said. "It's just not safe now."

As a kid Damion had known lots of ways to get around the neighborhood besides the road. Now all he had to do was remember one of them. But as he was walking back toward the Claremont Hotel, he found a better solution. A pickup full of men in work clothes had stopped while its driver asked directions to the street just beyond Damion's mother's.

"Can you use another volunteer?" he asked the guys in the back.

"Sure," said a skinny guy with a pockmarked face that looked vaguely familiar. He stood and leaned over to give Damion a hand up.

"Don't I know you?" he asked. "You must have been at the evac center."

"Yeah," Damion said as he climbed in. The truck lurched forward and they pulled up the street to the checkpoint.

The cops let them through without a hassle. The first part of the street looked almost untouched. Lawns were still green, trees sheltered the street, but both lawn and street were littered with blackened chunks of burned wood.

Then suddenly around a corner, they passed into a nightmare landscape. It was that quick. One minute there were green trees and beige and yellow houses, the next it was like being in the middle of a war zone. Hard to believe mere fire could have caused such complete devastation. Burned-out hulks of cars sat at the curb, nothing left but their metal skeletons. Cement foundations outlined houses no longer there.

The air stank of smoke and charred wood. Not the pleasant smell of a campfire, but an ugly mélange of things not meant to burn. Here and there the rubble still smoldered. The men in the truck were silent as they confronted it.

They were given shovels and instructions on how to handle the small fires. Told to call for help with anything that looked too big to handle. "Go slow," the driver told them, "remember that rubble is superhot. Sometimes stuff's compacted so much that the air can't get to it. You turn it over, the oxygen hits it and it'll ignite."

"And pay attention to the wind," the driver's companion cautioned. "If it starts to kick up again, we get out. Another Santa Ana and we'll be right back where we were yesterday."

Damion poked around with his shovel for a bit, then headed up toward his mother's house. There was no longer any question of whether the house might have survived. Surrounded by the smoky, reeking scene, he couldn't quite keep thoughts of his mother from his mind. She'd have died of smoke inhalation, he thought. Maybe it wasn't so bad.

"Be a man," he told himself angrily. "She chose to stay."

His heart sank when he realized how little was left from the fire. Not even refrigerators. It wasn't likely that the safe had survived. Everything was a dead loss.

It was hard to navigate with everything familiar gone. But he knew his parents' house when he saw the oversized fireplace and chimney. His heart seemed suddenly to grow and bang against the inside of his chest as he walked slowly toward it.

Beyond the chimney, the familiar million-dollar view was still there. His eyes stung with tears, but he told himself not to be a dope. He was here for the safe, for justice.

Still, he couldn't force himself to move forward. He

felt a growing horror at what he might find. Someplace in the debris was the safe. But someplace in the same debris was his mother. Even a coldhearted bastard like Chuck couldn't dig through those ashes.

He was about to give up and leave when a man in a bright yellow suit came down the street with a dog on a leash. Damion remembered hearing that they used dogs to search for bodies. He went up to the man.

"The guys at the roadblock said there might be a body around here, that house, I think," he said, pointing.

The man nodded. "Yeah, there was. We found it a couple of hours ago. I guess they just didn't get word yet."

Damion kept his face neutral and just nodded. Then poked around with his shovel while the man and dog continued down the street. Once they'd rounded the corner, he turned toward the pile of debris that had been the house where he'd grown up.

He picked his way carefully through the rubble. Twisted metal and blackened chunks of unidentifiable material were everywhere. But the piles were pitifully small to be all that remained of such a grand house.

He was on the edge of tears and it took all his willpower not to drop the shovel and flee. If the safe was there, it would be near the window on the right side of the house. He found a pretty good-sized pile of debris there, and at the center of it was the safe.

A sense of elation surged through him. The safe had survived. If the will was in it, he'd finally get what he deserved. Justice would be done at last.

He was glad he'd brought gloves. The safe was as hot as a pan on the stove. He turned the dial slowly to forty, back past twenty, stopping there the second time around, then back again to thirty-five. Turned the handle and pulled.

The door swung open.

Hot air poured out on his face, as if he'd opened an oven. He reached for the papers, then snatched his hand back. To his horror, a bright orange tongue of flame leapt up and grew in seconds to fill the safe. He reached desperately into the flames, trying to smother them. But they spread to his shirtsleeve.

He beat at the sleeve until the flames were out, then turned back to the safe. The fire burned low now, tracing glowing tracks along the edges of blackened pages. It had taken only moments for the entire contents of the safe to be reduced to the same black ash that covered the ground around it.

Knife of the Party

Annette Meyers

Minxie was always committing suicide, so when she died, no one was that impressed. This time, we all assumed, her safety nets—for she always prepared her suicides carefully—had failed her.

She was supposed to have been in Ibiza halfway across the world when she called Joel and left her usual suicide message on his answering machine: "I rue the day I gave birth to you, my ungrateful, ugly son. By the time you hear this, I'll be dead."

And she was.

But here's the thing. I'd brought Joel home from another tedious backers' audition and we were talking over how to change our presentation, you know, drop reference to the subplot and stick to the main story, that kind of stuff. I was really beat and still had about a dozen calls to make, but Joel said, "Come on in and we'll knock this off over coffee."

Let me tell you, when your writer wants to work, especially Joel, who's a great procrastinator, you take him up on it. So that's how I happened to hear Minxie's revolting lights-out message to her only child.

And I was there when Joel called her back. The poor guy always did, no matter how badly she treated him, and guess what? She'd left him the wrong number. Then there was all that hysteria about alerting the U.S. Embassy, which did not exist in Ibiza, and the Spanish police, and finally, nobody knew where the hell she was.

By this time there was a whole group of us trying to help, and then someone said, wasn't she at Dee Dee (Lady Stuart) Batton's house on Dune Road in East Hampton because it was in all the columns, but Minxie wasn't there either. And someone else said Minxie was really hiding out, after yet another face-lift, in her apartment on Sixtieth and Park, which turned out to be true.

But I'm getting ahead of my story. I first met Minxie Messerback at one of Mort and Poppy Hornberg's parties. It was a freebie—Mort was always amenable to them—at a little private club, charmingly called Privates, near the Plaza. We all had to sign a book with our names and addresses, and afterward we all got special invitations to join, for the modest sum of fifteen hundred dollars per annum. A mere bagatelle. I wonder how many who attended the party actually joined, for the club disappeared in less than a year.

I was still working as Mort's assistant at the time, although already counting the days I had left before I went out on my own.

So there I was holding up a pillar with Howie Heinz—remember him? No? Well, I guess it was a little before your time. Howie was a public relations specialist whom Mort had hired to try to improve his image. What Mort really wanted was for the *New York Times* drama critic to stop dumping on him, and lo and behold, the new show, which I thought was no better than a TV sitcom, had met with *Times* approval, in spite of the fact that Mort had a character come onstage clutching a toilet in his arms. Give me a break. Toilet jokes are a cheap laugh, but they always seem to bring down the house. And Minxie, who attended every Broadway opening religiously—on someone's guest list—was quoted as saying, "Show in trouble? Mort Hornberg and his toilet to the rescue."

Anyway, the party. Free booze flowed, but I wasn't having any. The new me was off alcohol because I was getting ready to produce my first show, and I had optioned Joel Messerback's new play, which we were setting to music. I'd gotten first dibs on two talented guys who had just become partners—Lou Cashwell, music, and Johnny Carey, lyrics. And Broadway wits had seized on the partnership and dubbed them Cash and Carry, which was fine with me and good for the project.

Anyway, Howie was off the booze, too, because he had a real full-blown drinking problem. He'd been in denial for years, but now he had a lousy liver and was warned that if he continued drinking, it would be over and out in no time at all. His friends, of whom I was one, sort of closed in around him, and although it was informal and unspoken, we all made it our business to protect him from himself.

So the two of us were standing there with our glasses of Perrier (oh, sparkle, sparkle), outsiders, watching the obsessively hilarious time the others seemed to be having.

"What do you think, Howie?" I said. "Isn't it a bore without the booze?" I'd always had such a good time at Mort's parties, but then I'd put away a couple of Stolies quickly, early on, so what did I really know?

"I had no idea," Howie said, lighting up. "They all look as if they're trying their damnedest to have fun, don't they?" He smoked Camels without filters and was so absentminded about the ash that his clothing was dusted with it, and once he'd actually set himself on fire when he dropped a lighted cigarette into his pocket. "I used to love these parties before I took the pledge," he said sadly. "Maybe I'm getting old." He was watching George, his longtime lover, who had not given up drinking, execute a tap routine with two other aging gypsies, which is what chorus dancers in the theater are called because they go from show to show.

"Not you, Howie. The rest of us, yes. Never you."

"Darling!"

We were suddenly confronted—did I say confronted? attacked is better—by a very slim woman in a cream silk tunic over cream silk pants. A matching turban covered her hair entirely. She might have been bald, but this wasn't so; I knew there were wisps of dark hair under it because we had the same hairdresser.

She was at least a head shorter than I, but managed to look tall, and even dangerous. *Whiplash* is the word that comes to mind. Maybe it was the extremely high cheekbones that jutted out from her face, which she highlighted with makeup. Or her narrow jaw, pointy chin, and high forehead. Her neck was long and covered by an Isadora scarf in—you guessed it— cream silk that flowed down her back.

One long elegant hand held a black cigarette holder, from which she occasionally took puffs as if it were an opium water pipe. In her other hand she carried a glass of clear liquid, but the fumes it gave off told me it wasn't Evian. It was pure gin.

She draped herself over Howie, "Kissie, kissie, pooh," and I could see he was flattered, for she was Minxie Messerback and she was a star. Or at least she had been. You can still see her old movies on TV, sort of a poor man's cross between Gloria Swanson and Joan Crawford. Only ten years ago you could find her doing her cabaret act at the hotel clubs, satirical songs and dance. There she'd stand in her signature cream silk, between two young stud types in tuxes, and sing stone-faced under her turban. The studs would pick her up, stiff as a marble column, and move her around, and all the time she'd be singing. It was an insane performance, just insane enough to garner a cult following. Some joker commented that if you cut her, she'd bleed gin.

Lately she'd had some success writing malignant fables for children, featuring a dreadful little girl named *Juicie Lucie,* the popularity of which I found bizarre, but then, what do I know about the tastes of children, or for that matter, publishing?

Turning her chiseled profile to me, Minxie made a grand gesture with her cigarette holder and said to Howie in her husky voice, "Who is your little friend?"

Now, let me pause here for a minute and tell you that *little* was never a descriptive word for me. I have always been tall, and swimming has given me good shoulders. I wear my thick sun-streaked hair high in front and long. Get the picture? I was, and still am, nobody's *little friend.*

Howie gave me a quick, nervous look as if he could read my thoughts, which he probably could because I never wore a mask, so he could see Minxie had stirred the killer in me. But she did that with everyone. I was thinking seriously about giving her the back of my hand. Swat!

"This is Sunny Browning," Howie said. "She's been Mort's assistant for years and she's producing Joel's new play."

"Oh, yes," Minxie said, turning partway to me without undraping herself from Howie. "Joel." She drawled it and it came wrapped with venom. "I suppose you know what you're letting yourself in for. No talent. No discipline. Chronically depressed, and—" she finished in a stage whisper "—so *ugly.*"

"Excuse me," I said, polite but furious. "Joel is very talented, and you should be proud of him. Any mother would be. And if he's depressed, I can certainly see why."

Sounds insulting? It was meant to be. Joel's mother was an infamous bitch. In a profile that appeared in the *New Yorker* some years ago, she had said she'd divorced his father, an internist, because he was "charmless" and "poor" and had wanted her to live with him in Harlem, which is what Minxie called the Upper West Side, an area of Manhattan that I am particularly fond of, populated by actors, writers, artists and musicians, and me, Sunny Browning.

Minxie married twice more, once to a wealthy industrialist who conveniently died six months later, and again to someone she'd met through Joel, an English title, whose tastes ran to prepubescent boys. They had separated.

These days, according to the profile, she lived in "a jewel box of an apartment" in the East Sixties with hotel service. Why are tiny apartments always referred to as jewel boxes?

Anyway, Minxie went back to doing her grape ivy number on Howie, but not before she gave me a look with those flat serpent eyes that would have melted steel. Then I remembered she'd been one of Howie's clients when she was doing her club act.

"Darling, you're not drinking," she said, sniffing his glass. "Naughty, naughty."

This is when George appeared, near panic on his face. "Don't do this," he said to Minxie. He threw me an anguished look.

"Howie," I said. It didn't take much for me to figure out there was a history here. I remembered Howie telling me that as a young PR man, he'd been assigned to baby-sit an actress who was a boozer and who always made him drink with her. His job was to get her to places on time, to carry her makeup case, which was actually a fully equipped bar. She didn't fly, so they crisscrossed the country blitzed on martinis until Howie had a breakdown.

"Oh, please," Minxie said, ignoring both George and me. "Good heavens, darling, we *must* have a little gin here." She snapped her fingers at a young man holding a bottle of champagne. "My friend here needs another drink."

"I'm not drinking, Minxie," Howie said weakly.

"Nonsense."

"You've got to do something, Sunny," George said. "He won't listen to me when she's around. She'll kill him."

Minxie laughed. "But you'll die happy, won't you, Howie darling?"

"Howie—" I said.

"Go away, little girl." When Minxie spoke, not one muscle on her face moved except for her dark red lips. It was as if she had lockjaw. "Come with me, Howie," she said, appropriating his arm.

"Don't do it, Howie."

"Sunny," Howie said. Against Minxie's steel will, keeping Howie sober was a losing proposition.

"Sunny!" Minxie grabbed it and ran with it. "What kind of ridiculous name is that? Come along, Howie." She sipped her gin and flashed me a look of pure loathing. "You're coming with me," she told Howie. "I have plans."

The thought did occur that a Minxie should not be telling a Sunny that she has a ridiculous name. And let's face it, Sunny *is* a ridiculous name, but not quite as ridiculous as the name on my birth certificate, which is Sunshine. If I didn't know better, I would think my parents were smoking pot when they picked my name. But what the hell, it comes with a lifetime guarantee that no one will ever forget it.

Howie and Minxie went on a binge to end all binges. Over the next two weeks they were put out of every club and hotel bar. Both ended up in New York Hospital, and only one of them came home. Minxie got on with her life as if nothing had happened; Howie Heinz was completely forgotten. But Howie's friends never forgot.

Now Minxie was dead, too.

Her funeral was an elaborate affair. Joel's friends all turned out for the service at Trumbell's because he'd asked us each personally. It was one of those rare beautiful April days in New York, dry as a bone. I had overslept and rushed out, stopping only at Starbuck's for a carry-along double espresso.

I walked through the park, past the Metropolitan with all its banners, and over to Trumbell's Funeral Home on Madison Avenue. Black limos were parked two deep for blocks uptown and down. Wooden horses barricaded the sidewalks, keeping the curious at arm's length. Groups of schoolchildren in uniforms sang what sounded like Sondheim's "Broadway Baby" in screechy little voices. And there were police everywhere. Obviously someone famous was going out in style.

A guard was putting an *X* next to my name on a list a mile long, when someone from CNN stuck a microphone in my face and said, "Ms. Browning, do you have any comment to make on the murder?"

"What murder?" I said.

"Move along," the guard said, and I was hustled into the subtly grand funeral home.

"The family's receiving in the Lincoln Room," I was told by a suitably somber-faced man, who pointed me toward the elevators.

I found Joel, as always, pale and rumpled, his hair

standing on end, in a vast room accepting condolences from two overprocessed ladies in spike heels and very tight skin. DeeDee, Lady Batton, and her sister, Irma, Countess de Porto. They were barely recognizable from the society pages because the photos in use were over thirty years old.

A man in a too sharp gray suit was sitting on a sofa near the door talking to a chunky, coffee-colored woman in an ass-hugging black dress, short enough to reveal highly muscled legs. I'd never seen either before, and since their attire bordered on inappropriate, I figured them for Joel's relatives on his father's side, of course.

Ah, that must be it, I thought. I marched right over to them, my hand out, and said, "Hi, I'm Sunny Browning, Joel's producer."

When their eyes raked me over like I was the catch of the day, I should have known they were cops. But I didn't until the suit said, "Mike Badillo, NYPD." He shook my hand, a good solid handshake. "This is my associate, Beth Williams."

"NYPD?" I looked around. Across the room I saw Joel's eyes pleading for me to come rescue him. The Lady and the Countess had brought him over to the coffin, which, would you believe, was open, at least the top portion was, revealing a seriously dead Minxie from midriff to coif. "Excuse me," I said, and made tracks to Joel's side. He took my hand and squeezed it.

I arrived in time to hear the harpies carrying on about something Minxie was wearing.

"It's mine," DeeDee said. "Remember when I bought it? It just disappeared. How long is it now?"

"Might have known," Irma said. "She always had sticky fingers. Remember when——"

Joel turned away, and so help me God, I saw DeeDee reach into the coffin and pry a ring from Minxie's finger. And then they didn't even have the grace to leave. I thought for a brief second about snatching it back, or making a scene, but came quickly to the conclusion that it wasn't worth it.

In my best funeral parlor voice I said, "Excuse me, but I must talk to Joel about the service." Whereupon DeeDee and Irma took their talons and went away, and I was left with Joel and a ringless Minxie.

The coffin was ornate, dark walnut with brasses. The lower, closed portion wore a blanket of pink tea roses. And Minxie in her cream turban lay like an Egyptian queen against the pink satin pillow. If I didn't know better, I'd say there was a smug little smirk on her face.

"Joel, police?" I said, trying to ignore her presence, which was intrusive even in death.

"They say she was murdered," Joel said. "Who would murder her?"

Who indeed? Aren't men foolish about their mothers? There would be a line from here to Atlantic City if one looked for someone who wished Minxie dead. Didn't he know that?

Me, I had an okay mother. The worst thing you could say for her was that she wasn't much of a cook, and we ate out all the time. She and my father owned Browning's, a bookshop on Madison Avenue, until they retired and moved to Hilton Head, where, after a few months of antiquing and playing golf, they went back into the book business.

Mort Hornberg arrived with Mickey Gray, the choreographer, and managed to find me in the crush. He whispered in my ear, "I'm absolutely devastated, darling."

"I'll bet," I said. "Where's Poppy?"

"She has a virus."

"Of course," I said. Poppy Hornberg was given to viruses that conveniently attacked in time for her to avoid most of Mort's theatrical obligations.

It was at this point that Joel's father, Dr. Herman Messerback, a kindly man with a shag of gray hair, made his appearance with Joel's half sister, an awkward child of nine or ten with dark kinky hair and thick glasses.

I was introduced and then drifted off to talk to George, whom I hadn't seen since he moved to the Cape. He had put on a spare tire of weight around the middle and grown a beard.

"I'm surprised you're here," I said.

"I had to come," he said. "Aside from the fact that Joel's a great guy, I wanted to make sure she was dead." He sauntered over to the coffin and stared down at her. "Bitch," he said. "Rot in hell." He looked at me. "I'd like to drive a silver stake through her heart to make sure. Can you imagine, someone in *New York* magazine called her the life of the party? She was more like the *knife* of the party."

I sighed, looked around, and caught the attention of the detective, who, by all that facial and body language, seemed to be trying to get me back to him. Now, what did he want? I wondered.

The room had suddenly become very crowded. Joel's friends and the people who knew Minxie undoubtedly, as George put it, wanted to make sure she was dead. I inched around an aging beach boy, Larry Morgan, former stud in black tux. He was going on about how much working with Minxie in her act had meant to him and his twin brother, Andrew.

I'll bet, I thought. According to Joel's agent, Wendy Peartree, Minxie had treated her backup dancers like sex toys, paid them poorly, and demanded constant attendance. They cleaned her place, did her laundry, drove her around, and carried her booze. Then when CBS produced her show as a special, she told Larry and Andrew that they were too old and did the show with two new boys.

When Andrew came to beg her to reconsider, she had him forcibly removed from her building. He was so distraught that he stepped off the curb, slipped on the ice, and fell under a bus. He's been in a wheelchair ever since. But hey, he put himself through law school on what he collected from the bus company and Minxie's building. Now he has a good practice in theatrical law. I knew he was here because I'd caught a glimpse of his wheels. He wouldn't have missed this for the world.

"Perhaps you can tell me who everyone is," Mike Badillo said.

"Oh, sure. I know most of the people here," I said. "Joel just told me it wasn't suicide." I looked around for Badillo's associate and saw her talking to Wendy Peartree.

"We're investigating a murder."

"She always took pills, but—I'm sure you know her history—never enough to kill her. And she always made sure everyone knew she was going to do it, so she could disrupt people's lives, especially Joel's, as much as possible. I always thought she'd outlive everybody. Of course, she never intended to kill herself."

"And she didn't."

"How did she die, then?"

"Why don't you let me ask the questions?"

"Well, okay, if that's how you want it, but I'd like you to answer just one for me. Pills are pills. What made you think it was murder?"

"Maybe it was the pillow."

"Huh? Pillow?"

"She could have done the booze and pills herself, but she needed help with the pillow."

"Pillow? Jeez," I said, nonplussed. "Someone snuffed the vampire with a pillow? Now, who would do that?"

"That's what I'm here to find out."

"So what do you want to know?"

"Who are all these people? Her friends?"

"Minxie? Friends?" I laughed. "She didn't have any friends. But okay, I think it's safe to say that everyone here wished her dead at one time or another."

"Including you?"

"Including me."

After I got finished telling him the Howie Heinz story, Badillo began pointing to people and asking me who they were. I'd just explained why Andrew was in a wheelchair when Wendy Peartree did something quite out of character. She burst into tears.

That stopped everybody cold for a minute, and then it was forgotten because we were respectfully asked to adjourn to the chapel for the service. I let the crowd separate me from Badillo and looked for Joel.

No sign of him, but Wendy Peartree, her back to the room, was staring out a window as the room emptied.

Now, I'm a sensitive person, and Wendy and I knew each other slightly from Smith, where we were both on scholarship. She was two years ahead of me. She wanted to be a writer, but then, a lot of us did.

Anyway, I came over and stood beside her, sending out empathetic vibes. We had a view of Central Park that looked like a rear-screen projection. It was so clear, I could almost see my apartment from where we stood. The Park was lush because of the persistently wet winter, and was practically dripping with pollen. But New Yorkers are never deterred. It was Sunday, so the Park was closed to car traffic—everything else was definitely possible.

I thought, maybe this is the perfect day to close the books on Minxie and move on with our lives.

I said as much to Wendy, who didn't respond. "Wendy?" I said. I touched her arm. It was as if she were not in her body. She looked at me and a stranger looked out of her eyes. It gave me the creeps. "See you later," I said, and I joined the last stragglers into the chapel.

An organ was playing tunes from Broadway shows; the place was packed and had an air of expectation. A celebration. I was standing in the back looking for a place to sit when I saw a hand wave to me. I followed it to an empty seat, realizing too late that the hand belonged to Detective Badillo.

"Who's that?" he asked immediately, picking up

right where we left off. He was pointing to an attractive man with neat gray hair and sharp blue eyes behind designer frames.

"Charles Newman," I said. "He's a celebrity editor." Which is why I recognized him. "He publishes Minxie's *Juicie Lucie* books." The surprising popularity of her books had turned a dying company around.

"She was switching publishers," Badillo said, so quietly I didn't make sense of it at first and had to play it back.

"She was? How do you know?"

"The agent."

"The agent? I didn't know she had an agent. I always thought they had come to her. Who is her agent?"

"The one you went to talk to," he said. "The one who had a crying jag."

I pondered that while the coffin was carried in and the outer doors closed.

A man of the cloth stepped forward and said a few words about Minxie going to a better place, which caused a ripple of suppressed laughter to float over the assembly. The two tucked and trimmed ladies chose this interval to totter down the aisle and look for seats.

I leaned over and told Detective Badillo about the ring snatch, and I saw him in turn repeat it to his cohort, who nodded several times. She slipped out of the row and took a stand in the back near the doors.

Joel got up and thanked everyone for coming, breaking down at the end and having to be led off the platform. Then it was over.

In the rush for the door, and with a little clever broken field dancing, I managed to lose the detectives.

The elevator was packed and a crowd was waiting for the next one, so I slipped down the double flight of stairs. There were still hordes of people around, gawking, but at least the tinny-voiced schoolchildren were gone. Minxie hated kids, Joel had once told me.

I confess I was feeling a little depressed and I couldn't really say why. Except maybe if Minxie was murdered, it stood to reason the murderer could be someone I knew. Minxie had literally made my skin crawl when I first met her, and I was glad she was dead. Maybe that's what was depressing me.

We were all going to meet at Joel's house in Chelsea a little later, but honestly, I needed a drink. I was near the Hotel Mark, so I walked into the bar, sat down in the farthest corner, protected by a giant fern, and ordered a Stoli martini, straight up.

I was well into my second and starting to feel mellow when I heard someone say, "You're sure she didn't have time to change it?"

The response was teary but clear. "It's over, Charles. They're ours now. She was a monster."

I peered through the fronds. Wendy Peartree and Charles Newman, Minxie's erstwhile editor. They were holding hands.

And that's all I heard because wouldn't you know a dentist from Oregon came in with his wife and another couple and sat down between me and the others and proceeded to tick off every goddamn thing they'd done so far today. Lord, I always thought the Mark was safe from dentists.

I couldn't get out of there fast enough, and I wasn't the only one. Wendy and Charles Newman were gone. What were they cooking up? I wondered.

I asked Joel about it later. He was sitting cross-legged, like a giant Buddha on a straw pallet. He'd redone the entire house Japanese with shoji screens and tatami pillows, low couches and tables. His latest lover was a Japanese interior designer.

The result was so uncomfortable, I couldn't find a place to sit, so I knew I wouldn't stay long, unless I adjourned to the kitchen, which I eventually did.

Joel said, "The stories weren't Minxie's to begin with. Wendy wrote them. She was here doing some secretarial work and left them for me to read. They were so clever, I showed them to Minxie, and you can guess the rest."

I could. "Poor Wendy. Why didn't she get a lawyer?"

"Minxie threatened to kill herself. She'd already sold them and there was so much publicity. I asked Wendy not to sue, and said I'd make it up to her, which I did. I made her my agent and she turned out to be good at it. And she's going to own those books now."

"She is?" Curious. I always thought Wendy was in love with Joel. In fact, everyone thought that, I bet even Joel. I wondered if he knew about Charles Newman.

"Yes. I made Minxie put it in her will."

That's when I adjourned to the kitchen, where I poured myself some coffee. Lacquer trays with Japanese food were being prepared with exquisite artistry by women in white kimonos.

What if, I thought, Minxie intended to change her will? I was sitting on a stool thinking about it when who should come into the kitchen but Detective Badillo.

"I can't find a place to sit," he said. He poured himself some coffee.

"Grab a stool."

We sat there for a while watching the Japanese ladies work. It was hypnotic.

"So what do you know?" he said.

"Nothing much." I was thinking that the police had so many suspects, they had no clue . . . and if they couldn't come up with an eyewitness, which they obviously couldn't because there'd been no arrest, then someone might actually get away with it.

"You have any thoughts about the *Juicie Lucie* stories?" Badillo said.

"They are nasty little pieces. Just like Minxie. Why?"

"She was leaving them to Wendy Peartree."

"No shit?"

"Yeah."

"It was in her will?"

"It was in the last one she signed. She'd called her lawyer to make a change the morning she died, but never got to sign it."

"Did the change have anything to do with the *Juicie Lucie* stories?"

"How'd you guess?"

"Minxie was a monster."

"Is that all you have to say?"

"Yeah," I said.

Listen, this is the way I figure it. I'm going to have a hit show with Joel. He's important to my career.

Minxie was a monster. If she'd lived, she would have tried to ruin Joel, and I might have gotten caught in the fallout.

So how's this scenario? My best guess is, being Minxie, she called Wendy and told her that she was writing a new will and that Wendy would never get her stories back. Minxie was probably leaving them to the Skinhead Society of North America, or something else not on Wendy's list of favorite charities. Wendy went to talk her out of it and things got a little out of hand. But hey, Minxie had taken the pills already and drunk the booze, and was more than halfway there anyway. Except . . . something was bothering me.

I said good night to Joel and the others. On the way out I saw Badillo was eating a salmon roll. "By the way," I said, "when Minxie was found, where was the phone?"

"Lying next to her on the bed."

"Cordless or plugged in?"

"Cordless."

"So the question is, was she talking to someone? Did she make a call after she called Joel and told him she was killing herself?"

"She couldn't have with that phone," Badillo said.

"Why not?"

"No battery."

It was only later, after I got home, took my shoes off, and poured myself a glass of Merlot, that I got it.

Minxie hadn't called Wendy to torture her or otherwise. She'd called Joel and delivered the last straw. It wouldn't have been difficult for Joel to put an old message on his answering machine and get me there to hear it. All those years of taking Minxie's emotional abuse finally drove him over the edge.

Or, giving him the benefit of the doubt, maybe Joel went there to reason with her about Wendy's stories, but Minxie was vicious. He had made Wendy all sorts of promises. There was nothing else for him to do. He held the pillow over her head until she stopped breathing and then left the phone on the bed thinking it was working.

The police, of course, would assume Minxie made the call to Joel from another phone, and I suppose she could have. But I don't think so.

I finished what was left of the wine. I had a show to produce, so there would be no more grape for me for a while.

And, you may well ask, what am I going to do about Joel? And Minxie's murder? You got it. Nothing. Not a damn thing.

The Dog Who Remembered Too Much

Elizabeth Daniels Squire

"Mama's gone, Peaches," Lola said to me, "and I need your help."

I held the phone tight, and a shiver of sadness went through me.

I knew Lola meant that her wonderful eighty-three-year-old mother, Bonnie Amons—my next-door neighbor—had died. Lola liked soft-pedal words—"gone" or "passed on" for died, "indisposed" for vomiting all over, and so forth.

Bonnie's death was my fault. Now, why on earth would I feel like that? I'd been good to Bonnie. I even helped train her dog. "I heard she was much worse the last few weeks since I've been away from Asheville," I said. I looked out into my sunny garden where a robin took a morning dip in the birdbath. Bonnie's garden adjoined mine on the right. That blooming apple tree was on her land.

"She'd been declining," Lola said. "Even her mind was going. She talked about changing her will to leave Doc James everything she had if he'd just get her well. Of course, she couldn't do that without a lawyer." Suddenly Lola sounded smug, but then properly sad again. "You're never ready for loved ones to go, are you? And I arrived to look in about eight this morning and . . ." She sighed.

I figured there was no easy way to say what she found. But she hadn't called me right away. My watch said quarter to ten.

Strange, I thought, that Bonnie got so sick so fast. Three weeks before, she'd been a little vague about time, she'd been almost blind, but there was still a lot of spunk in the old gal. She did have to take heart medicine, but otherwise she was full of ginger. Still, she *was* eighty-three. And nobody lasts forever.

"And now," Lola blurted, "somebody is trying to shoot George."

"Shoot George?" Why on earth would anybody want to shoot my neighbor's little black and white volunteer dog? I say volunteer because he simply appeared a year or so ago. And Bonnie couldn't bear not to feed him, so George—which is what Bonnie named him—moved in and became her mainstay.

"But everybody loves George," I said. "What on earth happened?"

"Right after I found Mama"—silence while she pulled herself together—"Peaches, she had plainly passed on. I found her and then I called Doc James and Andrea Ann." Andrea Ann was Lola's older sister.

"George barked to go out and I let him out and then

I heard a gunshot. But thank the good Lord I hadn't closed the door tight, and George came running in and had one of his shaking fits."

I knew it didn't require a gunshot to scare the dog. He had those shakes with new people, especially men, and especially men wearing boots. Somebody had mistreated that dog. But somebody had been good to him and trained him right, because he was an affectionate little dog who would sit or come on command. I figured we'd never know the whole story.

"I didn't see a living soul," Lola said, "but the mountain is in back of Mama's house here. Somebody could shoot down from among the trees and then slip away."

"It's probably some crazy mean kid," I said, "with a new gun. What do you want me to do?"

I said that bit about a kid to ease her mind, but I found myself wondering: Was there someone from that dog's past who wanted him out of the way? Silly idea, I told myself. But the idea grew: Was there some guilty secret the dog knew? Oh, come on! What imagination! First I'd asked myself if it was my fault that Bonnie died because I wasn't around to look in. Then I wondered if a little dog knew guilty secrets. But I never entirely dismiss my wild ideas. Some of them turn out. If you have a lousy memory, and I admit to that, sometimes you just know something without remembering the little signs that made you know it. I file my strange ideas under "Way Far Out," but I don't erase them.

"People will be coming and going here," Lola said, "paying respects to Mama. Would you take care of George till I get time to take him to my place?"

"And are you going to keep him for good?" I asked.

"I don't know," she said. "Mama would want him to have a good home, but Victor doesn't care too much for dogs."

I didn't like Lola's husband, Victor. Why did my wonderful friend Bonnie's two daughters both marry stinkers?

Unsuccessful stinkers. One from the city, one from the country. Andrea Ann's Arnold had run a tired trailer park out in the county where he grew up, except he'd finally sold it and put a down payment on a house near Bonnie's (which is to say, near me) and announced he was going to be a salesman. Now they were neighbors. And Arnold had to shave more often. Funny thing, though, Arnold had always had bedroom eyes even without shaving. Gave every woman he met the once-over like he was checking her out for sex, like his imagination was extra good in that department. Carnal Arnold. From the day I met him, I'd remembered his name that way.

Lola's husband, Victor, had a craft shop in Asheville. He'd always shaved. In fact, he overdressed. Slick Vic. He wore suits with vests to work. But most of his mountain-type "handmade crafts" came from Korea. He couldn't understand why, in an area with so many real and beautiful crafts, his shop didn't do well. Also, Victor was selfish and wanted to be the center of everything. And Lola was, I am sorry to say, a doormat. A mealymouthed doormat. Victor and Lola were made for each other. But not for a little dog with boot-kicks and God knew what else to get over.

"I'd like to have George," I said. "He has character. I'll come get him right now."

"Now, where has that dog gone?" Lola groaned as she let me in the front door. Why on earth had she worn a pink satin blouse to drop by her mother's in the morning? It went with her teased hairdresser hair and her carefully painted rosebud mouth. On a woman of fifty-plus. No doubt Slick Vic liked it.

We traced George to Bonnie's room, where the unmade bed looked so forlorn. Doc James must have arranged for the funeral home to come and get the body. Lola seemed too upset to have thought clearly and worked that out. Doc was getting a little senile himself. At least, I didn't think he'd come to see Bonnie as often as he should. But Bonnie would never change doctors.

George stuck his little black nose out from under the dust ruffle when he heard me and gave the single bark which means hello. "Good dog," I said to encourage him.

I looked around the room and choked up. The picture of praying hands, as worn as Bonnie's, hung as always on the wall above the old brass bed. Across from it was the plain bureau with Bonnie's hairbrush and comb and the old crazed mirror that had belonged to her mother. On the bedside table was a framed picture of the two girls as kids, Lola and Andrea Ann. Pouting in Sunday dresses. Also a glass of water, Bonnie's bottle of heart pills, and a box of dog biscuits. Everything was just like it had been at my last visit when I'd slipped in early before I left for my plane. I was glad I'd said that good-bye.

I walked over and picked up the pills and sighed. Heart medicine almost killed my father. As-much-as-you-need can save your life. More-than-you-need is deadly poison. "Lanoxin" (Digoxin), the label said, Rite-Aid. "Bonnie changed pharmacies," I said out loud. "I used to get her pills for her sometimes from Barefoot and Cheetham when I got my thyroid pills." Who could forget a name that made a picture like Barefoot and Cheetham? The two are actually old mountain names. Several in the phone book.

"Rite-Aid is a chain, so it costs less," Lola said primly. She stood near the bed nervously, watching me. Twitching like she wanted me to hurry up.

George edged out from under the bed. His small straight tail began to wag. He fastened his bright little black eyes on me.

"Bonnie really counted on George," I reminisced. "He even helped her remember her pill." Silence. Lola didn't like to admit that before the dog came, her mother sometimes forgot to take her heart pill at all. Which was dangerous. So I had come to the rescue.

I take pride in the fact that my friends count on me for memory tricks. In fact, I'm writing a book called *How to Survive Without a Memory*. My only problem is that sometimes I forget to take my own advice. But the dog-pill trick really works. A dog's stomach can tell time as well as an alarm clock. Give him a treat at the same time two or three days running, and he'll come ask for it on the button after that. Especially if he's a hungry type. And before George showed up on Bonnie's doorstep, goodness knows how long he'd been hungry.

George nudged my leg to be patted. I stroked his velvet head.

"Yes," Lola admitted, "George was a help, although my Victor was always afraid the dog was going to give us fleas."

Fleas! I'd taken on the job of seeing that George never had any. Bonnie's daughters never took time for that. Lola was always off at Victor's beck and call.

Andrea Ann, who was a trained nurse, did look in more often. She kept an eye on her mother, now that they'd made up a long-standing fight. You see, Andrea Ann had thought her mother had ruined her marriage by not lending her money. A dumb idea, but Andrea Ann had spells of dumb. And she had a talent for getting mad. Angrier Ann. She had evidently forgiven her mother, but she wasn't about to take on dog care.

Sometimes I wondered if Andrea Ann had any warm feelings—even for people, much less dogs. She'd told me that when she was a child she'd dissected small animals—mice, chipmunks, and once (to my horror) a squirrel—because she wanted to know what was inside. Which maybe made her a better surgical nurse, especially since her patients were anesthetized while she was with them. Human interaction was not required.

I don't think Andrea Ann knew how to show love. And Lola wasn't much better. George was the one who quivered with love whenever Bonnie came near. Who jumped with joy when she fed him. George knew she'd taken him in and saved his life. Fleas, indeed!

"Why, George told your mother by his bark whether a friend or a stranger was at the front door. He went crazy over strangers."

"And she felt safer that way, Peaches," Lola admitted, shrugging those satin shoulders.

"And George may be small and scared of strangers," I added, "but he can be fierce. He used to come steal my cat's supper. Now I put it on a high shelf."

"Mama called him a feist." Lola eyed his bowed legs, white chest, and funny little black body. "But he looks like a mongrel to me."

Out in the country, feists are kind of a breed. Not all exactly alike, but all small and fierce when they need to be. That's where the word *feisty* comes from. The dictionary says so.

"It's our mountain thriftiness, I guess," I said. "To breed a fierce watchdog in a small size that won't need much to eat."

George came out from under the bed and began to bark. Someone at the door? Andrea Ann should certainly be here by now. We went to look. No one was there. George raced back into the bedroom. He stood by the bed and barked. All of him quivered, and he pranced up and down, stamping first one front paw, then the other.

"Oh! It's time for your mother's pill!" I could have cried. He was barking, as always, because it was time for the treat that Bonnie gave him each time she took a pill. George wanted his dog biscuit. I gave him one for old times' sake. I looked at the pills. Take one at 10 A.M., the label said. And sure enough, the clock said ten. George was going to have to be deprogrammed so he didn't bark every day at ten o'clock.

I picked him up and he wriggled with delight and licked my nose.

"Where's Andrea Ann?" I asked. Now she and

Arnold lived just a few houses down the street, and Lola said she'd called her sister before she called me. Andrea should have arrived.

"She said she had to get dressed," Lola said. "She and Arnold." Arnold the new salesman. Shallow and insincere. He'd kept trying to talk Bonnie into selling the large tract of land with a lake and a little cabin on it, out at the edge of town. Bonnie'd never gotten there the last few years. But she was attached to that place. Carnal Arnold was too thickheaded to understand that. Or maybe he and Andrea Ann had wanted to borrow the money that Bonnie could get by selling the land. They tended to gamble. They'd been on vacation to Acapulco and Atlantic City and I forget where else.

You might think I don't like anybody the way I talk about Bonnie's girls and their men. I like most everybody. But something had gone wrong with those girls. I never knew their father. He was gone by the time I moved in next to Bonnie. Maybe he was the bad apple. Bonnie refused to talk about him.

"Do you think your father is still alive?" I asked Lola. "Do you need to let him know?"

She glared at me. "That," she said, "is not your business." At the same moment Andrea Ann walked in the door. No pink satin for her. Nurse's white and laced shoes. Andrea was the practical type. Dumb spells and all. Her mother said she never wasted a thing. Even saved odd bits of string. She glared at me too.

So I took a hint and went home, carrying little George against my shoulder.

I put my old barn coat on the floor for him to lie on.

Silk, my cat, who used to belong to my mother, came through the cat-door. My father didn't really want Silk, and I seem to inherit animals. Silk and George were friends from outdoors. No problem. I poured myself some cornflakes, added milk. I did some wash. I answered two letters. George was restless. He knew something was wrong. He kept going to the door and asking to get out. He didn't know how to use the cat door. "You've been out," I said, remembering the gunshot, "and it nearly killed you." I looked out the window. I saw Lola talking to Carnal Arnold on her mother's front porch. Even from a distance I could see her preen and him leer. A car drove up and out got Victor. A traffic jam. About time that joker got there, it was early afternoon.

All of a sudden George began to bark again. It wasn't quite his stranger-at-the-door bark. But insistent. He didn't go to the door and hop up and down to get out. Still, I glanced outside. Nobody. I looked at the clock. Two o'clock. Not the right time for the pill routine. What on earth was he trying to tell me? I gave him a dog biscuit. He stopped barking.

Then I heard a thump on the side of the house, over toward the bedroom—the side away from Bonnie's house. I went in the bedroom to investigate. Both animals followed me. I looked out the bedroom window, past the stained-glass cardinal fastened to the glass. Nobody in sight on that side of the house. Though there was a hedge. Someone could have slipped behind that. Nothing seemed to have fallen in the bedroom. The picture of an old man playing a mountain dulcimer hung securely in place. So did the picture of the barn owl. No explanation for the noise.

Only then did it occur to me that that thump was designed to get me out of the kitchen. That someone actually banged the side of the house.

I hurried back in the kitchen, and George began to run toward the cat door. I saw what he was after—a big piece of juicy raw hamburger. I ran so fast, I grabbed it before he did. I wiped the floor with my sleeve before either animal could lick any juice. I put the meat in a square freezer box and called the police department.

I was lucky to reach an old friend, Lieutenant John Wilson—whom I call Mustache, for obvious reasons. "I hate to hear from you," he said, "in case somebody else has been murdered." He said it like a joke. But of course, it wasn't. I've been mixed up in several murders. Not, thank God, on the wrong side.

"You're right. My next-door neighbor, Bonnie Amons, has been murdered," I said. "If you'll get right over here, I can tell you how to prove it, even though she was eighty-three and everybody thinks she died of natural causes. Or," I said, "I can give you the proof if you come at five-thirty."

"I can't come now," he said. "I can't even talk long now. I'd have to send somebody else. I'll come at five-thirty or quarter of six."

"Nothing is going to change before then," I said. "But don't be late."

You can bet I took good care of George for the rest of the afternoon, and Mustache arrived as promised, about five thirty-five.

"OK," he said, "tell me your theory. I bet it's something that nobody but me would ever believe. But I've had practice." He sighed. I know he wishes I wouldn't get mixed up in strange deaths. Like finding my poor aunt Nancy in the goldfish pond or stumbling on the fact that a serial killer was coming up I-40 our way and had my father on a list. Mustache wishes I wouldn't throw him curves. He has an orderly side that wants the world to make sense. You can tell by his crisp blue suit. No wrinkles. And by his straight firm mouth and intelligent eyes.

On the other hand, if he stuck to the tried-and-true way, he probably wouldn't have that scar next to his eye. He probably wouldn't have that wry manner— that was kind of nice. "Why do you believe that your neighbor, Bonnie Amons, was murdered?"

I introduced him to George. "This little dog belonged to Bonnie Amons, and he was trained to bark for a dog biscuit at ten o'clock every morning," I said. "That reminded her to take her heart pill."

George eyed Mustache's feet. No boots. George stood his ground.

"Now, someone has trained this dog to bark for a dog biscuit more times a day than Bonnie was supposed to take pills. Today he's barked at ten and two, and I'll bet he'll bark at six. That would make a regular pattern." Even my friend Mustache looked doubtful. Mustache looked at the kitchen clock. Quarter of six.

"And then, if you want to be sure of the whole pattern, let your police gal who works with the drug-sniffing dog keep George for a day and see," I said. "If she gives him a dog biscuit after he barks for it, he'll keep on barking at regular intervals, and you can use that for evidence."

"I might laugh at that evidence," Mustache sighed,

"except I know you. But we need more. That dog-alarm-clock stuff could be laughed out of court."

"Well, I'm willing to bet an autopsy on Bonnie Amons will show she's been taking more Lanoxin than she should, maybe three times as much," I said. "The amount will match the number of times a day that George barks in a certain way. I showed Bonnie how to train this little dog to bark when she was due to take her medicine, but now her daughter, Andrea Ann, has trained the dog to bark more often. And I believe the overdose killed my friend."

"Well, you know about heart medicine, all right," he sighed, and pulled at his mustache, "since the attempt last year to kill your father with it. So you think this Andrea Ann killed her own mother?"

"Sure," I said. "Andrea Ann had a fight with her mother because Bonnie wouldn't lend her money. Then Andrea Ann made up and helped nurse her mother. Maybe just in order to kill her. Andrea Ann is a little strange. But very determined. She didn't like to live in a trailer park."

"But how could anyone prove Andrea Ann was the poisoner, even if the autopsy and the dog check out? And we can't even ask for an autopsy without some proof that something is wrong," He chewed the end of his mustache. "I hate to let you down," he said kindly, "but this one may be too preposterous if all you have is the dog and speculation."

"Luckily," I said, "Andrea Ann thought the dog could incriminate her by barking too often. She thought I'd figure out what happened. She had one of her dumb spells. So she gave me proof.

"Here," I said, "is some hamburger laced with

poison. I'm sure of it. If you look in Andrea Ann's refrigerator, I think you'll find unpoisoned hamburger that matches it. Andrea Ann never could bring herself to waste anything. She may possibly have thrown out the poison, but she can't have thrown it far. She's needed to be over at her mother's house with her sister, looking innocent. She could slip out while her sister was busy flirting with her husband and drop the poisoned meat into my kitchen, the louse. But she didn't have time to go far away. And she didn't expect to have to use poison. Earlier she had shot at George, but she missed. Then she probably poisoned this meat with what she had handy—some household pesticide. You'll find the evidence. I have faith."

But Mustache was staring at the clock. The hands said six. George was lying quietly on the floor by my feet. I sighed. So OK, my imagination led me astray. But I didn't believe that. George yawned.

And then he stood up and began to bark. He jumped up and down and ran back and forth. He stamped his feet.

I handed Mustache a dog biscuit. "Here, you give it to him," I suggested. He did, and George wagged his tail and stopped barking.

I am happy to say that when Mustache got himself a hurry-up search warrant, there *was* hamburger in Andrea Ann's fridge, and it matched. Modern science can spot those things. The rat-poison box was still in her garage. She was overconfident. So sure that once the dog was dead, nobody could spot those extra pill-barkings. So sure she could prevent us from discovering the secret of the dog.

Mustache found one thing I missed. Andrea Ann

was going to three different pharmacies to get Lanoxin, using stolen and forged prescription forms she got from her nursing job.

As for George, he settled in with me and is a big help. I used to take my thyroid pills when I thought of it. Or else I didn't. Sometimes it was hard to remember. Now I take them every day at 10 o'clock.

Waiting for Pixie

Mignon F. Ballard

She was the only mother in the school parking lot who
never looked at her watch. The woman in the blue
station wagon smiled into the sun, sassy green scarf
cresting immaculate white blouse, blond hair in a tidy
twist. She reminded Millie of the confident hostess in
that old TV commercial: "I shampooed my carpet
only thirty minutes before dinner guests were
due . . ."

This was the third day Millie had parked next to her
while waiting for her daughter Anna to shoot from the
building with the screaming, squirming throng of first
graders released at two o'clock. Millie was one of the
early mothers who arrived ten or fifteen minutes
before the bell and waited, steeped in soggy Septem-
ber silence while cartons of once frozen yogurt oozed
with thawing broccoli in the trunk. It was a long,
boring wait, and probably unnecessary. A penance.

The first day of school she'd arrived five minutes late to find Anna crying and forlorn under the shedding sycamore at the edge of the school yard, and tasted guilt as caustic as acid. She'd lingered longer than she meant to with a customer who couldn't decide between the hand-stitched crib quilt or the calico bunny at the gift shop where she worked, then got stuck in traffic. It had taken two chapters of *Uncle Wiggly* and a game of Go Fish to make Anna smile again.

The family had lived in Atlanta less than a month, and while Bailey, their eight-year-old, had already become friends with the boy across the street, Anna knew no one her age. Most of the others in her class had gone to kindergarten together, formed secret-sharing friendships. It would take longer for Anna.

Millie lifted heavy hair from the back of her moist neck and drummed on the steering wheel. She liked her part-time job and the extra money, and knew she was lucky to find work in such a short time, but there never seemed to be enough hours in a day. She glanced again at her watch—ten minutes to go. Three loads of laundry waited to be folded, and she was supposed to make sandwiches for Bailey's Cub Scout pack. Millie had a cramp in her foot and nothing to read.

She stepped from the car onto melting asphalt. A ghost of a breeze whispered past her face, then abandoned her to the sun. Even the door handle was hot. Millie tapped lightly on the window of the blue station wagon. The glass was cool and clean, unsmeared by chocolate-covered fingers. A golden-haired doll dressed in frilly pink sat like the princess she obviously was on the backseat. The woman inside reached across to open the door. She looked like Donna Reed playing Princess Grace.

"Hi, I'm Millie McRory. We seem to be habitually early." Why did she feel as though she'd stepped into a Disney movie?

Her neighbor smiled a frost-free greeting. Time didn't matter. Neither did melting yogurt, slushy broccoli. "Do come and sit with me, please! It's a long wait, isn't it? I'm Vivian Baldwin. You're waiting for a first grader? Whose class?"

"Mrs. Garlington's." Millie hid the ink smudge on her blouse with her purse.

"Really? Mine has her too!" The woman's face softened. "Her name's Pixie . . . Well, that's what we call her; it's really Charlotte. Isn't it awful how nicknames get started? But honestly, *Charlotte!* Such a heavy name for a tiny baby . . . and she was such a little elf."

Millie laughed. "That's why we decided on Anna; not much you can do with that."

"Does your Anna like school? Pixie can't seem to get enough of it." Vivian studied the closed door of the building. As soon as the bell rang, it would swing open to free the wild swarm. Was she timing it to the last second?

"Does recess count? She loves playing on the monkey bars, chasing people," Millie said. "I guess we should've named her Cheetah."

Vivian held to the steering wheel: right hand at two o'clock, left hand at eight. Millie almost expected her to chime on the hour. "Pixie just loves stories," Vivian said. "She'll listen to Dr. Seuss for hours. And dress-up! What a mimic—a little mother! Puts twelve dolls to bed every night."

Millie sighed. They once bought a doll for Anna. She named it Superman and tied it to the chinaberry tree. Millie guessed it was still there. "Well, it takes all kinds," she said.

The bell rang and Vivian touched her arm with a cool hand. "If you're early tomorrow, come over and chat. It will give us a chance to know one another."

Millie spied Anna lagging behind the rest, shedding a fistful of dog-eared papers. "There's mine, the litterbug with brown braids in the red pants with paint on them."

"Pixie's always last." Vivian groaned. "She loves school *that* much."

Anna's face was damp and she smelled of mud and ripe bananas. Millie kissed her. "I love you," she said through a mouthful of wispy hair. "How was school?"

"Rotten." She wiped her nose on the back of her hand. "I hate that Wilbur!"

"Wilbur who?"

"Wilbur . . . I don't know. He gul-lups."

"Gullups?"

"Yeah, gul-lups, like big loud noises when he drinks his milk. He sat next to me at lunch. I moved. Yesterday he wet his pants."

"Do you know a little girl named Pixie?" Millie asked.

"Sure."

"Like her?"

Anna grinned. "Sure. Me and Pixie beat up on Wilbur at recess. He cried."

Millie almost missed a traffic light. "Anna! It isn't fair for two—*Pixie!* Are you sure?"

Anna sniffed. "Sure I'm sure. Mary Dean Higgins threw up at lunch."

Millie turned in to the vague new street they now called home. Pixie wasn't a common nickname, yet there must be more than one.

The next day Vivian told her Pixie couldn't stand jam or crunchy peanut butter. She demanded a complete change of clothing at the least sign of dirt, and slept with a golden-haired doll named Lucinda.

That afternoon Anna bounced happily to the car with a frowny face on her numbers homework and clay in her hair. "Why are you always the last one out?" Millie asked, waving grimly to Pixie's mother.

"Not. Pixie's still in there. The teacher kept her."

"Why?"

"Throwing mud."

"Anna, are you sure your friend's name is Pixie?"

"P-P-*Pixie!*" Anna sputtered, spitting all over the windshield.

"All right! Never mind. What's her last name?"

"I don't know. Just Pixie. She lives right next to the park. In a green house. Her dog's named Hey You."

Dog? Millie sighed. There were two Pixies, she was sure of it. She had seen the green house—a modest cottage, toys in the yard. There had to be two.

The following day Vivian admitted that Pixie slammed her head on the floor during tantrums, wrote her name in toothpaste on the bathroom mirror, and kicked the pediatrician. Millie smiled. Several days later, slowed by traffic, she arrived at school a few minutes late to find a swarm of buzzing children shouting encouragement to a utility pole. Her heart almost stopped. Swinging in midair, climbing hand over hand up the guy wire, was a fragile fair-haired child whose underpants had never seen bleach. She led her own daughter, protesting, to the car. "Anna, who is that?" Millie nodded toward the acrobat.

Anna shrugged. "Pixie."

Millie wasn't surprised. She opened the door for Anna and darted a look at the woman in the blue station wagon. Vivian Baldwin watched the child slide down the wire and tumble giggling to the ground. The woman's features were composed, her eyes calm, her serenity unruffled. Maybe she's one of those people who never get flustered, Millie thought. Or maybe she's on Valium.

By the end of the next week, Millie knew Pixie's first words, *Daddy home;* her favorite toy, a musical lamb; and the exact date of her successful potty training. She learned that Pixie liked bubble baths, ballet lessons, and vanilla ice cream, and disliked boys, thunderstorms, and large dogs. The wide-eyed doll (Lucinda?) on the backseat wore something different every day and had eight changes of clothing—Millie had counted them—but had not been moved from her original position.

"The leaves on the sycamore seem to be turning brown all at once," Vivian remarked one day as they waited in her station wagon. "In a few more weeks they'll all be gone."

Millie nodded. They had exhausted the subject of the weather—wet summer, dry fall—the convenience of the neighborhood where Millie lived, and the funny things their children said. Other than that, she didn't seem to be able to come up with a topic of common interest. Vivian didn't work outside the home and never appeared to be concerned about what to have for supper, the washing machine that overflowed, or any of the necessities of living that consumed Millie's day. The Braves were in the playoffs again, but Vivian wasn't a sports fan, and she didn't seem familiar with any of the authors Millie mentioned reading. Books were definitely out. What on earth did this woman do with her time?

Millie stared at the door of the school. "Aren't they running a little late? Seems they should be out by now."

Vivian smiled. "I expect they'll be along in a minute. They're probably having assembly today, or maybe they had a fire drill."

"Oh, good grief! How could I forget?" Millie glanced at her companion's face. "The fire station."

"What?"

"The first grade went to visit the fire station. Didn't you sign a permission slip? They'll be a half hour later today."

Vivian Baldwin frowned. "Oh, yes . . . that. I'd forgotten." She closed her eyes and leaned back in the seat. "Well, it shouldn't be much longer—and it is cooler now."

Millie looked at her watch. "I have to pick up Bailey. The elementary school lets out in ten minutes." Why couldn't they house the primary and elementary schools in the same complex? Irritated, she reached for the door handle. "Sometimes I think there should be two of me! Bailey's so reckless, I'm afraid he might—"

Vivian stared at her with a fixed expression.

Millie hesitated at the door of the car. "Vivian, is something wrong?"

The woman opened and closed her handbag, her mouth a stiff line. "What? What did you say?"

"I said I'm going to pick up Anna's brother. I'm such a fool about children and traffic . . . Are you sure you're all right?"

Vivian whispered something and turned away. Her fingers knotted around the steering wheel.

Millie closed the door, leaned in the window. "I'm sorry, I didn't hear you."

Vivian brushed an imaginary hair from her face and fingered the tiny pearl buttons on her dress. Her nails, Millie noticed, were trimmed to the quick. "I said, you're right. You can't be too careful." Her smile seemed forced.

"Well, I'd better run. I'm playing it close as it is." Millie stiffened against the sun-warm car. She hadn't realized how tense she had become. "Look, would you mind . . . I should be back in plenty of time, but if the children get here before I do, could Anna please wait here with you? I shouldn't be more than fifteen minutes."

Vivian's eyes went past her to the door of the school. "Anna? Yes, of course."

"You know her, don't you? Brown pigtails, dirty face." Millie attempted a laugh. "Tell her I won't be long."

"Wait!" Vivian leaned across the seat, laid a slender

white hand on Millie's tan one. "There's no need for you to rush back. Let Anna come home with us. You said she and Pixie were friends."

Millie hesitated, not knowing why. Anna was fond of Pixie, and she did need a friend.

"Please?" Vivian smiled. "Let them play awhile. I'll bring her home in an hour or so."

Millie hoped those cool blue eyes couldn't read her uncertainty. Her husband, Ted, teased her about being overprotective, but with all the drugs and guns, and people doing such awful things to one another, you didn't know whom to trust. "It's kind of you, but—"

"Really, we'd love to have her. I feel I've known you much longer than—what is it now? Almost a month! I'd like to get to know Anna too."

Millie bit her lip. Bailey would be wondering where she was . . . No, he wouldn't! He'd be racing around the school yard, yelling, chasing, acting wild, not looking where he was going. And she was already late. "All right, if you're sure," she said. "Just don't let her overstay her welcome. I'll look for you around four . . . and, Vivian . . . thanks! Oh—you do remember where we live, don't you? The second house on—"

The driver behind her tapped the horn. Millie was blocking the drive with her fanny. Vivian smiled and nodded, waved her away.

Millie felt herself flushing. She was being silly and irrational. One of those smothering mothers! Anna had been complaining she had no one to play with, and now that the child had found a friend, she wanted to bind her with apron strings.

As Millie pulled out of the parking lot, Pixie's

mother raised her fingers in a friendly flutter. She was still smiling.

It was not until she was pouring Bailey his second glass of milk that Millie remembered: She didn't know Vivian Baldwin's phone number, nor had she given her hers! Would Anna have learned it? She doubted it. They'd only lived here since August. Millie hoisted the Atlanta phone book onto the kitchen counter and shuffled through its pages. There must be over a hundred Baldwins! She ran her finger down the list looking for the street next to the park. What was it? Nancy Creek? Yes, that was it. But no Baldwins lived on Nancy Creek, or at least none that were listed.

Relax. Vivian knows where we live, Millie reminded herself. Hadn't they talked about the neighborhood, the advantages of a dead-end street? But would she remember? There was something spacey about the woman, something almost childlike.

She thought of the small green house with the toys in the yard. Next to the park, Anna had said. It was also on the way to the library. And didn't she have a couple of books overdue? What a perfect excuse! She could drop by a few minutes early and collect Anna. *Just happened to be in the neighborhood,* she would say. *Thought I'd save you a trip.*

Leaving Bailey with their neighbor across the street, Millie tossed her books onto the seat beside her and drove the few blocks to the library, slowing as she neared the park. The green bungalow looked scruffier than she remembered. A child's bike sprawled across the steps. A large cedar took up most of the yard where grass grew in patches, and a small green tent sagged in its shade. Millie smiled. Anna would love the tent. She pictured the two girls inside—eating Twinkies, probably. Vivian didn't seem a Twinkies kind of mother, but this was definitely a Twinkies kind of yard. She parked the car out front by the rusting mailbox. A dog barked somewhere in back. Hey You?

But other than the dog's yapping, the place seemed quiet, deserted. Of course, they could have stopped somewhere. Maybe Vivian took them next door to the park. Millie looked at her watch. She would spend some time at the library and come back later. What if Anna saw her here hovering? Her daughter hated hovering. She was getting ready to pull away when she heard the woman's voice.

"They're not here." She was a large woman, one of those who ought not to wear shorts, but does anyway, and she stood there with her empty garbage can—the kind on wheels.

"I beg your pardon?" Millie hesitated, her foot on the brake.

"I thought you were here to see the Hollinses." The woman's eyes narrowed and she poked her face closer. "They don't ever get home till around five-thirty—more like six."

Millie felt she was being assayed and had come up lacking. "Actually I'm looking for the Baldwins. Isn't this where they live?"

Tight Shorts glanced behind her at the green house as if it might have changed while her back was turned. "Here, you mean? No Baldwins on this street, and I've been here over fourteen years."

Dear God. Millie drove away so fast, she almost ran over the woman's foot. She'd made a mistake, that's all. Anna had said a green house. Maybe it was purple.

Blue. Surely somebody at the school would know the Baldwins, where they lived. Maybe she could catch them before they went home for the day. The library was closer. She would call from there.

A red light caught her at the corner. Two boys on bikes wobbled past. *Hurry, oh, please hurry!* Somebody had yanked out her insides and replaced them with mud. Her legs wouldn't work, they had no bones in them. If anything happened to Anna, Millie would detonate. There would be nothing left but tiny, meaningless pieces, and no one would be able to put her together again. Ever. She would be like Humpty Dumpty—bits of shattered shell.

The librarian at the front desk read her face, and not only let her use the phone, but looked up the number. The line was busy. Millie counted to ten and dialed again.

The school secretary listened politely as Millie stammered her predicament. "Just a minute, Mrs. McRory, I'm going to let you talk with our principal, Mrs. Thompson. Hold on."

Millie held on. The world had been created in less time than this. Had they been disconnected?

"Mrs. McRory?" The principal's voice was so soft, Millie thought she might smother in it. "With whom did you say Anna went home?"

"Pixie. Pixie Baldwin. She's in Anna's class."

She heard a faint rapping, like a pencil hitting the top of a desk. "There's only one child called Pixie in the first grade, Mrs. McRory. Pixie Hollins. Are you sure she's not the one?"

Pixie Hollins? Well, of course! Her mother probably remarried or kept her maiden name. But then why did her neighbor say there were no Baldwins on the street? "Her mother's name is Vivian—slender, blond, drives a blue station wagon. We visit in the parking lot every day, and she offered—"

"Mrs. McRory." The principal took a deep breath and hesitated. "Mrs. McRory, I'm afraid we have a problem. Pixie Hollins's mother works until five o'clock and the child is picked up by a nursery van after school. I believe you've been talking with someone else."

"Then who . . ." Millie sagged against the counter, pressed the receiver against her face.

"First let me call the Hollins home, and the childcare center as well, just to be sure. I could be mistaken." Mrs. Thompson's voice was smooth, like that of a pediatric nurse calming a frightened child. "If you'll give me your number, I'll call right back."

During those few minutes Millie recalled the brief conversation in the parking lot. If only she hadn't been in such a hurry to get Bailey! The news was filled with stories of people who kidnapped children— horrible people—yet Vivian Baldwin seemed gentle, almost ethereal . . . Oh, God, what had she done? Millie's head felt light, hot. She wanted to cry. The librarian was eyeing her with concern.

With her finger, Millie traced a design on the countertop, wishing she could relive the last two hours, have another chance. When Mrs. Thompson called, she knew what the principal would say.

Mrs. Thompson spoke gently. "The Hollins child was absent today, Mrs. McRory. Your daughter didn't leave school with Pixie Hollins, but I think I know where Anna is. If you'll meet me here at the school, I believe I can take you there. We're going to find her now, don't worry."

"But where? Look, shouldn't we call the police?"

The principal hesitated. "Very well, I'll call them, ask them to meet us there. Now, you will drive carefully, won't you? I'll wait for you out front." In spite of her caution, the woman's voice urged, *hurry*.

Don't worry? How could she not worry? She had let her little girl go off with a stranger. Anna was so trusting, innocent. Millie's hands trembled as rage surged through her like an electric shock. She would kill Vivian Baldwin if she'd hurt her child—and she wouldn't need a weapon. Millie had never felt anger like this before. It frightened her.

Millie ran to the car; the library books were still on the seat. Of course the principal could be calm, it wasn't her child who was missing. It was hers—Millie's—and it was all her fault. Oh God, what was Ted going to say? If only she could get in touch with him! But her husband had been out of town on business all week and was now on his way home—somewhere between Nashville and Atlanta—and she didn't know where to find him.

A woman in a white Chevrolet waved to her as she pulled into the school parking lot, then reached across to open the passenger door. Millie slid in beside her. The principal was red-haired, raw-boned, and angular. Thank heavens she wasn't the motherly type! As it was, Millie's voice shook as she turned to the older woman. "Where is Anna? Do you know who took her?"

Mrs. Thompson made a sharp right turn into the street and raced under the yellow light at the corner.

"We did have a Pixie Baldwin a few years ago," she said. "First grader, charming child. She was killed in an accident—running across the street to her mother's car—darted right past the crossing guard. Happened here at school, on that busy side street. By the time I got there, it was too late, but I'll never forget it. Never."

Millie buried her face in her hands. Something hot and heavy rose in her chest and plummeted to her stomach. That poor woman! And she had said that about Bailey being careless!

"Pixie's mother had been to a meeting that day and was a few minutes late. She saw it happen. Helpless. Didn't cry—not then. Only begged, 'Let me do it over! Please, let me do it over!' As if we could turn back the clock. How I wish we could!"

Millie felt the principal's hand on her shoulder as they stopped for a light. "I'm afraid she's taken Anna home with her," the woman said. "I've asked the police to meet us out front, let us go in first. You'll have to pull yourself together now—for Anna's sake. We'll be there in a minute."

Millie tried to picture her daughter. Was she alone? Crying? Frightened? Vivian probably had told her she was Pixie's mother, invited her home to play. Anna had never seen Pixie Hollins's mother. Of course she would accept, eager to spend an afternoon with her new friend.

Millie found herself rocking, urging the car forward. "I'm sorry about her little girl, but she can't have mine. She had no right to take mine! She won't hurt Anna, will she? What was she doing at the school every day?"

Millie noticed the principal's assessing glance, probably to see if she was *pulling herself together.* "I hardly think the woman's dangerous," Mrs. Thompson said. "I heard she had a complete emotional breakdown after Pixie's death—she was their only child. Vivian was in a hospital for a while. I believe she's still in therapy."

"But how do you know she wouldn't hurt Anna? You can't be sure! They're never sure." Millie thought of all the murderers she'd read about whose neighbors were surprised, shocked, at the things they did. How would she react if anything happened to one of hers? How could she stand it? Would she do something like Vivian Baldwin had done?

"To tell the truth, I didn't know Vivian had been released," Mrs. Thompson went on. "Apparently her doctors must've thought she was well enough to adjust." She turned in to a tree-lined drive. A police car waited discreetly at the curb. "Did you say she's been at the school every day?"

"At the same time." Millie met her eyes.

"She's doing it over," Mrs. Thompson said.

Millie stared at the sedate Georgian house with ivy climbing its walls and had to restrain herself to keep from dashing to the door, screaming for Anna. While the principal spoke with one of the officers, she wanted to grab her child and run—away from this house, away from the strange, grief-stricken woman who lived here.

Two uniformed men waited at a distance as Millie and Anna's principal walked to the door. The women could be neighbors making a social call, a committee from the church. The doorbell chimed—light, happy

222

notes—bars from a familiar waltz. "The Blue Dan-
ube"?

Vivian Baldwin showed no surprise to see them on
her doorstep. She merely stood there smiling in her
beige knit dress with a yellow flower in her hair. The
rooms behind her were silent.

Millie wanted to shake her. If the principal hadn't
restrained her with a touch, she would have shoved
her way inside. "We've come for Anna, Mrs. Baldwin," Mrs. Thompson said. "Is she ready?"

"Anna? Why, yes, she's in the kitchen. We're having
a tea party. Please come in." She stepped back,
allowing them to enter, and Millie noticed the doll in
her hands: Lucinda, the blond, blue-eyed passenger
with the glamorous wardrobe. Vivian was changing
the doll's clothes; she stroked the bright yellow hair as
they followed her down the hall.

Millie heard voices in the kitchen. Soft voices.
Anna sat across the table from a pleasant-faced older
woman who rose as they entered. Anna was eating a
large piece of chocolate cake. "Hi, Mom!" She stuffed
in another gooey blob and smiled.

Millie gripped the back of her daughter's chair. If
she touched her, she would melt. "Hi, honey." Her
voice seemed to come from far away. Behind them,
Vivian Baldwin with her blue-gowned doll disappeared down the long hallway.

"You're Anna's mother." The matronly woman
glanced from Millie to Mrs. Thompson. "And
you're . . . ?"

"Estelle Thompson, her principal. We were concerned. I'm afraid there was a misunderstanding."

"Eva Blackstock. I'm Vivian's mother." The woman held out her hand. "I'm so glad you came! I just called the school and they told me you were on the way. I can't tell you how sorry I am about this . . ." Her voice dropped. "I had no idea—came home from running a few errands, and, well . . . My daughter's never done anything like this before."

Millie watched Anna scoop the last of the icing from her plate and resisted the desire to enfold her daughter's small, chocolate-covered face, hold her close. She tried to speak. Couldn't.

"I tried to find you in the phone book," Mrs. Blackstock said, "but your number wasn't listed, and Anna couldn't remember it. We weren't sure of your address." She sank onto a chair. "I hate for this to happen! Vivian spoke of you often. I thought she met you through her volunteer work." Her voice faltered. "It's the first time she's showed an interest in making friends, meeting people . . ."

Estelle Thompson had stepped outside to talk with the police, and the two women looked at one another across the table. Millie wiped her daughter's face with a tissue. "Please. It's partly my fault; I should've been more careful. And thank you for looking after Anna." She smiled. Her world was whole again. "I left my son with a neighbor, and I imagine Mrs. Thompson needs to get back to the school . . ." Millie looked away. Words. Empty words. Instinct compelled her to move toward the door, just as the desperate emptiness in Vivian Baldwin made her wait in front of the school each day for a child who would never appear.

Mrs. Blackstock followed them, touched her arm. Her eyes pleaded. A mother's eyes. Millie had seen that same expression in her own visor mirror as she rushed to meet Estelle Thompson.

Millie drew her daughter to her as Mrs. Thompson drove them back to the school. She mustn't let Anna know how frightened she had been. "Did you have a good time?" she asked, smoothing the hair from Anna's face.

"Uh-huh. They got a dollhouse. A great big one! And about a million, jillion dolls! It was neat." She frowned. "But I wouldn't want to stay there."

"Why not, Anna?" Millie's smile felt pasted across her lips like a bandage. "Why wouldn't you want to stay there?"

"Because those are that other Pixie's things, not mine. And she's selfish too—wouldn't even let me play with her old lamb!" Anna yawned. "Hey, Mom, can Wilbur come home with me tomorrow?"

Sign of the *Times*

Patricia Sprinkle

That Wednesday morning, I arrived a trifle late for the weekly editorial meeting of the *Stateston Times*. I'd barely rushed past Junior, our receptionist, and laid my file of local news and the week's crime report on the conference table, when Lamar Ledbetter, our editor, glared across the table at the woman he adores and declared, "I don't see how I can possibly help you."

"But you must!" Cass Higdon said desperately. "It's happened twice in two weeks!" She slewed her eyes toward me. "Abby, at least tell Sheriff Burton to look for a connection."

I opened my mouth to protest. Joe Tadd Burton may be my first cousin, but he hasn't taken an order from me since we were six.

Before I could say so, Graham Taylor loped in— late, as usual, carrying an untidy stack of files. "Connection between what?" He set down the files while he fetched coffee, toppling baseball scores and promotion ideas all over the rest of our editorial offerings.

Ted Butler, our publisher, fastidiously straightened Graham's files, then fingered the gold sunburst charm at the open throat of his creamy silk shirt. "Stephie Wooten was robbed yesterday—"

"While," Cass butted in, "she was down at Diamond's spending the thousand-dollar shopping spree she won in our drawing last week." If Cass didn't stop twisting her fingers like that, she was going to slice herself on one of those silver rings she's started wearing since she became High Priestess of West Georgia.

Ted went on as if she hadn't said a word, "—and Cass thinks it's related to her horoscope column. She predicted last week that Sagittarius would have good fortune, and Stephie is a Sagittarius."

"Poor old Stephie. Did somebody take all her designer dresses while she was out buying more?" Ruth Reems caught my eye across the table and let one eyelid droop.

Given the length of her lashes and the amount of mascara she wears, Ruth's lids practically droop of their own accord. With a wide white streak in her dark hair, all that makeup, and a husky voice that sounds like she was weaned on whiskey sours and cigarettes, you'd never guess Ruth is a pillar of the Baptist Church—or, as Joe Tadd says, a sizable column. Ever since Ruth's husband told her she isn't fat, merely voluptuous, she has thrown caution to the wind and too many calories down her gullet.

Ruth covers religious and cultural news for the

Times—which in Stateston are frequently synonymous. She is also a terrific listener, so people pour their hearts out and she churns out stories that would make Robert E. Lee in the town square weep, if statues could read. On the other hand, she is a realist and—at times—a downright cynic. Stephie Wooten is our town's rich girl, having inherited her daddy's pulpwood, banks, and bonds. She needed to win that shopping spree like I need to win a steady job or Ruth needs to win a year's supply of Windermere ice cream.

When Graham finally got his coffee sweet enough and made his way back to the table, Lamar rubbed the back of his thick pink neck the way he always does when irritated. He used to do the same thing during third grade multiplication tests. "You're late," he growled.

Actually, we'd all been late. I'd had to stop by Joe Tadd's for the crime report, Ruth had an author interview, Cass went to the Lutheran Women's annual prayer breakfast for Ruth, and Lamar had to get his Cadillac serviced. His snarl had less to do with punctuality than with Graham's passing up the empty seat by me, inching his lanky body past Ted, and dropping into the chair beside Cass without taking his green eyes off her scoop-necked blouse.

I've known Graham, Ted, and Lamar forever. I can remember when Graham had hair and played sports instead of writing about them, Lamar edited the high school paper, and Ted still used his childhood nickname and delivered his daddy's newspaper instead of publishing it. For the life of me, I can't see what those men see in Cass Higdon—except their vanished youth. Sleek brown hair curling around shell-shaped ears, big brown eyes, an uptilted nose, and curves in places any adolescent boy can draw aren't everything.

When Cass divorced that Alabama stockbroker last year and came home, though, Ted and Myra had just split up and Myra had quit as women's editor. (Myra's such a bitch, Ruth and I heaved a sigh of relief. Even Ted didn't deserve to be stuck with her all his life.)

Anyway, Lamar hired Cass, and he and Graham started circling and sniffing her like bird dogs in heat. Graham spruced up his wardrobe. Lamar took to using Brut and getting his rough black hair styled instead of merely cut. Even Junior combed his ponytail.

Looks to me like grown men would prefer women with common sense, steady work habits, and blooming health, but if I'd ever found one who did, I wouldn't have been there that particular Wednesday morning with a file on Stateston's latest crime wave.

I decided it was time I added something to the conversation. Facts, for instance. "It wasn't just dresses they took. They got Stephie's jewelry, including her mama's ruby necklace. *And* the silver service her great-grandma hid from the Yankees. They also—"

"Where the Sam Hill could they hope to sell that stuff around here?" Lamar's big face was flushed with indignation.

"Where could anybody sell poor old Mr. Whitacre's stamp collection around here?" Cass dabbed her perfect nose with a pink tissue. "But it got stolen last week, didn't it? You'd think we lived in New York City!"

Please don't get the idea that we are a bunch of hick

reporters for a rinky-dink paper in a nothing town. Stateston had twenty-five thousand citizens at the last census, and since Yankee traders started dotting our landscape with factories, we've added several thousand more. As Joe Tadd says, the place has gotten so big, we can't trust a stranger to be a cousin anymore.

The *Stateston Times* is a fine paper, too, with three national awards to its credit. I joined the staff right after I got my journalism degree from Northwestern, back when Ted's daddy—who was much sweeter than Ted, but not half as handsome—was still alive. After he died, Ted came back from the navy to take over the paper. Nobody was surprised. We'd all known getting an Emory law degree and becoming a navy lawyer was just Ted's way of passing time.

Ted persuaded Lamar, who was writing for a Cleveland paper, to come home as editor, and Ruth, who's a few years older than us and past president of every women's group in town, to write religious and cultural news. Ruth knows everybody who matters in Georgia.

Graham came back just before Cass, after ten years as a pro basketball player. He'd played for the University of Georgia first, and since the university also gave him a journalism degree (please note the verb), Ted hired him as sports reporter as soon as a vacancy could be arranged.

Why did we all come back to Stateston? I think it's because when you grow up in the South and live other places, the soles of your feet get sore from dragging all those roots around. It's a relief to plant them where people know to put ice and sugar in tea and—even if they worry about cholesterol—still toss a slice of fatback in the vegetables.

That Wednesday, Graham looked around the table in bewilderment. "What about Mr. Whitacre's stamps?" Graham collects stamps himself, but we couldn't expect him to be up on the news. Except for sports and weather, he never reads a lick of anything.

As crime reporter, I started to enlighten him. "Mr. Whitacre's stamp collection and all his Civil War stuff got stolen last week, while he was up at the Atlanta opera. The thief—"

This time, Cass butted in. "He's a Scorpio, and I'd told Scorpios to enrich their lives through the arts. Ruth wrote about the opera coming to Atlanta, so he took his cousin from Macon. God, what's going on?"

Ruth shifted her bulk in one of the hard wooden chairs Ted keeps promising to replace but hasn't. "Honey, don't blame God for this. He's got better things to do than read your horoscopes."

Especially, I added silently, since God knows the horoscopes aren't written by an honest-to-god charlatan, just a flirty woman with a hankering to see her words in print. Out loud I said, "If you're worried, Cass, why don't you give up the horoscope column and stick to women's news?"

I may have sounded a tad waspish, having been interrupted twice in three minutes. Cass lifted her lashes like I'd been downright rude. "I can't give up my horoscopes, Abby! People depend on them!"

She had a point. Last November, Cass had begged Lamar to let her "spice up the paper" with a weekly horoscope. Since the man was already besotted with her, he agreed. We all figured she'd just copy horoscopes from the *Atlanta Constitution* or somewhere.

Instead, she'd ordered books on astrology and actually read them. And while at first she wrote a lot of what Ruth calls "Cass's cutesy counsel"—like "enrich your life with the arts"—in late December, she started getting lucky. She said the full moon would bring double good fortune to Libras, and Meg Bates gave birth to twins two months early, in time for a double tax deduction.

Cass told Gemini to seek treasure close to home, and old man Wier found a case of Jack Daniel's buried under straw in his barn in time to invite his cronies in for a Super Bowl party. His brother Jake, the town drunk, probably hid it there before he died, but folks were glad Mr. Wier found it. After his bout with cancer last summer, most folks suspected that was Mr. Wier's last Super Bowl.

When Cass counseled Aries to expect a legacy, Miss Ada Potts down at the public library got a call from a Valdosta lawyer saying a distant cousin had left her a thousand dollars—just in time to pay for a bus trip to Lake Junaluska with the Golden Olders from the Methodist Church.

The most romantic story was repeated again and again over at the Katty Korner Kafe: After Cass told Cancer to pursue romance on Valentine's Day, Missy Butler, Ted's bucktoothed cousin, received a dozen roses from "A Secret Admirer." Tinker Boggs, who inherited the Chevy place, had been blushing and shuffling his feet around Missy for weeks, so—pursuing romance—she called to thank him. Tinker never quite admitted to having sent the roses, but he did finally get up his courage to ask Missy out. In April, when Cass told Virgo to solidify casual relationships, he proposed. Missy, reading that Cancer should take serious thought for the future, accepted, and in June, Ted gave the bride away amid a suitable shower of birdseed, favorable augurs, and publicity.

Even Ted had been a Cass fan since January, when she had told Capricorns to watch for good business opportunities. Ted, who had just gotten a tip on the stock market, decided to take an unusual risk, and made a killing. After his guest editorial praising "our very own local astrologer and financial whiz, Ms. Cassandra Higdon," people started reading their horoscopes with the attention women usually give the Bible, and men the sports pages.

Even children got hooked on horoscopes after Cass told Taurus high expectations would be fulfilled and Billy Soat's bull won first place in the 4-H cattle show.

All through March's drizzle, April's azalea and dogwood dazzle, and May's sweet corn, Ted and Cass huddled over the business pages each morning, while most evenings Lamar squired around a woman who got more attention than a bloomin' homecoming queen. I could—and did—point out until I was blue in the face that less than ten percent of Cass's specific predictions were accurate. Ruth could—and did— point out that most of the ones Cass got right could be put down to coincidence, personal endeavor, or—she added with a wink at Graham—crooked cattle judges. Who do you think believed us? Nobody but a few newcomers, who claimed that only old-timers' horoscopes really came true.

Since the first week of May, however, horoscopes hadn't been quite as popular around our office as they were around town. That week, Cass told Pisces to slow down and smell the roses. Lamar, a Pices, invited her to spend Saturday with him at Callaway Gardens. It poured rain. Graham—also a Pisces—heard Lamar repeating the advice, put a thousand dollars at enormous odds on Slow and Sweet in the Kentucky Derby, and won. Graham took Cass to lunch to celebrate, and they didn't come back all afternoon.

Lamar got a bit frosty after that. Graham—always one to grab a dropped ball and run with it—started inviting Cass to high school baseball games. Cass treated them both just like she always had, sweet and helpless. If she knew she'd come between men who'd been buddies since kindergarten, she gave no sign. All summer she went to ball games with Graham and concerts with Lamar, just like everything was hunky-dory. (She and Ted stopped doing the financial pages together about that time, too. Ruth and I saw them together occasionally at lunch, and decided that since his divorce was now final, he had little money to invest. That Myra is a shark!)

I wondered sometimes if Graham and Lamar knew Cass was also frying other fish. One weekend in Columbus, I spied her in a restaurant with Tom Johnston, a lawyer about her own age who'd just moved to Stateston. Even at that distance and from behind a potted palm, he was gorgeous. When I told Joe Tadd about it later, he said Cass was smarter than she looked if she knew to do her real courting out of town.

Now we were in August, with days so hot that even dogs wouldn't claim them. Tempers were short. I hoped Cass would show some sense.

Which brings me back to that Wednesday morning —and murder.

After Cass insisted she couldn't give up writing the horoscopes because everybody depended on them, the devil got into me and Ruth about the same time.

"I'll bet Mr. Whitacre's just *sick* about losin' his stamps and swords," Ruth drawled. "His granddaddy started that collection, and he had some irreplaceable specimens."

"Don't forget his cannonballs and Jefferson Davis letters," I added, "and Joe Tadd told me this morning that Stephie Wooten is threatening to kill whoever broke into her house."

I watched the others carefully as I said that. It had occurred to me that everybody around that table knew when Stephie was going to shop at Diamond's. We'd decided last week to give the shopping spree winner front-page coverage, so I'd called Stephie to set a time to meet her there for pictures. Our editorial "offices" are just one big room with short glass partitions. We have few secrets.

Nobody looked guilty, though, and I was ashamed of myself for even thinking such a thing. Why should any of them steal?

Lamar earns a decent salary, and even though Wal-Mart put his daddy's drugstore out of business, they paid Lamar enough for the land they built on to keep him in new Cadillacs every two years.

The paper doesn't make Ted rich, but his daddy, Theodore E. Butler, Sr., owned a good many acres of timberland, as well. People can say what they want about pine trees, but as my own daddy used to say, they are the same pretty green as money. Except for a stiff alimony payment to Myra every month, Ted doesn't spend much. I've wondered a few times lately if he's salting his money away to see the world. Ted is lean, light, and attractive, if you don't mind short, arrogant men. I've occasionally imagined what it would be like to see the world with him—but when you and a fellow dissected a cat in formaldehyde together in tenth grade, it's hard to get him to look at you romantically later.

Graham wasn't as fortunate as the rest of us. His daddy drank up whatever he made at Wier's Sawmill. Still, Graham went to college on a basketball scholarship, made a bit of money playing pro basketball, and married a rich woman who died three years ago. If a white Mercedes and annual gambling trip to Las Vegas mean anything, he didn't need Stephie Wooten's jewelry nor Mr. Whitacre's collections.

Ruth, of course, I dismissed without considering. She's so straight, she makes the rest of us look positively kinky, and while she doesn't say much about it, I know she inherited enough money from the sale of her daddy's seed and feed store to keep her comfortably even if she weren't married to the high school principal, which she is. I also know something that not another soul in town suspects: Ruth's parents came from Maine. What would a Yankee be wanting with Confederate swords and Jeff Davis's letters?

There was one more thing, though—something Sheriff Joe Tadd had told me that morning, and which I'd twice been about to say when I was so rudely interrupted: At both Mr. Whitacre's and Stephie's, the thief left a scrap of paper with their zodiac sign on it. Somebody was pointing at Cass's horoscopes, all right. But why?

Before I could try a third time to tell about the signs, Junior called from the front desk, "Abby, Joe Tadd wants you on the phone. Right now."

I pushed back my chair and grabbed my notebook and pencil out of habit. "He probably thinks I've forgotten we're going out to Aunt Edna's for supper."

Joe Tadd's voice was gruffer than usual, which meant he was hunkered over his desk, beefy shoulders in their khaki shirt curved over the phone to keep curious deputies from listening in. "Abby? They's been a suicide. Car left running in a locked garage. I thought you might like to get on out there to look over the scene and get a head start on a story. Just don't get in anybody's way."

"Who is it?" I tried not to sound thrilled. After all, somebody had taken his or her life. But we don't get many mysterious deaths in Stateston. We get our share of shootings, of course—southerners have always been trigger-happy—but this was the first time in the two years since Joe Tadd was elected sheriff and Ted made me crime reporter that we'd had what I would call an honest-to-God interesting death.

"It's Tom Johnston, that young lawyer fellow from Vidalia."

"The one I saw Cass with?" I spoke in a whisper. Junior had developed a sudden industry about emptying wastebaskets nearby.

"Yeah. But don't tell her or anybody else about this yet. Just get yourself over to his house. Got a pencil?"

I jotted down the address and grabbed my pocket-book, notebook, pencils, and camera gear. We have a photographer on call for the *Times,* but I prefer to take and develop my own shots. It's something I take pride in.

At the front door, I told Junior, "Tell Ted and the others I've had to go after a story. Be back when I can."

Tom Johnston had bought a house in one of the new sections of Stateston, which was surprising. Most houses out that way had not only men, but women and little children in them. He'd known enough to plant his red and white petunias and dusty miller around the mailbox, where anything else would be fried to a crisp in the August sun, and he'd put red, pink, and white impatiens in between the boxwoods facing north. He had even kept up his watering all summer, because his lawn was green and his flowers blooming. A most domesticated home for an unmarried man.

All that beauty, however, was marred today by bright yellow strips of police barrier tape draped from tree to tree, as if teenagers had decided to roll him in living color.

He didn't look any better than his house.

Tom Johnston had been the kind of man my mother is still waiting for me to bring home: tall, with yellow hair and blue eyes a woman could die for. Except he had died first. Slumped over his wheel like a sack of cornmeal. One look at his face, and I hoped never to see such a sight again.

The entire garage was filthy with an oily gray film

that clung to the rakes, Weed Eater, and a once red lawn mower. It all but covered the blue BMW's temporary license plate, and had even dulled poor Tom's once bright hair.

By the time I had photographed him from the side, through the windshield, and over his shoulder, my morning Wheaties had started to heave. I backed outside and breathed deep while I shot the garage door and the back of the car. While focusing, I tried not to look at the garden hose snaked from the exhaust pipe along the side of the car and draped in the left back window.

"Mind if I look around the house a bit?" The reporter side of me wanted to push myself forward, but as cousin of the sheriff, I was reluctant to ask for special favors.

The officer in charge nodded. "Okay, but don't touch anything."

She hadn't told me anything I didn't know already. The reason Joe Tadd lets me this close to a crime scene is what we call our china-shop rules: *(1) Look, but don't touch. (2) You are responsible for anything you break, including a premature story.*

Tom Johnston had been more domestic outside than inside. His rooms were sparsely furnished with what looked to me like the wrong end of a divorce settlement. On the kitchen table—a small scratched maple one his mama had probably had in her attic—a paper lay open. Beside it sat a wine-red mug of black coffee, half-drunk, and two thirds of a piece of toast. A big roach waved his antennae at me from atop the toast.

I raised my hand to swat it, then remembered I was to touch nothing. Joe Tadd had better hurry, though, if the toast was a clue. I photographed it, just in case.

Automatically I bent to peruse the paper, which was ringed with coffee as if Tom had set his mug on it a couple of times while reading. It was this week's *Times,* open to the comics and the horoscope.

I could almost see the picture: Tom sitting happily with his coffee and paper in the morning sunshine, reading the funnies and his horoscope, then rising half through breakfast to kill himself.

Why didn't he finish his coffee?

And what on earth did Cass tell him to do?

Since I didn't know Tom's sign, I scanned her entire horoscope for any advice to kill oneself with carbon monoxide. Cass said some asinine things, but nothing quite so tacky as that. The closest I could get was Leo: "Take a loved one on a special trip." It was a stretch, I'll admit, but at least it could be read to mean "Get in your car and head for the world to come." Presuming, of course, that Tom Johnston interpreted "a loved one" to mean himself. I wasn't sold on that theory.

Having exhausted the possibilities of the breakfast table, I turned to the kitchen counter. What I saw there turned me cold on that hot August morning: two birthday cards sitting right in front of the microwave. They proved that Tom Johnston *was* a Leo. Since they were already open, I bent and read the signatures: "Love, Mom" and, in a child's pencil-gripping scrawl, "I love you dady, Ben."

The last brought tears to my eyes. They made it hard for me to focus, but I took a picture anyway.

Young Ben deserved to know his daddy had been proud of that card.

Behind the cards sat a florist's vase with a single red rose, but no card. I didn't need a card. When you've lived in a town like Stateston all your life, you recognize florists by their bud vases. Was there a house in town that didn't have one in that exact shade of green? I had two at home and three at the office, above the coffeepot. When I was done at Tom Johnston's, I'd call Dixie Darling Florists and find out who ordered that particular flower.

Joe Tadd arrived while I was back in the master bedroom, taking pictures of anything I felt could be of conceivable interest to my readers.

Who am I fooling? Some of my readers would be interested in everything from the cockroach to the dead man's underwear drawer. I had shot the things that interested *me:* the coffee mug and the newspaper, the cards and the rose, the bill of sale for the BMW— which I found tucked between the pages of a library book down behind the bed.

Okay, I'll admit that in order to get the last picture, I used a corner of the bedsheet to hold the book, and another to very carefully lift out the contract. The reason I took a picture was, the contract was dated last Saturday, and signed—to my utter amazement—by Cass Higdon. Tom took his final trip in Cass's car.

That's why I was a bit antsy when I heard Joe Tadd's size thirteens clumping down the hall. Quickly I closed the book with the contract inside and pushed it back over the side of the bed, where I'd found it. Joe

Tadd found me busily photographing the dead man's collection of change and business cards on his dusty dresser.

"So what have you uncovered and shoved back into place?" he greeted me. Have I mentioned that knowing me all his life has not made Joe Tadd a gentler, kinder man?

As he had known I would, I turned a fiery red. But I wasn't going to tell him what I'd found until I had talked with Cass—and maybe Lamar. Joe Tadd didn't sign my paychecks.

"I found a roach eating toast on the kitchen table," I replied as tartly as I could muster. "If you want to save those particular crumbs of evidence, you'd better get hopping."

"That toast's told me all it's going to tell." Joe Tadd ran a practiced eye over the dresser and turned toward the bed—the only other furniture in the room, unless you count a straight chair that had no more secrets than a single woman in her own hometown.

He found the book in a matter of seconds, of course, and turned to ask, "What the Sam Hill're you grinnin' at?"

"You used the same corner of the sheet I did. I keep telling you I know as much about your job as you do."

"You've already read this, I suppose."

I nodded.

He shook his head. "I never figured Mrs. Higdon was that sort of lady. I suppose that nightie's hers, too." He jerked his head toward a cloud of pink I hadn't seen before, flung carelessly behind the door. "That little lady's got some explaining to do."

* * *

Her explanation rocked us all. Cass had given Tom the BMW as a joint birthday/wedding present! Without saying a word to anybody, they'd gone over to Phenix City, Alabama, on Sunday, stood in front of a justice of the peace, and gotten married like they were teenagers afraid of being stopped.

She had a license to prove it.

She also had a will, dividing poor Tom's estate evenly between his son, Benjamin Clayton Johnston, and his wife, Cassandra Higdon Johnston. Poor Ben had lost his "dady," but he was now a rich little boy. Cass was a rich little widow. Turns out Tom Johnston was part of one of the big Vidalia onion families, and merely hadn't gotten around to buying new furniture since his divorce.

Once Tom was taken out of the car, however, the coroner decided he'd died not from carbon monoxide but from a hole in his skull as big as a golf ball. Once Joe Tadd found the golf club that put it there (neatly wiped and replaced in Tom's own golf bag), he had no alternative but to arrest Cass. He had a murder, and no other suspects.

Cass protested mightily that she had loved Tom, and would never have hit him over the head for *money*. Nobody believed her. A woman who sneaked off and got married to a man who got himself killed and left her money within the week—why, she might do *anything!* Besides, who but Cass had any reason to kill such a nice young man?

Tom Johnston, I must insert here, *was* a very nice young man, but nowhere near as nice as he became the week after he died. Folks in Stateston don't merely speak well of the dead, we give them a Protestant beatification.

So Cass might—and did—explain until she was puce in the face that her aunt lived in Phenix City and they'd gone over there to get married so she would have some family at her wedding. It did no more good than bathing a bitch in heat. People around here know better than to believe people who don't stand up in front of a preacher.

As if being suspected of murdering your husband weren't bad enough, Cass lost her horoscope column, too. She conscientiously wrote her next column Wednesday night in jail, but Lamar and Ted decided not to run it.

When she got bailed out, Cass resigned, went back to her own apartment, and refused to answer her phone.

That meant somebody else had to cover the fifteenth annual Junior League cook-off on Friday. Ruth was trying to wind up several stories early so she and Bert could go see their grandbaby before Bert's new school year began. Lamar was covering national and international news. Since he couldn't possibly ask a former basketball star to cover a "damned bake sale," guess who got assigned the story. I'll give you one clue: It wasn't Junior.

Wearing a new taupe chino suit and what Mama calls my balky face, I parked my Toyota in the First Presbyterian parking lot and shouldered my camera. If you're wondering why the cook-offs are held at First Presbyterian, you don't go to a church that regularly feeds four hundred people every Wednesday night.

First Presbyterian has one of the few kitchens in town where a bevy of belles can whip up special recipes all at the same time without stepping on one another's toes or getting shut down by the health inspector.

One of the first people I met inside the newly decorated white and green fellowship hall was Myra Butler, looking lean and chic in a taupe suit cut so well that it made me despise mine forever. Myra is what novelists would call a willowy redhead. I call her a dyed witch myself, but only in private. She's too old for Junior League, but have you noticed how the League keeps upping the age so nobody in this generation ever has to leave? I figure they'll have a senior chapter of the Junior League before we all die out.

Anyway, Myra—presuming that being either the former women's editor or, more likely, the former wife of my boss gave her special privileges—leaned down, put her sticky red lips near my ear, and murmured, "I'm so glad you came, Abby. I was afraid they might make Cass come in spite of—everything." Her pause before the last word said more than the rest of them combined.

Ignoring her, I started toward Missy Butler Boggs, who was heading my way wearing a cute little pink plaid outfit just right for an afternoon in the kitchen with the Junior League. Heaven help me, I was beginning to think like a women's section editor!

Stephie Wooten sidetracked me, floating up in a totally wonderful (and inappropriate) ivory silk pantsuit the exact shade of her salon-perfect hair. I say floating, because she was surrounded by a cloud of cinnamon and anise—presumably less vile when baked together than when inhaled.

Stephie went to school with my big sister, so I've known her since I was skinning my knees on roller skates. She still makes me feel childish and awkward. She's got that kind of beauty and grace. Plus the money to keep up beauty and grace years after Father Time has let the rest of us down.

She greeted me like a long-lost cousin—which we probably are. "Abby! Do you know if Joe Tadd has any notion yet about who robbed me? Because if he hasn't, I've been thinking. Cass was the one who predicted I'd be lucky, and she knew when I'd be out of the house . . ." She widened her light gray eyes and waited for me to catch up with her own quick mind.

I set down my camera with a thump. "I don't know a blessed thing about it, and I've got a story to write. Who's in charge?"

Stephie took a step back, a mass of injured feelings from the top of her moussed head to the tips of her sixty-dollar nails.

Tough. In that moment I had decided at least to give Cass the benefit of a doubt. It wasn't a noble decision. I'd just be dadgummed if I was going to side with the likes of Myra Butler and Stephie Wooten.

With relief, I saw Dixie Hollingsworth of Dixie Darling Florist near the kitchen door. I excused myself with the good manners my mama taught me, and hurried across the room.

As soon as I was close enough to speak without being overheard, I asked, "Dixie? On the day Tom Johnston died, who sent him a single red rose?"

Dixie has the memory of God. I watched calendar pages flip behind her eyes as she ran her mind down an invisible order book. Finally she shook her head.

"Nobody. I never delivered a rose to Tom Johnston in his life. A planter once, when he was in the hospital with his appendix. Pothos, kalanchoe, and a small Chinese evergreen. From his secretary. That's all."

"He had a rosebud in one of your bud vases on his kitchen cabinet. No card. Who bought roses the day before he died?"

Again the calendar pages flipped, the order book was read. She puckered her lips and counted on plump fingers with blunt, natural nails. "Graham sent a dozen to Cass Higdon at the office. Now, if you want pink, Stephie Wooten ordered a dozen for her women's luncheon."

"No, red is fine." *They* gave me plenty to think about.

The obvious conclusion was that Cass had taken one of Graham's roses home to Ted on his birthday, then killed him later. But what if somebody wanted to frame Cass for the murder? What would have been easier than to take one of her roses and a bud vase from the shelf in our office, and leave them for Joe Tadd to find?

Nothing—if you happened to work for the *Stateston Times.*

I left while the cakes were still rising, the aspics congealing, and the Junior League squealing and cooing over appetizers and dips. I had enough pictures of wide smiles and straightened teeth to fill a month's columns, and I could write the story in my sleep. I'd probably have to. I'd been doing some thinking, and I wanted to talk to Cass.

She almost didn't let me in. I'll never know whether it was my personal charm or the smell of Missy Butler

Boggs's cinnamon Toll House cookies wafting through the door, but finally I heard the chain rattle and knew I'd won.

Cass looked dreadful. Her hair hadn't been combed and the mascara under her eyes looked as old as she had been when she first came to work on the paper. She'd aged considerably since I saw her last.

"What do you want?" Her voice was hoarse, her eyes suspicious.

"Just the facts, ma'am. Nothing but the facts." I pushed gently past her and took a chair. She didn't have the strength, I judged, to physically throw me out.

When she'd sat down on the sofa, twisting her hands until they were rosy, I came straight to my first point. "Are those the roses Graham sent you Tuesday?" I pointed to a vase on her coffee table.

She gave the wilting flowers half a glance, and nodded. "Yeah."

"Where's the other one? Dixie said she sent twelve."

Bless her soul, if a jury had seen her turn and start to count them, they'd have acquitted her right there. Joe Tadd, however, would take more convincing.

"Tell me about the horoscopes," I interrupted as she reached rose number nine.

She turned back to me, looking blank. "What about them?"

"How did you think them up? Where did you get your ideas? And don't give me any hocus-pocus about the stars. You don't know any more about the conjunction of stars than I do, which isn't much."

She opened her mouth to protest, then collapsed

against the cushion like a balloon that has suddenly lost air. "From books, magazines, things I read during the week. You know, like I read Ruth's column on Ted's desk saying the opera was coming to Atlanta, so I put in that somebody ought to get some culture." Her mouth twisted in a sad smile. "I said it nicer than that, of course."

I nodded. "Of course. And how did you decide who got what dosage—I mean, what sign got which particular advice?"

She shrugged. "Most of the time, I just put my next idea under the next sign. Sometimes I'd switch them around, if I'd said something similar not too long ago."

"And they always appeared exactly as you wrote them?"

When her eyes flickered, I knew I was on to something. Cass was having an unusual experience: a new idea.

"I . . . I don't know. I never compared what I turned in with what came out in the paper."

I took her back to the office late that evening, when every decent soul in Stateston was in bed. We pulled up her columns on the computer hard drive and compared them with the printed versions. They were identical.

I still wasn't satisfied.

"Did you back them up on a floppy?"

Cass nodded, looking embarrassed. "I know Lamar told us not to ever take our stories out of the office, but I thought if I ever left the paper, I might want to take the horoscopes with me, to show another editor what I could do." She sighed. "Then when I did go, I forgot them." She fumbled in the back of her bottom drawer and pulled out a box of disks.

I was already busy at the keyboard.

The next morning the staff of the *Stateston Times,* including Cass and Junior, met in the boardroom with a special guest, Sheriff Joe Tadd Burton. At every place was a neat stack of typed pages and copies of the paper, going back several months.

Joe Tadd waved in my direction. "It's your ball game, Abby."

I cleared my throat. This wasn't just any story. It was the scoop of a lifetime. So why did I feel so miserable?

"Well, we all know that Cass has been accused of murdering her, ah, husband." I looked quickly from Lamar to Graham. Lamar was rubbing his nape like he'd been stung by a wasp. Graham was drawing basketballs all over the margins of his papers. Neither man looked at Cass. Cass looked at the table.

"Either she did it," I continued, "or somebody wanted to make sure it looked like she did it. If the latter is true, then the most likely person is one of us, because we're the only ones who knew that Cass would be leaving early that morning to cover the women's prayer breakfast for Ruth. That assumes, of course, that somebody knew about her marriage, and where Tom lived. Right, Joe Tadd?"

Joe Tadd nodded his big head. "That's right, cuz."

I swallowed hard. "Also, somebody had to hate Cass enough to want to frame her." I looked around the room, but only Junior's eyes met mine. He'd better close his mouth, if he didn't want to catch flies.

"But even before the murder, something odd was going on. At first Cass had an uncanny streak of lucky predictions—twins, Ada Potts's legacy, Mr. Wier's liquor, Billy's winning bull, even Missy's marriage."

"Don't forget the stock market and the Kentucky Derby," murmured Ruth, forgetting to wink.

"Right, but they were two lucky predictions that couldn't have possibly been fiddled with." Now I had all their eyes fixed in my direction. It ought to have been a heady sensation. Instead, I felt ready to toss my Mini Wheats.

Joe Tadd, bless his heart, came to my rescue. "Abby, let me take it from here." He took a deep breath and began speaking in his best testifying-in-court voice. Practicing, I guessed. "In front of you are copies of some of Cass's horoscopes as she turned them in, and as they later appeared. Let me call your attention to one for February second, in which Cass originally predicted that Gemini would receive a legacy. You will see that in the paper, Aries is to get the legacy instead."

We all nodded. Who could forget Ada Potts's delight? We'd run her picture on page two, climbing aboard the Golden Olders bus.

Joe Tadd rumbled on. "Earlier, on January twelfth—"

Ruth was already running red nails down corresponding pages. "Cass said for Taurus to 'look for treasure deep within,' but *we* told *Gemini* to seek treasure *close to home!*" Her wide-lashed eyes swept the table. "Who's been messing with these horoscopes?"

Since nobody rushed in to volunteer, I picked up

where Joe Tadd left off. "Late last night, Cass, Joe Tadd, and I started putting a few things together. Lamar, you're in the best position to have edited these horoscopes." He turned bright purple.

I hurried on. "And Graham, your daddy worked at Wiers' Sawmill, and used to drink with old Jake Wier. You could have known about that Jack Daniel's in the barn, or even put it there. You also collect stamps, so you'd know how valuable Mr. Whitacre's really are. And you judged the cattle show. You also ran the Diamond's Department Store promotion, so were most likely to be able to rig the drawing so that Stephie won."

Graham's face wasn't quite so handsome when beet-red. "Hell, Abby, I hadn't read the column when I picked that damned bull." (That, I believed. See above, about his reading habits.) "And that drawing was held right here, in front of the whole staff and all the bigwigs from Diamond's. I didn't even pick the winner. Dick Diamond did!"

"What was done with the box of entries afterwards?" Joe Tadd asked with surprising mildness.

Graham paused, uncertain. Junior raised his hand, still too young to speak up in a roomful of adults without permission. "I took it down to the dumpster and tossed it in. You told me to," he appealed to Ted.

Ted fingered his lucky sunburst and nodded. "Sure I did. Not much point in keeping a box of losing entries hanging around, is there, Joe Tadd?"

"Did anybody check the entries just before the drawing, to make sure the ones in the box were the ones you'd been putting in all week?" Even I shifted uncomfortably under Joe Tadd's stern look. He was getting more like a sheriff and less like a cousin every day.

When nobody said anything, he shook his head. "Easiest thing in the world to write the same name on duplicate forms and replace the originals. No matter which slip is drawn, Stephie wins—although Cass had originally predicted that Pisces would have good fortune. Why, I wonder, was that changed to Sagittarius?"

Junior flushed with excitement. "Because somebody wanted Miss Wooten to be out of the way so they could rob her house! Hey, why are you all looking at *me* like that? I didn't do it!"

"No," I muttered, looking at the table. "It had to be somebody who knew when Stephie's birthday was. Somebody, maybe, who went to school with her. Like you, Ruth."

Ruth rumbled comfortably. "Honey, I can't remember my own children's birthdays, much less those of classmates I haven't sent a card to in a hundred years. But wait, birthdays *are* printed in our church newsletter each month, aren't they, Ted?"

Ted shrugged. "I seldom read church newsletters, Ruth."

I had to swallow half my internal organs before I could speak. "But you do read every single word that gets printed in this paper before it goes out. Like Lamar, you could have edited the computer copy. You also have a lawyer buddy in Valdosta who remembers helping you do a good deed for a dear old woman in Stateston last winter, faking a legacy so she could take a special bus trip. If pressed, Graham might remember your telling him how hard Billy Soat worked on raising that bull after his dad lost a leg at the sawmill, and the Atlanta opera might remember selling you two opera tickets that Mr. Whitacre received anonymously in the mail the same day the paper told Scorpios to get themselves some culture. Only Cass had originally suggested that Leo get culture, you will note." I held up a printout from her disk.

"Ridiculous, Abby!" He looked around the table, sighting down his aristocratic nose. "Can any of you imagine me—*me*—fixing cattle shows or sending anonymous opera tickets? Why on earth should I do good deeds for—for *her?*" His voice was harsh.

"Because you loved her." Ruth's voice was deeper than ever, her eyes pink with unshed tears. "God help you, you loved her, too."

Ted put his hands on the table and started to push back, but Joe Tadd already had a beefy hand on his shoulder. "Just a minute, Mr. Butler. You need to know that Tom Johnston's lawyer will testify he told you Tuesday at the health club that he'd drawn up Tom's will, and you seemed surprised Cass was married. An officer is at your house right now with a warrant, looking for Mr. Whitacre's Civil War collection and Miss Wooten's silver. If he doesn't find them, I have a warrant for your safety-deposit box. Now, you want to tell us the story, or let us put it together piece by piece?"

Ted shook off Joe Tadd's hand like it was a heavy buzzard. Shoving back his chair, he stood—short and slender in the morning light. His hands shook as he addressed Cass, but his voice was cold and steady. "You showed an undeniable flair in picking stocks, my dear. How unfortunate that I mistook your interest in my stocks for an interest in myself." He walked proudly to the door, Joe Tadd right behind him.

Cass slipped out a minute later. Graham and Lamar watched her go with hungry eyes, but they stayed with the rest of us—mostly, I think, because we are all people who need other bodies around us when we grieve. I couldn't have gone to my desk and faced a keyboard right that minute if my job had depended on it.

"Well!" Ruth finally found her voice. "What do we do now?"

Lamar stood and sighed heavily. "I have a paper to put out. I guess I can tell you now—a month ago Ted sold me the *Times,* in a very private deal. Said he wanted to be able to clear out when he got ready. I never thought this would be my first story after he left. Abby, write it up, will you?"

I nodded. "Sure, Lamar, as soon as I think up a lead."

Lamar trudged out to his desk without another word.

"But why would Ted have stolen all that stuff?" Junior demanded, bewildered.

I shrugged. "To discredit Cass's horoscopes?"

Graham shook his head. "You heard what Lamar said. I think he was stockpiling assets Myra couldn't get at. He probably thought Cass would run with him. Poor old Theo." Graham stared morosely at the scarred tabletop.

"Who's Theo?" asked Junior, still puzzled.

"Ted," I replied shortly. "He was called Theo until high school, when we all found out that 'theo' means god. He took so much teasing, he changed his name."

Ruth pursed her lips in a ghost of her usual wry smile. "Too bad, Abby. You could have begun your story, 'Theo Butler did it.'"

The Murder Game

Jean Hager

═══════════

"Reddick, I want you in my office! Now!"

"Yes, sir!"

Charles replaced the receiver, his heart pounding double time. This is ridiculous, he told himself as he took several deep breaths.

He'd been working on his first job, as personnel manager in a ninety-five-bed hospital, when that arrogant jerk who now occupied the president's office was a pimply-faced adolescent. For the past fifteen years, he'd held his current position as vice president in charge of special projects at Houston's Hope Medical Center, the largest hospital in the state. And for all of those fifteen years, he'd loved his work and had planned to put in another eight or ten years before retirement. He couldn't have foreseen that the former president, the man who'd hired him, would be forced out by the governing board and Derek Dishner brought in to turn the hospital into a lean, mean machine with a fat, black bottom line.

Dishner had been on board for two months now, and in that time he'd managed to humiliate, alienate, and scare the crap out of every employee who'd had any dealings with him. That included anyone with any management responsibility, from the five vice presidents down to the head X-ray tech. But the VPs had taken the brunt of Dishner's abuse. By the end of Dishner's second week, it was clear that he perceived the VPs as loyal to the former administration and, therefore, part of a sloppy paternalistic system that had to be rooted out. He probably wasn't going to fire them; that would result in bad press and possibly lawsuits. Instead, he had set out to make their work life so hellish, they would have to resign. Then he could replace them with a handpicked team of barracudas who shared Dishner's lack of regard for the people under them.

Charles stood, buttoned his suit jacket, straightened his shoulders, and left his office. "I've been summoned by The Man," he told his secretary as he passed her desk.

He received a sympathic grimace in return. "Do you want me to stay until you get back?"

"No. I'll see you tomorrow." It seemed much later than five, Charles reflected, as he strode down the carpeted hall to the president's office. Days that had flown a mere two months ago now dragged endlessly. He'd become a clock watcher, a trait that had formerly infuriated him in an employee.

As Charles entered her office, Verna, Dishner's secretary, who was as anxious as everyone else about her job security, looked up and stage-whispered, "He said to send you right in."

Charles stiffened his spine and tapped on the dark, polished door, waited for the snarled "Come," and stepped inside. The president occupied a large corner office overlooking a beautifully landscaped courtyard adjacent to the pediatric wing. According to the hospital rumor mill, Dishner had ordered bulletproof glass installed in the large windows. Good thinking, Charles had thought when he'd heard it.

Dishner glowered at Charles from behind a massive mahogany desk as he jerked his head toward a chair. Charles sat down without speaking. Damned if he'd fawn over the SOB like Bill Stacey, the vice president in charge of the physical plant and grounds. Not that he thought any less of Stacey for it. The poor guy was sixty-one years old and still more than a year away from a decent pension.

Dishner tossed a thick, stapled sheaf of papers across the desk, and Charles grabbed it before it hit the floor. Dishner's face was flushed, but then it usually was. He suffered from high blood pressure. "How do you explain this?"

"Pardon me?"

"Your people screwed up royally. Again."

Charles glanced at the top sheet. It was an application for a federal grant prepared by Myra Peterson, manager of the rehabilitation center, one of the departments under Charles's supervision. They'd been getting the grant for six years. An annual application signed by the CEO was required by federal statues, but it was strictly routine. It would be dropped in a file in Washington and promptly forgotten.

"I checked this over carefully before I routed it to you," Charles said. "It seemed in perfect order to me." Myra could put this stuff together with her eyes closed. The former president had barely glanced at such routine paperwork before signing. Charles kept these thoughts to himself, however. Pointing out how things used to be done was a sure way to send Dishner into orbit.

"Well, *I* won't have time to check it over carefully," Dishner mimicked, his tone dripping with sarcasm. In other words, he didn't trust Charles's judgment on a routine grant application. Dishner never missed an opportunity to insult a VP. "It reached my desk this morning and the deadline for filing is tomorrow."

"That's when it has to be postmarked," Charles said. "My secretary will take it to the post office first thing in the morning."

Dishner cursed and got up to pace behind his desk. His face was red enough to catch fire. Charles spent a moment imagining flames spontaneously bursting from his boss's flesh. But Dishner was still ranting, and Charles forced his mind to focus on the words.

"A thorough once-over would take at least a week," Dishner snapped, then paused to glare at Charles. "I'm going to sign it this time."

You bet your bippy you are, Charles thought. If he refused to sign, he'd have to explain to the board why the hospital failed to get grant money they'd been receiving on a regular basis.

"But hereafter," Dishner was saying, "I'm not putting my name on anything unless I've verified every detail."

What a pompous liar. It would take twenty men full

time to verify every detail in the papers that crossed the president's desk. The truth was, Dishner was alway looking for an opportunity to call a VP on the carpet, and the grant application had provided one.

"I'm sorry." Charles hated the sound of his own voice. He had yet to have a meeting with Dishner when at some point he didn't feel compelled to utter those words. "It won't happen again."

Dishner slapped his palms down on the desk and leaned forward, thrusting his flushed face nearer Charles's. A perfect target for a fist in other circumstances, Charles thought regretfully. "You're damned right it won't! Tell Peterson I want these things a month ahead of the deadline or she'll be looking for a job."

"I'll take care of it."

Dishner snorted contemptuously, making it clear that he questioned Charles's ability to take care of the most minor problem. "No wonder this hospital is in the red. It's run by a bunch of jerk-offs who don't know their butts from a gin whistle." Charles stared out a window at the courtyard beyond, unwilling to open his mouth for fear of what might come out. Insubordination could be grounds for dismissal. Finally Dishner waved his hand and barked, "Get out of my sight, you pathetic idiot!"

Charles walked stiffly from the office. In the hall, he realized that his shirt was wringing wet beneath the arms. He took off his jacket and headed for the parking garage.

Ten minutes later he entered The Lion, a neighborhood bar and grill where he could usually find some of his colleagues after work. Charles often stayed for dinner. Since his divorce three years ago, he ate most of his evening meals out. The only time he attempted to cook these days was when his boys came to visit, which was rare now that they were both at UCLA.

Looking around, he spotted the four other hospital vice presidents at a table. He paused at the bar to order a drink, then joined them, bourbon and water in hand.

Charles surveyed their glum faces as he pulled out a chair. "Long day, troops?"

"What *day?*" muttered Gary Gilbeck, VP of finance, otherwise known as the CFO. "It's been at least a month since this morning." He clasped his hands in mock prayer. "Tell me this is Friday."

"Nope." Lauren Millhouse, vice president of marketing and in-house publications, and, at thirty-nine, the youngest of them all, stirred the ice in her glass with a scarlet-nailed finger. "It's Wednesday."

Gilbeck swore. "I can't stand it."

"Actually, today was almost bearable for me," said Maisy Calhoun, former trauma nurse and, for the last eight years, vice president in charge of nursing services. "I didn't see hide nor hair of our little Hitler."

Bill Stacey raised a hand to catch the bartender's eye and extended two fingers to indicate a double. When his drink arrived, Bill took a healthy slug, then said, "That snake called me everything but a billy goat today."

"So what else is new?" Lauren asked.

"Yeah, join the club," said Charles.

Maisy was watching Stacey worriedly. "Hitting it a little heavy, aren't you, Bill?"

"What are you, my mother?" snarled Stacey.

"You won't be able to drive home if you don't slow down," Maisy warned.

Stacey shrugged. "So maybe I'll hit a tree doing ninety." He took another swallow. "Come to think of it, that would solve a couple of problems. My wife would get three hundred thou in insurance and I'd be out of here."

"Ye gods," Gilbeck sighed. "We're having us a real pity party. Are things truly so bad?"

A four-voice chorus answered, "Yes!"

"Have we no pride?" Gilbeck grumbled. "Why don't we do something about it?"

"What do you suggest?" Stacey inquired. His words were slightly slurred, Charles noticed.

"Well . . ." Gilbeck frowned. "How about mass resignation? The SOB's already in over his head. Let him try to do the job with five new VPs who don't know 'come here' from 'sic 'em.'"

Maisy laughed harshly. "Easy for you to say, Gary. You're forty-three years old. You're still marketable. You and Lauren. The rest of us can't afford the luxury of pride."

Lauren bristled. "I worked sixteen-hour days to get where I am. No other hospital would hire me at anywhere near my current level."

"I'm past worrying about my pride," Stacey said. "I've got to hang in somehow for another fifteen months, till I meet the rule of eighty." The hospital pension plan paid out full benefits only when an employee's age and years of service added up to eighty. Taking retirement prior to fulfilling the rule of eighty would get you a pittance. Even with Social

Security, you'd live in virtual poverty for the rest of your days.

"Maisy and Bill are right," Charles agreed. He was fifty-three, Maisy fifty-seven. Younger than Bill Stacey, but not young enough to be snapped up by another large hospital at anywhere near the comfortable six figures they now earned. At his age, Charles knew he'd be lucky to find any kind of job.

Lauren, who was busy making intricate folds in a paper napkin, looked up at him with brown eyes full of compassion. God, he still wanted her, after all this time. Their affair, three years ago, had been the happiest few months of Charles's life. Then his wife had found out about it and sued for divorce, and Lauren had ended the affair, saying if she was out of the picture, Charles could mend his marriage. Charles hadn't wanted his marriage back. He'd wanted Lauren. But she'd held firm to her decision to end the affair. For months he'd kidded himself that, in spite of the fourteen-year age gap, he could win her back, once his divorce was final. It hadn't happened, but they'd established a friendship of sorts.

Last year he'd gotten his hopes up again when she'd had to bring her manic-depressive mother to live with her. Every other week there was a crisis, and Charles was always there with a sympathetic ear and a shoulder to cry on. Lauren had come to depend on him. But after her mother's death, Lauren had pulled away from him again. He'd tried to believe she just needed time to deal with her grief, but recently she'd told him she was seeing someone else.

Since then, when he couldn't sleep, he'd lain in bed and indulged in bizarre fantasies—like kidnapping her and making her his love slave. At times, he felt almost desperate enough to try anything to get her back.

Lauren made a final fold in the napkin and set her handiwork on the table in front of her. Gilbeck reached over and picked up a perfectly formed rose. "What's this paper thing you're always doing?"

"Origami."

"Come again?"

"Origami. It's the Japanese art of paper folding," Lauren explained. "I used to bite my fingernails. I tried everything to stop, but nothing worked until I took up origami."

Charles smiled, remembering the things she used to do to stop her nail-biting when they were together. She'd painted them with horrible-tasting stuff, worn gloves all the time or Band-Aids on every finger. She'd even threatened to start smoking so she'd have something to do with her hands, but he'd talked her out of that one. Finally she'd taken a class in Japanese origami, and now she made birds, animals, and flowers from any paper that happened to be around when her hands got restless. The activity was as unconscious as her nail-biting had once been.

"Speaking of things Japanese," said Maisy. "Aren't they the ones who perfected the art of sticking metal wires into their victims to torture them while they die a slow death?"

"Yeah," said Gilbeck, an evil smile curling his lips. "Imagine Dishner with wires sticking out of him. I like that better than mass resignation. Wonder where we could find an Asian torturer."

"Hiring your basic hit man would be simpler,"

Stacey slurred. He laughed raucously, causing several people to turn and look in their direction.

Gilbeck pretended to consider the idea. "What would a hit man cost us?"

"Get with reality, you guys," Maisy said. "Hit men always get caught and spill their guts. Look at what happened to that ice skater."

"I dunno," Charles joked. "Gilbeck may be on the right track. There's plenty of brainpower at this table. Surely we can devise a foolproof method of murder."

They all got into the game then and spent the next half hour coming up with ever more outlandish methods of murdering Derek Dishner. By the time Charles had dinner and left The Lion, he was feeling quite relaxed. The murder game had, at least, given them a vehicle to let off some steam.

The next evening, as soon as the five of them were gathered at their regular table in The Lion, Maisy said, "I talked to a lawyer this afternoon to see if we had grounds for a lawsuit, just in case Dishner comes up with some devious way to kick us out. Like restructuring and eliminating our jobs."

Charles had given some thought to consulting an attorney himself. "And?" he asked.

Maisy shook her head. "We'd have to prove discrimination against a particular class of people. Because of age or sex, for example."

"Don't waste your money on lawyers, Maisy," Gilbeck advised. "It's obvious Dishner wants to be rid of all of us, regardless of age or sex."

Having created a cat out of her paper napkin,

Lauren dropped it on the table and crushed it with her palm. "You won't believe what that disgusting pig did today. He called me into his office and made a pass. Ugh!" She shuddered with distaste.

Maisy frowned at the younger woman. "What did you do?"

"Pretended I didn't take his meaning. What should I have done?"

"Maybe you ought to make a date with him," Stacey said. "It's one way to keep your job."

Lauren looked over at him sharply. "Oh, please . . ."

"You could charge him with sexual harassment," Gilbeck suggested.

"I don't want to be a hero," Lauren said sourly. "I just want to be left alone to do my job."

Enough of this gloom and doom, Charles thought. He rubbed his palms together. "Only one thing left. We get rid of him."

"We could put strychnine in his coffee," Gilbeck offered. "It's a horrible way to die, I'm told," he added with a devilish chuckle.

"Poison's too easy to detect on autopsy," Maisy said. As a nurse, she was the medical authority in the group.

"I've got it," Stacey put in. He was pacing himself this evening, still nursing his first drink. "We replace his blood pressure pills with placebos, and he strokes out."

Maisy shook her head. "Too iffy. He'd probably notice he wasn't feeling right and see a doctor who'd prescribe a different medication."

They played the game awhile longer before going their separate ways.

An almost cheerful atmosphere encompassed the group when they gathered Friday evening at The Lion. They looked forward to two whole days away from the hospital and the constant anxiety of knowing that a summons from Derek Dishner could come at any moment.

"I did a little research last night," Stacey announced as soon as their drinks arrived. "My son is a pharmacist, and he left some books behind when he moved into his own place. It's amazing how many medicines can kill you. Antidepressants, for example. Taken in combination with blood pressure medication, a single dose of an antidepressant can be fatal in minutes. The blood pressure falls so low, the heart stops. It'd look like simple heart failure." He lifted his glass to Maisy. "Even you have to admit it's perfect, Maisy."

"Only problem is," Maisy said reflectively, "it would have to be a powerful antidepressant like Haldol or Thorazine. You can't get that stuff without a doctor's prescription."

"Aren't you forgetting?" Gilbeck inserted. "We work in a hospital. We're surrounded by all kinds of drugs."

"But they're locked up," Maisy said. "Only one nurse on each shift has a key, and she has to account for every pill, capsule, and drop at the end of her shift."

"Shucks," Charles said. "I knew there had to be a catch somewhere. Nice try, though, Bill."

Lauren left first, saying she had plans for the evening. As he watched her hurry away, Charles's gut twisted with jealousy. She probably had a date with the new guy tonight. The party broke up soon after that. Everybody was eager to get a head start on the weekend.

Monday morning arrived far too quickly. Charles had an 8 A.M. appointment in Dishner's office, and dreading it had thrown a pall over him all day Sunday. He went to work a half hour early and fortified himself with three cups of coffee in his office. At five of eight, he walked down the hall to the president's office suite.

He reached the outer door simultaneously with Verna. "Eight-o'clock appointment," Charles explained as he held the door for her to precede him.

"Oh, yes," she said a little breathlessly. "I remember seeing your name on his desk calendar." She turned on the lights and stashed her purse in a desk drawer.

While Verna got ready for the day, Charles crossed his legs, jiggled a foot, and flipped nervously through a magazine. After a few minutes, he got up and walked around the office, hands in pockets, jangling his keys. Verna watched him silently. Finally he sat down again and picked up another magazine. Charles continued to sigh and flip through magazines as several more minutes passed.

"He should be here any moment," Verna said finally. "Would you like to wait in his office?"

It was obvious his fidgeting was getting on her nerves. He slapped a magazine back on the lamp table and opened the door to Dishner's office.

"I'm going to run down the hall to use the copy machine," Verna said, hurrying out.

Charles found the light switch and turned it on. As the door swung shut behind him, he froze and a shrill yelp of shock escaped him.

Dishner was slumped behind his desk. His head lolled against the high back of the chair, his eyes fixed, unseeing, on the ceiling. For a moment, Charles's mind went totally blank.

The first thing he was aware of thinking was that Dishner still had on the gray suit and blue tie he'd worn the previous Friday. Dishner's skin was as gray as the suit, the flesh of his face slack.

Charles's next thought, as he continued to stand paralyzed just inside the door, was, This has to be a dream. He squeezed his eyes shut, but when he opened them again, Dishner was still there. Then he thought about the Murder Game the VPs had been playing at The Lion. But that was just a *game.* Surely none of them would really translate the game into reality. They weren't killers, were they? No, of course not. The silent reassurance released him from his paralysis.

He went around the desk and felt for a pulse, an automatic reflex despite the fact that it was evident Dishner had been dead for some time. Dishner's skin was cold. Charles struggled to stifle the flash of relief and, yes, gladness that rushed through him. Dishner would never hassle anyone again.

He dropped the cold, stiff wrist abruptly, turning away. As he did so, he caught a flash of white from the corner of his eye. A square of notepaper had fallen under the desk, one corner sticking out just far enough for Charles to notice it. The paper marred the otherwise perfectly ordered office. Perfect, that is, unless one noticed that the occupant wasn't breathing. Charles stared at the paper, thinking that Dishner might have left a dying message. He picked up the paper. It was blank. Absentmindedly he stuck it in his jacket pocket. Then he went out to summon help.

The pathologist issued his report Tuesday afternoon. It gave the cause of death as congestive heart failure. Charles was still at his desk an hour after his secretary had gone home. He'd had a very full day. In fact, he couldn't remember when he'd last worked so hard; but instead of being tired, he was exhilarated. With Dishner gone, he felt like a man released from a prison cell. The governing board had met that morning and named Bill Stacey acting president. The general feeling was that they'd take their time about finding a permanent replacement, provided Stacey instituted cost-cutting measures quickly.

Dusk gathered outside Charles's office window. A couple of the other VPs might still be at The Lion, but he didn't stir from his chair. Something had been niggling at the back of his mind all day.

He propped his head in his hands and closed his eyes, tried to clear his mind of the many details of the workday. Behind his closed eyelids, he could still see Dishner's gray, staring face.

Dishner had had high blood pressure.

He should have died of a stroke, but he'd died of heart failure. Charles told himself it didn't matter what he'd died of, the man was gone. But he couldn't turn off the stream of questions.

Hadn't he heard something else about heart failure recently? At The Lion, he thought.

Charles went back to the last time the group had gathered for drinks. It was Friday, and they'd all been feeling good because of the weekend. Stacey had said something about reading one of his son's pharmacy textbooks. He'd remarked upon the fact that so many medicines could kill you.

Suddenly Charles had it. According to Stacey, a single dose of an antidepressant taken in combination with blood pressure medication could be fatal in minutes. It'd look like heart failure.

But you couldn't just walk into a drugstore and buy antidepressants off the shelf. And as Maisy had pointed out, at the hospital such powerful drugs were kept under lock and key. In the room where the drugs were kept, people were always coming and going. For someone bent on breaking into the drug cabinet, the chance of being seen was too great. Besides, if any drugs were missing, he'd have heard about it by now. He brought himself up short. What was he thinking? He didn't really believe any of his colleagues would do anything so rash and risky as breaking into the hospital's drug supply, much less commit premeditated murder.

Forget it, he told himself. Just be happy that Dishner would never browbeat anybody again. Why look a gift horse in the mouth?

He pulled open his bottom desk drawer and reached in for a file he wanted to take home with him. Instead, his fingers closed on the scrap of paper he'd dropped into the drawer yesterday morning, the one he'd found in Dishner's office. He started to toss it in the wastebasket, but stopped when he noticed that the paper had been folded several times, then smoothed out again. The fold lines were still barely discernible. Curious, Charles refolded the paper along the same lines, then unfolded and folded it again in a different order. After yet a third refolding, he held a paper swan in his hand. He set it on the desk and stared at it as several seemingly unrelated facts came together in his mind.

It occurred to him that the most commonly prescribed drug for manic-depression was lithium, a powerful antidepressant. Lauren's mother had been severely manic-depressive. Then he recalled Lauren's haste to leave The Lion the previous Friday evening. To go home and get ready for a date, he'd assumed. But maybe the date hadn't been with the man she'd told him she was seeing. And maybe she'd only stopped by her house to pick up something before returning to the hospital.

According to the pathologist, Dishner had died sometime Friday evening.

Charles thought about these things for a long time. Then he had a new thought. It was shocking to realize that he was capable of entertaining it. Was he truly desperate enough to stoop so low?

He thought about it some more. Then he picked up the phone and dialed.

"Hello." She sounded breathless, as though she'd had to run to catch the phone.

"This is Charles. Have I got a deal for you."

MALICE

DOMESTIC

Anthologies of Original
Traditional Mystery Stories

1

Presented by the acclaimed Elizabeth Peters.
Featuring Carolyn G. Hart, Charlotte and Aaron Elkins,
Valerie Frankel, Sharyn McCumb, Charlotte Maclead
and many others!

2

**Presented by bestselling author Mary Higgins
Clark.** Featuring Gary Alexander, Amanda Cross,
Sally Gunning, Margaret Maron, Sarah Shankman
and many more!

3

**Presented by Agatha Award-winner Nancy
Pickard.** Featuring Wendy Hornsby, Dorothy
Cannell, Deborah Adams, Camilla T. Crespi
and many more!

616-02

**Available from
Pocket Books**

POCKET
BOOKS